Hammer and Lock

A Texas Romance

By Louise Crouch

For more from Louise Crouch please visit
http://loucrouch.wordpress.com

Dedication

To my family for their love and support

To my children for their patience

To my husband for saying yes

Table of Contents

Chapter 1

My sincere condolences. The question lay not in the substance of the words inked in neat masculine script, but the identity of the author. Evelyn Lockwood pocketed the week old letter as the stage coach doors swung open. Aunt Eustace's freckled hand snatched at Evelyn's doe skin gloves and squeezed.

"Welcome back to Dew Springs, Evelyn."

Texan dust stained the hem of Evie's green satin skirts as she strode across the timber boardwalk to the lawyers office. As she passed, the postman's letters cascaded to the slats, the mercantile busybodies paused and a wolf-whistle escaped the doors of the Nine Lives Saloon.

"It must have been a while since a Lady; a *real* Lady has walked these streets, Aunt." Evie paused outside the lawyers' double glass windows to tuck a stray honey-coloured curl into the bun that rested at the nape of her neck.

"I dare say it's been a while since they have seen a *lady*, the likes of you Evie," Aunt Eustace said.

Evie Lockwood flashed a pair of jade green eyes at the spry fifty-five year old in an attempt to hurry Eustace along. Evie had travelled from New Orleans via rail and stage and now stood metres from the answer to all her burnings questions, waiting for her Aunts' dawdle to hasten. Evie would have this resolved by noon, then lunch at the homely café and be on the Coach shortly after. Evie inhaled slowly as she tugged on her brocaded corset, the sharp odours of manure and sweat mingling to clog her throat.

"You've been away so long, you might need it dear," Eustace jibbed.

Evie glared through the shop glass window that advertised the newly printed *Texas Almanac for 1873, an Emigrant's Guide to Texas*. Evelyn refused to acknowledge her Aunt and the trickle of sweat that slipped through her corset. By noon, she reminded herself and tugged on the door.

Mr Thomas Franklin Esquire stopped Evie in her tracks. His thick fingers locked together on the solid oak desk, a wiry brown moustache accentuating his chubby features. With quivering jowls and another stern "No," the lawyer, refused to divulge the "issue" in Evie's fathers Last Will and Testament.

"Had I known you were arriving today, Ms Lockwood, I would have arranged for this meeting at a more appropriate time. I understand you would like the matter settled efficiently, Ms Lockwood so we will reschedule for after lunch. Half past two should be sufficient time. "

"I don't know why you had to summons me to Dew Springs for a simple reading of his Will. Surely you could have sent word or travelled to N'Orlins, yourself?" Evie said.

Two days back in her home State and already her tongue had twisted. Her heart begged to hear the sweet creole or baritone jazz of her adopted city. Franklin raised a bushy eyebrow and gestured to the door. Resigning herself to his adamant refusal, Evie sighed.

"Half past two it is Mr Franklin."

Evie and Eustace spent an early lunch at the café waiting for the time to speed by. Instead it dripped, hauntingly, and achingly past. Evie spent half the time in deep reflection and the other half glancing at the grandfather clock ticking away at her torment. She missed her father. She had grieved for Earl when she'd read the telegram. Eustace had wept as only an older sister who outlived a younger sibling could. Earl had made his apologies for missing Christmas last year, but had never hinted at an illness. Would he have told her? Evie had loved her father, however as the years had stretched so had their relationship. As with Earl's visits, the letters between father and daughter had travelled the distance, their frequency in decline.

Earl's letters read like a bank journal or a newspaper, numbers of stock, the weather, and the crops. Evelyn's were no better, succinct sentences of her relevant milestones. No apologies, no explanations and no mention of her mother. Edwina Lockwood died during childbirth with Evie's never-to-be brother and suddenly Earl had a ranch to run with a two year girl to raise by himself. His sister, Eustace had come running, unable to have any children of her own, Eustace had collected husband after husband, until Evie came along.

When Eustace had arrived, her pomp and splendour had crept into every corner of the homestead. Until, Evie turned eight. In one swift day, Earl had bundled Evie up and sent both her Eustace back to New Orleans. The clock struck one, and a bead of sweat trickled down Evie's back.

Eustace muttered inappropriate curses under her breath and smiled when Evie arched an eyebrow. Eustace dabbed at her brow, smoothing back wisps of silver hair into her stately bouffant, modelled on Marie Antoinette. Eustace portrayed herself as just as profligate and promiscuous as the late Queen of France; however Evie knew her Aunt was quite the opposite. Time had dealt Eustace a kind hand, a handsome woman, who looked regal rather than ravaged, and twice as stylish as her peers.

Evie's teaspoon clattered on her saucer and she watched her Aunt engage other patrons in small talk about the town, an upcoming ranching Festival and the gossip of Evie and Eustace's arrival. Their long vowels and slow drawl about small town ideas grated in Evie's ears. Throughout Evie's upbringing, Eustace had instilled Evie with a healthy respect for wealth, how to earn it and how to keep it. Evie had made substantial financial gains and now stood to befall a very large windfall on her latest investment in the Jay Cooke and Company.

Unfortunately Evie's plans to snare "new money" shipping magnate Lewis Myers had to be postponed with her summons to Dew Springs. Not that a minor delay would halt her progress, she would simply sell the Ranch and return to New Orleans in time for the latest round of society balls and engagements.

The heat reduced Evie's need for gloves and she tucked them away at quarter past one. Evie wondered how large the windfall would be when Jay Cooke and Company expanded the railroad further west. It seemed to Evie that civilisation in this country rivalled an inferno, starting on the east coast and the embers blowing west across the country. Some embers struck fuel and burned brightly leaving great cities such as Philadelphia, Fort Worth and New Orleans, in their wake. Some embers petered out and left ghost towns and dust bowls thirsting for the rail to revive them. Dew Springs was one of the latter.

At ten past two Evie and Eustace exited the café and strolled along the sparse boardwalk that separated civilisation from muck. A shoulder clipped Evie's elbow followed by quick apologies woke her from her daydreams.

"Ma'am"

A dark brown Stetson swept back from a proud brow and eyes the colour of melted chocolate ran down her physique.

"I …um" Evie stuttered.

A firm hand clutched Evie's and dropped a moist and inviting kiss to the back, "Well Evie-lyn Lockwood, pleased to make your acquaintance again."

"Pardon?" Evie mumbled, her brain taking longer to decipher the twang.

"Richard Kline. It's been a while," Richard Kline smiled as he straightened his gingham covered shoulders. He stood a half a foot taller than Evie which is no mean feat thanks to Earl's generous height. He tugged suggestively on his leather thong tie and tucked one thumb into his waistband, "Too long a time. So you're back in town, to inherit what's… I should say, the Double E Ranch." The long notes of his words teased her ears.

"Yes, it seems so". He was the cleanest man she had seen in days, but she couldn't place the face or the name, "Have we met before?"

"Yes Evie-lyn."

Only Texan's could turn her perfectly respectful name into a dinner-time catcall.

"Yes Ma'am, sometime back when you were knee high to a grasshopper." He took the time to run his devil-brown eyes over her dress, stopping short of licking his lips, "Took a spell from my Ma's tree one day, nearly knocked you out cold. Earl nearly knocked my head clean off my shoulders when I brought you back." Evie racked her brain, but the memory remained stubbornly absent. Lost for words again, Mr Kline steered her back into the present day, "Four Star Ranch, we have your rear boundary."

"I see."

Evelyn flicked her skirts and followed the movement with her eyes if only to break the vicious blush rising from her neck to her cheeks. He introduced himself to Eustace and Evie quickly assessed the man in front of her. Tiny laughter lines appeared beside his eyes and his thin lipped mouth twisted to the side into a smile, no a definite smirk. The sharp, if slightly effeminate, planes of his jaw drew her eyes back.

"If you have any trouble out there, do not hesitate to holler for me. I'd be only too pleased to be bumping into you."

Richard dipped his hat low and swept backwards, allowing her the sight of his physique in double-stitched denim and tan boots.

At quarter past two Evie sat recomposed in Mr Franklin's office waiting for the lawyer to commence proceedings. Eustace fell into deep small talk, her blue-grey eyes never leaving the blushing cheeks of Mr Franklins, while Evie poised herself, smoothing her skirts and refusing to sweat.

A holler from the front room, fractured Evie's calm, announcing the arrival of a third party. *A third party?* Evie took two deep breaths to resettle, preparing to face a widow, a whore, a step-mother, when muddy black boots appeared in her view. At her leisure and with a distasteful pucker on her lips, Evie assessed the new comer. The boots enveloped faded denim jeans, held up by a gun belt of all things. A black shirt stretched taught across broad shoulders and tucked haphazardly at odd points along the man's waist. By the time Evie's eyes had met the divine jaw line of Cade Hamerton, she realised her initial assessment had turned into outright appreciation. His wide heart shaped mouth softened the strength of his dimpled chin and the proud nose that would seem too large on any other face. Blue eyes penetrated Evie's calm exterior and his flat expression managed to dismiss her instantly.

Hamerton roughly shook hands with Franklin before reclining against the book shelves, frustratingly on the edge of Evie's peripheral view. He slowly placed the dirty boot against the legal books stacked there. Only after Hamerton stopped moving, could Evie take breath again. She glanced at Eustace whose idea of support included a sly wink. Evie dared a second glimpse in Hamerton's direction to observe the brute had crossed two thick forearms upon his chest. Even reclining his figure dominated the room. He hadn't even removed his hat!

"Ms Lockwood, Mr Hamerton, let's begin with my condolences to you both for your loss."

Evie cautiously nodded. How did he know her father? Was he a bastard son from another mother? No, the slight freckling across his nose and the russet coloured three day growth placed him at least three years older than her, maybe five. Business partner?

Hamerton nodded.

Evie frantically racked her brains for any recollection of her father mentioning a partner, hired hand or a trail boss, but nothing. She noticed the handle of a pistol peeking at her from this far hip. What business partner needed a gun! For the reading of the Will no less! Well, business partner or not, whatever her father had bequeathed to this Hamerton, she could handle. Hamerton might even buy the Double E from her if she could haggle a decent price. Maybe bid Hamerton against Kline and she could name her price! The butterflies in her stomach calmed ever so slightly.

"Now to commence…"

"To hell with the formalities Franklin, just cut to the chase. I have stock to attend to."

Evie eyes popped the same time her jaw dropped and Eustace chuckled ever so slightly in the corner, "I beg your pardon."

"Listen, lady," Hamerton's last syllable, rolled in a deep and rough southern drawl that dragged down Evelyn's spine.

"Of course Cade, of course, there's no need for cursing, I shall cut to the chase," Franklin's jowls quivered.

Evie, stunned to her boots, at the complete lack of manners from Hamerton, regarded the cowering Lawyer. She had eyeballed, threatened, huffed and puffed to get her way and

Franklin refused to bend. Hamerton threw some cuss words at the man and he turned to jelly.

"Now, the nuts and bolts are as follows, I hereby bequeath in whole the working yards and range of the Ranch known as the Double E..."

Here it comes, thought Evie.

"....Some 15,000 acres in total, including all outhouses, the pump, barn, tools, dairy, stockyard, and...."

15,000 acres, is that how big it is? Dollar signs flashed in front of Evie's eyes, how much could she get for an acre? She would have to see the lands office on the way out.

"....to Cade Troy Hamerton."

Evie's lips puckered and her throat closed tight, "Pardon?"

"Hold on Ms Lockwood,..."

Hold on? That's exactly what Evie was doing; white knuckled to the oak arm rests. Eustace looked like she would faint.

"To my loving daughter..."

Loving? Evie drove her thumb into the oak.

"I hereby bequeath, the homestead and house yard in whole, boarded by the white fencing including the hen house, "

Hen house, oh Lord! How could she sell a hen house?

"...further Evelyn Francis Lockwood shall receive the current and future stock to be born on the Double E, hereby to be known as the Angus Breed Stock including the Angus bull Jorge...."

Silence settled awkwardly in the tiny space of Franklin's office, broken by the crack of wood on timber as Hamerton slammed the office door.

Chapter 2

As Evie unravelled her honey gold braid in the Blue Bell Hotel bath, she tried to find a positive in her father's bizarre bequeaths. After Hamerton's violent exit, Franklin summarised that Evie owned the homestead and all the entailed within the house yard including the chickens. Furthermore she owned the Ranch's newest edition, an Angus Hereford bull, named Jorge. Earl's trouble with tick fever, drought and famine forced him to revise his business plan. He'd spent his last dime on bringing the beast out direct from Scotland. In turn, Earl bequeathed his daughter the current and future Angus breed entitled her to all the unborn stock, currently residing in his, or more correctly, Hamerton's heifers. Franklin failed to explain just how Hamerton came to inherit the remainder, although Evie guessed her father had become indebted to Hamerton somehow.

Hamerton. The smallest sliver of a childhood memory tickled Evie's mind. There had been dozens of boys around the Double E in those days. Drifting in and out of stables and homestead alike, cow pokes and waddies, some boys were different every day. Evie had only been young; she couldn't remember one of the boys' faces or names. Like an echo of a ghost, Evie remembered one boy who, wherever he walked, a shadow followed with whispers in his wake. Was Cade the man this boy grew into? Do the shadows and whispers still dog his footsteps? The way Franklin shook and shivered at the Cowboys' demands made Evie think they did.

If Cade had been that boy, how did he come to such financial wealth to be indebted by her father? Did he swindle Earl and hence, herself out of the Double E? She would make a time tomorrow to visit the Ranch and under the guise of making Hamerton an offer, she could review the books. Myers would have to wait a few more days.

Myers. Evie had to force the image of the suave shipping magnate into her brain. Thick wavy black hair he wore slicked back and his dark all-knowing brown eyes. Tall, no wait, average height. Cade's six foot and more height dwarfed Myers. *Myers.* Shipping entrepreneur, industrialist, and warehouse mogul. Not only did he own the majority of warehouses along the docks, he had branched out into the shipping lines. His wealth grew daily and so did the line of wedding bell chasers. Evie would have to rush back to New Orleans to secure her future and Myers. Tomorrow she would hire a wagon to the Double E and face Hamerton. A brief image of his roped forearms resting across his broad chest flashed in front of Evie. Time to vacate the bath.

Upon returning to the bedroom, Evie sagged on her bed, while Eustace sat at the tiny corner desk scratching away at her correspondence to Jeffery Willington Senior, her latest potential husband.

"Had enough of the bath dear, I shall have this sent off in the morning before we leave. I have decided not to completely unpack and get comfortable here." As she said the words Evie noticed her Aunt had barely removed a single item from her luggage. "After this afternoon, it might be prudent to stay out the homestead from here on…"

"Stay at the homestead! Did you see that man?"

"Yes, Evie, I did…" Eustace pursed her lips, like a cat sizing up a saucer of milk.

"Aunt, I am referring to his behaviour, his manner and his aggression. How uncivilised and arrogant can men get. Even that Richard whatever his name is …"

"Dear Evie, this is Texas. In my short time here, I learned that the men are like the countryside, big, beautiful and wonderfully unpredictable."

"Aunt Eustace!" Evie chastised.

"Calm down my dear, we've travelled off the track a bit; I wanted to suggest that a decent time spent looking over Earl's books might offer up a few indications as to what happened out there and how this Hamerton ended up with your inheritance. Furthermore, I took a wander down to the town cemetery and it seems Earl is presently absent, ergo laid to rest at the Ranch. So if I should wish to pay my respects it will be at the Double E."

10

"I see Aunt, although there is no reason why we have to stay out there."

"Evelyn," her Aunt took a sterner tone, "If you do not intend to reside or take possession of what's left of your inheritance, how will you ever convince Hamerton to pay his highest price? Supply and demand Evie. Any trader will pay a higher price for what is no longer available. You legally own that Bull and that homestead and you go out there with the appearance of taking possession of those items for your own benefit. Only then will Hamerton see that he will have to buy them from you at *your price*."

"Yes indeed." Evie didn't want to talk anymore. She berated herself for needing Eustace to spell it out. Distracted she snuggled down under the coverlet and wished she had chosen a hand maid for the journey and told Eustace to stay at home.

In the morning, Eustace had reconstructed her splendid hairstyle and left Evie alone to finish her breakfast. Her aunt returned with a wagon and a driver to take them out to the Double E. While the driver loaded their luggage and Eustace paid the bill, Richard Kline appeared on the steps of the hotel, tucking his tail and buttoning yesterday's gingham shirt.

"Evie-Lyn, had enough of Dew Springs already?"

Without asking, Kline started lifting her trunks onto the wagon.

"On the contrary, I am…" Evelyn cleared her throat, "taking possession of my inheritance"

"Taking possession. Is that right? The way I hear it, there ain't much left for you to be taking possession of, Evie-Lyn."

A blush crept up Evie's neck and stung her cheeks; she should have guessed small town talk would be quicker than the wind. Damn that Hamerton for gloating!

"Not yet, but when I am done there will be."

There, let the gossips send that around to Hamerton's ears.

Kline offered her his most crooked smirk yet, "Well now, if you need a hand in that direction, don't hesitate to holler." He dipped his hat to Eustace before crossing the street to the Stables.

"Nice man, isn't he?"

Evie didn't reply, she just mused over his thinly veiled offer. Hamerton and Kline had history? Could she count on Kline as an ally?

The journey out to the Double E ranch soothed Evie's soul a little as she adored the rainbow of wildflowers that littered the edge of the track. The wide rolling prairie fields spread out either side of the travellers, interrupted here and there with groves of oaks and elms. Evie's gaze followed the perfect white clouds floating elegantly across the big blue Texan sky.

Evie's daydream broke with the noise of the cart wheel's striking wood. The sound brought flashes of memory from the narrow timber bridge she had walked as a child. The crystal white stream bubbled and frothed underneath the planks as their driver, Charles, manoeuvred Whiskey and the Trap right to the door.

Evie stood back, while Charles unloaded the cases and measured up the homestead. The grey paint now peeling, framed with bright white wash on the window and door frames. On the front porch sat one rocking chair with matching handmade side table and another chair just to the right. Evie would bet her chickens that Earl sat there every afternoon to watch the Hands come in from the range. She strolled into the hall and wandered in and out of the two sitting rooms on either side. In the first sitting room, the stone backed fireplace looked well used and the chairs comfortably lived in. In the second, a scarred timber table stood surrounded by four chairs with faded and threadbare upholstery. Behind the table noises emanated from the kitchen and Evie ventured on to investigate.

A chubby dark face starred at her from the bench, with both arms covered up to the elbows in flour. A tiny olive skinned face peeked at her from behind the cook.

"Can I help you?" bellowed the large woman in her later years.

"Ruth?"

"No Ruth has passed on girl, I'm Maybelle. If you're mistaken me for Ruth, you must be -"

"Evelyn Lockwood."

12

A petite olive skin face stepped out from behind Maybelle and transformed into a beautiful young girl, Mexican or Indian Evie couldn't tell.

"This is Pearl, Ms Lockwood. We are both sorry for your loss. This house loved him dearly."

Pearl's face took on an unearthly grimace and she arched an eyebrow at Evie before storming out the back door.

"Never mind her, now how can I help you Ms Lockwood."

"My Aunt Eustace and I have come to stay, well move in, and take residence….." Evie stumbled, "I wanted to introduce myself. I will take stock of the house first and then come and discuss how the house should run now that I have returned. "

"Oh will you now?"

Evie paused at the reply. Eustace had servants back in New Orleans, why did Maybelle seem so shocked at Evie's request?

"How about you go find yourself a room and I'll make you lunch, but the running of the house is up to you. I cook and wash and nothing else. You're Daddy and Cade never asked me to do more and nor will you."

With that Maybelle went back to beating the dough on the bench. The silence stretched out so long, that Evie began to feel awkward, in her own home, nonetheless. Evie swallowed her pride and decided to head upstairs. Her father had built the house with more bedrooms than fate would have it. Evie bypassed Earl's room, smiling at the crooked bed and cowskin rug stretched tight across the floor. The second room stood bare, with the exception of a white painted bed and matching set of drawers. The third door she opened as if guided by the years gone by and Evie recognised her room as a child. Earl had left the single bed in the middle surrounded by the wooden nightstand and dresser Earl had made himself. The sting of tears began to well behind her eyes at the reminder of his heartless rejection. Evie moved onto the fourth room only to discover the door locked.

Evie twisted the handle again and butted her shoulder against it to make it move. It didn't and she turned away in defeat only to run face first into the solid chest of Hamerton.

Chapter 3

"Looking for this?" His caramel tones caused goose bumps to dance over her skin. He leaned over, sending one thick bicep past her ear to unlock the door. As the room fell into view, Evie quickly identified the occupier of the room. Why did the smell seem to tempt the flight of butterflies?

Evie cleared her throat, "Since I intend on residing in my inheritance, I will formally request you vacate."

Her father had let this man, live in the house! Hadn't Maybelle mentioned that Cade hadn't asked her to do anything? He must have conducted himself as man of the house immediately after her fathers' death. Or worse, during his illness!

He entered the room leaving her gawking after him on the threshold, "Vacate?"

A thick bubble of sound came forth from his throat that resembled a laugh. No a scoff! As she watched, Cade began pulling his shirt up from the waistband throwing flashes of hard muscled skin her direction. When his fingers began tugging at the buttons, Evie bolted into action.

"Now listen here, this is my house." A twang crept into the words and she fought it back.

"What happened to that great southern hospitality? Lose it in N'Orlins." He scoffed again and more buttons fell aside.

"You will leave, because I have asked you to leave. You heard Franklin this is my inheritance to do with as I see fit. I don't know and don't care what my father let you get away with, but it will not continue now that I am here. "

"And what are you going to do about it?"

He tossed his cream Stetson onto the bed revealing deep russet coloured locks that brushed the white collar of his shirt.

"I'll remove your possessions one by one and send them out that window if I have to."

Evie hadn't planned on just how angry he could make her. She was supposed to be negotiating a deal with this man, not tossing out his belongings.

He tugged his shirt open and loosened his belt, as he strode towards her, for a moment Evie realised of what he could or might do to her if he really wanted to. Evie froze as Cade's frame filled the doorway, placing his hands on the door jamb either side of her heart shaped face. The white shirt fell apart to reveal the powerful chest underneath covered with a light dusting of fuzz. Her eyes betrayed her and she followed that light trail of fuzz right down the middle until it circled his belly-button. The sight sent shivers down to her toes and she swallowed hard when she looked up into those piercing blue eyes.

"You kick me out and I will put the other half of your inheritance in this room instead."

Evie tried to scoff at the thought of him manhandling a full grown bull up the stairs and for a second she didn't doubt he could do it.

"You wouldn't dare!" She put on her best scowl and crossed her arms.

"Try me Darling." He said and he moved forward forcing Evie to retreat to let him pass.

He grabbed a towel from the hall cupboard and headed downstairs. Evie threw herself back against the wall and rested her palms on her stomach, anything to stop the butterflies! She hadn't realised her eyes had closed until she heard Hamerton's determined footfalls advancing. Within two strides he had closed the distance. Evie bit her bottom lip and tried to look composed. Without words, he reached behind her to lock his bedroom door and descended the stairs out of sight.

What the hell am I going to do with him?

By the time Evie had returned to her normal self, Maybelle had shared that Earl had succumbed to influenza and in the last few days had refused anyone's help. Eustace had agreed to take Earl's bedroom and let Hamerton stay where he was. She offered the smallest words of comfort,

"The situation will sort itself out."

Maybelle offered little information on Hamerton himself, except that he had grown up on the Double E, the son of a cowhand, who for some reason, had moved on leaving Cade behind. Cade had earned his place in Earls' staff and been indispensable ever since. Mabelle validated Evie's theory that Hamerton had been running the Double E before Earl became sick.

Evie retired to the study after that and lost herself in the piles of paperwork that her father had accumulated over the years. Mabelle brought her lunch to the pokey little room and Evie set to work locating and assessing Earls accounting journals. At the conclusion of stacking each mountain by year, in order of month, Evie finally began to read each journal. In short order, she found regular monthly repayments without an explanation. Her father had taken a loan? Within the next few journals she found the repayments of the loan had doubled. As Evie read on, she realised the effect of double repayments on her father's income was slowly bankrupting him. *Hamerton*!

She threw the books aside and rubbed her eyes. A deep orange filtered through the dusty curtains and Evie rose from her paper mountain, sending her arms skyward, and chest forward, the bones in her corset rising up her ribs. She would be sore tomorrow. She took a few tentative steps out on to the porch just as the air began to cool. A low bellow echoed through the afternoon chill from the stockyards.

"That's the better half of your inheritance." Cade's deep timbre resounded from behind.

A chord struck in Evie's heart as he sat down on the table *beside* the rocking chair, to pull his boots off, she focused on the cattle yards.

"Jorge?"

"Yeah and he sounds hungry."

Evie heard the screen door open and the Hamerton muffled compliments to Maybelle's cooking. Evie would have to broach the loan somehow, but for now her curiosity had peaked.

"Hungry?"

Evie walked to the end of the porch and peeked around at the stock yards. From this distance she could make out the lumbering shape of a massive beast stirring at the gate. Why did he come to the gate? Shouldn't he be out on the range, tending to his...*ladies*?

17

The stock yard stood completely fenced off from the barn in which the dairy cow indignantly chewed her cud, her ears twitched with the buzzing insects, grunts and snuffles answering Jorge's bellows. Evie stood on her tiptoes to see that a bucket of corn husks had been stacked nearest to the stockyard gate. With all the courage Evie could muster, she approached the bucket of husks. Selecting the choicest produce in hand, she approached the Angus bull.

Jorge's snuffles produced tendrils of slobber that dribbled down Evie's delicate hands, as the bull inhaled husk after husk. The dairy cow lifted her head and snorted abruptly, and Evie edged towards her second guest, husk ready in outstretched palm.

The bucket now empty, the dairy cow returned to her stall and Jorge ambled away bellowing his appreciation. Evie's shoulders relaxed and a smile crept onto her face. A small victory, but a victory nonetheless, she mused. Evie turned to the ranch house, the paint peeling, white picket fence, her chickens roamed loose in the front. She recalled frantic boot steps and childish giggles, Aunt Eustace's mock scowl at the dinner time grime that would follow Earl inside. Evie's ribs swelled for a moment, until she noticed the hulking silhouette, on the porch. Evie clenched her fists.

By the time Evie had washed up for dinner, taking extra measure to set her expression to stern, Eustace had already set the table. Evie took her seat adjacent to the head of the table, Eustace opposite and Hamerton at the far end.

"So you and my brother were close then?" Eustace asked.

"Yes Ma'am." Hamerton said and then shovelled peas, potatoes and a huge slab of beef into his mouth.

"Maybelle tells me that you grew up here?"

"Yes Ma'am."

Evie's brow crinkled at his reticent answers. She reached for the beef and the table rocked gently to one side. Evie clicked her tongue and helped herself to the potatoes.

"You must have some stories to tell about my Earl then?" Eustace kept prodding.

"Yes Ma'am. Always good for a laugh, hardworking, respectful, honest." Hamerton heaped another forkful of beef into his mouth and nodded.

"So you must have worked very hard for him in all that time then?" Eustace asked.

"Ma'am, should you have questions about Earl, then ask away. If you'd like to get to the point, I'd appreciate that just as well." Cade leaned casually back and placed his hands palm down on the table.

Evie though to ask about the loan but thought better of it. Even she knew if you accused a man of being dishonest, you needed evidence.

Aunt Eustace nodded quickly and with a mismatched gingham napkin dabbed at her thin lips.

"I am curious about my brothers bequeaths."

Hamerton rose sharply from the table, plate in hand. The ceramic clinked into the sink. Noises of swishing water returned to the table when Hamerton didn't. Eustace and Evie entered the kitchen.

"Yes." Eustace answered.

Cade's broad back rolled and dipped with his ministrations. He grabbed a pot from the bench.

"He owed me."

"He owed you?"

Evie couldn't believe her ears; his debt repayments had bankrupted her father.

"Owed you for what?" Eustace levelled at him.

Hamerton shook the residual bubbles from his solid fingers, "For stock, Ma'am. Your brother suffered some heavy losses and lost almost half his herd. I was his partner for some of it and suffered losses of my own. Earl brought me into the business rather than loose the Double E altogether." He sent a cutting stare in Evie's direction.

"Why you?" Evelyn asked the tone a little thicker than she'd have liked.

"Because your father needed someone to take over the Double E for when he could no longer run the Ranch. I was already the Leading Hand, it was a natural choice."

Evie's eyes regarded Hamerton's boots as she clenched and unclenched her jaw. Hamerton's watchful gaze spurred the anger on, and Evie inhaled slowly before she returned her own heated glare to his steady blue eyes. Eustace walked between them,

"Well for that I thank you Mr Hamerton. I feel as though I might retire early tonight, Evie come dear and help me."

Questions like bubbles fizzed in Evie's brain as she helped her Aunt upstairs in a haze. When Evie returned down stairs, the table had been cleared and the early evening cricket chirps drifted through the screen door. Hamerton's figure reclined in darkness, steam warped tendrils of coffee into the darkness,

"Not what you wanted to hear, Darl'n?"

Evie flicked at her skirts, her hands safely occupied instead of stinging his cheeks.

"What do you really want to know Evie?" He asked, the deep silk tones softened with the shadows.

"Why did you become his partner?"

"I told you, he had suffered losses,"

"Yes, but if he was losing stock and cash already, why buy in? Why not buy him out entirely in the first place."

"That's a cut throat way to look at it."

In the half darkness, Hamerton's head swivelled, his eyes pits of polished cobalt, traversed Evie's profile. The cool night air lingered across Evie's skin, and she fought the urge to shiver.

"It would have been a better business decision. You said so yourself, you took loses as well." She leaned forward against the porch rail, the gentle breeze bringing flavours of oak moss, sage and coffee.

"I owed him. Simple as that."

"You owed him; I thought you just said…"

Evie's hem swished along the slatted porch, the small light of the homestead sent the angles of Cade's jaw into sharp relief.

"How much of your father do you remember before you left Evie?"

Evie paused, whirlwinds that stung the eyes and clogged her throat, heat so suffocating her lungs burned for water, empty plates and rumbling bellies. Edwina Lockwood had perished out here,

"I remember the heat, the hunger… dust."

"Your father Evie, not the Double E."

Evie sighed as she crushed flaked paint chips between her thumb and forefinger,

"You say that I left the farm. He sent me away."

"He travelled to see you every Christmas."

Evie let the paint fall to the grass below. Hamerton had brought up all those childish feelings she had pushed aside,

"Why don't you tell me what you saw of my father?"

"He loved you. He missed you. Raised me like I was his own, because of it."

"He never mentioned you." Even in the darkness she realised her words had landed like an arrow, because Cade's bulky shadow trembled. "I mean to say we never really talked about the Double E. Mainly about New Orleans…"

That's exactly how it had gone, every visit Earl had made to the city, Evie showed the City to him, taking her father out to lunches, dinner, the theatre. He had talked about heads of cattle and she had glazed over the details. Maybe he had mentioned Hamerton?

"Ever wonder why he never asked you to come back?"

He drew a long steady sip of coffee. The evening breeze dragged the sweet bitterness to tease her. Evie wiped her dusty fingers on her skirt, her palms damp, cheeks flushed with colour,

"Because he finally had his son."

Evie clutched at her ribs, her throat constricted. What had Hamerton done to bring this out in her? Her heel clipped into each other as she tore from the porch, all the way upstairs to her bedroom. Eustace caught her at the door.

"Seems you managed to charm the beast,"

"Only one of them," Evie blinked, and tried to pretend like those words had not come from her mouth.

Eustace chuckled, "Goodnight Evie."

Chapter 4

Evie watched the first golden rays turn the fields into rivers of fluffy wheat and green oceans of sorghum and corn. Chickens clucked to fill their lay boxes, the dairy cow lowed to the rising dawn and Evie realised her time at the Double E had to be cut short. She made her bed, the crisp linen folded evenly against the haphazard and roughhewn frame of the handmade structure. Evie trailed her fingertips along the planed edges, not a shadow of a splinter to be found. She needed Hamerton to make an offer and return to New Orleans as soon as she could. Eustace launched at Evie after breakfast of eggs and toast, Maybelle remaining silent as Evie sliced her bread either dangerous thin or obscenely thick.

"By all means Aunt Eustace, pay your respects. I will see to it,... later,"

Evie eyed the family plot through the kitchen window. The too fresh wooden cross sparkled in the early sunlight and Evie tore her eyes away. Her lashes blinking away any moisture that threatened.

"Have it your way, Evelyn," Eustace clucked her tongue and carried her dishes to the sink.

Maybelle's brown eyes darted from Evelyn to Eustace and back again. The clinking chink of chip ceramic roused Evie's daydreams. Like looking through a sepia mirror, Evie's selfish feelings had tainted her father's good name and the happy memories they had shared. She couldn't face him or his grave today.

Within an hour of review amongst her father's journals the tears that threatened broke. She sucked in a few sharp breaths, the dampness cool against her flushed cheeks. Evie's hands came to rest on her hips, the corset rigid and tight. A cool breeze flirted through the doorway of the study, and Evie couldn't resist. A few hours of the morning still remained so Evie took a stroll around the Ranch. She stopped by the barn and disturbed Pearl milking the dairy cow,

"She likes the corn husks, are you the one who sets them aside?"

The young girl carried the milk pale straight passed Evie with a word.

Evie sighed, her shoulders suddenly too heavy for the brilliant day that had arrived. Evie kicked her skirts along the ground, careful to avoid the thistles and diverts that loomed in the house yard. Around the side of the homestead, the old horse stables had been expanded. Instead of the small three bay wooden shacks that Evie remembered, a huge newly built structure stood in its wake. Evie walked closer and caught sight of Hamerton ducking in and out of the fenced off area that had been added to the side. Perhaps this is where Earl's money had gone?

Evie froze. Could she face him again? If only she managed to sneak inside and take a peak without Hamerton seeing her. Evie snatched at an innocent grass strand and twirled it between her fingers. Hamerton walked in and out of sight again, his face turned away from Evie. He seemed preoccupied. Evie found herself pushing the doors aside and tiptoeing into a wide alley of multiple bays. One side filled with six or more fillies. She caught sight of Hamerton outside, guiding a Stallion into the fenced area. At the sound of his return, she hid amongst the saddles hanging at the end.

Hamerton opened the bay of a beautiful palomino filly and lead her out to the stallion. Evie didn't have to wait long before he entered her vision again. He stood with his back towards her, resting one of his black boots on the lowest beam. Evie didn't have to guess as to what was happening between the filly and the stallion because Cade's wicked smile gave it away. He stripped off his leather vest and rolled his sleeves up over his coiled forearms before mucking out the stalls one by one. Hamerton whistled some tune or ditties she hadn't heard before and Evie decided it was time to move.

As her hand reached the door, the whistling abruptly stopped. She retracted her hand, straightened her skirts before turning around,

"I came to make a deal."

"A deal?"

The shovel rested idle against Hamerton's inner thigh. Evie blinked away the image of how tight the fabric clung there and concentrated on his eyes. Pools of deep sapphire blue reflected the image of frightened little girl and Evie straightened her back. Suddenly the stallion gave a snort and Evie stared as the two horses nibbled each other's necks in post coital satisfaction.

"A *monetary* deal," Her voice boomed louder than intended.

Cade smirked, "Go on,"

A broom whisked away the finer stranglers of straw and Evie watched the ropes of muscles bunch and ripple under his sweat stained cotton shirt.

"I understand that you have built a life out of the Double E, a life I would not be able to build for myself," She decided honey would gather more flies than vinegar, "I have come to offer you my share of the inheritance for your purchase."

"Your share?"

The broom shelved as Hamerton neared, dusting muck from his hands as he walked.

"For a fair price."

"And what's a fair price, Darling?"

A curl of his russet coloured hair fell forward across his brow and a fleeting urge to smooth it out of the way riled Evie's composure.

"Well how many ladies has,... um.... has Jorge....seen to?"

The sassy know it all girl Evie portrayed in New Orleans hadn't the nerve to discuss these issues with a man like Cade. Thank goodness the stallion had cooled his amorous behaviour.

"Ladies? Seen to?" Cade's lips kicked up at the corner, dimples rent the sundrenched skin, making his teeth all the whiter, "Well I won't know that for sure until the calving takes place, and some will drop within days of each other and some within weeks. Then the calves have to been weaned before they are worth anything. Some calves won't survive. Then the weaners have to be driven up the trail and some won't survive that. So how do you put a figure on maybes?"

Evie saw his point. She would have to do her homework. Right now she was falling behind in the knowledge stakes. How many heifers did he have, when would they calve, what's a weaner?

"Well, I will be making the same offer to Richard Kline tomorrow."

"Kline?" Hamerton shoulder's straightened his dark brows flat.

"Yes, he's the closest neighbour, it make sense."

"Business sense?" Sapphire pools revolved into icy pits, "Kline has no business with the Double E."

"Well that's no concern of mine, if Kline is willing to pay the right price; he *will be* doing business with the Double E and yourself."

Cade suddenly dominated Evie's field of vision, his lips once full now thinned to pale lines, his nose, once or twice broken, exhaled in long slow breaths. A wave of coloured flushed into Evie's cheeks, she swallowed, flavours of juniper, wood smoke and moss danced across her palette.

"Your father wouldn't let it happen, you can't...."

Evie felt the heat infuse into her blood, "Well Hamerton, I'll allow you first option, first thing Monday morning. After that Kline will have my full attention," Evie wound her skirts around her fingers and strode to the door,

"Be careful what you wish for, Darling."

The stable doors slammed as Evie's footfalls ate the distance to the homestead. She wished for New Orleans bustles, strings of haphazard jazz, the throng of culture and wealth that impressed and awed from every angle. Myers, don't forget Myers, Evie. Time ticked with wedding bell chasers that caroused and seduced, and a dilapidated homestead with a few chickens and unborn stock would not land Evie, the shipping magnate.

Hamerton took dinner to his room that night and the following morning, Maybelle stood fortified in the kitchen, the small Pearl dashing out from under foot with a royal scowl across her stunning features. A faded scar run from cheekbone to hairline, deepened with the girls determined frown.

"Cade left at first light. Set a fire under that boy, you did Ms Lockwood."

Eustace mumbled into her breakfast of pancakes and bacon, and Evie pushed the pieces around her plate. Whatever money he

26

had skimmed from father would be used to pay out Evie. A bitter taste clung to the back of Evie's throat.

"Today is Sunday Miss, if you aint going to eat it, don't make the rest of us late. The Lord is waiting, Ms Lockwood."

Sunday? Church in Dew Springs. Evie carried her plate to the sink, a playful cowpoke hound stoically sat at rear door, grey tail wagging at great speed as Evie approached. The moment the bacon strap left Evie's plate the house erupted in bellows and huffs,

"What did you do that for? That good for nothing animal hasn't been taught any manners yet. Pearl, if that pup finds his way back here again, you tell him, he'll be facing my wrath. You hear me Pearl?"

The girl had vanished and Evie washed her plate, biting her tongue as Maybelle peered out the rear door, towel across her shoulder, hands on hips. Pearl resurfaced just as the wagons left the Double E for the arduous trip to town. It was here amongst the other patrons that Evie caught a moment to speak with Kline. He took one look at Evie in her bright blue satin dress and matching bonnet and whistled loudly.

"Why Evie-Lyn you look very much the Lady today." His eyes ran over her slowly taking particular interest in her décolletage.

How could she forget this dress sat tighter around her bosom than any of her others? Evie had wanted to make a favourable impression on the man, served her right if she had far exceeded her own expectations. Hamerton arrived at the back of the freshly built Church just in time for the sermon to start. Evie took it in her stride that he examined her physique with the same masculine hunger as Kline. Today her dress matched the exact shade of his eyes, venomous cerulean.

"Thank you Mr Kline,"

"Rick, please call me Rick, now what can I do for the Lady today."

He held out an elbow and she graciously took it, refusing to look at the last row of pews.

Cade Hamerton took his seat at the back and heard not one word of the Preacher's sermon that morning. Every fibre of his being focused on the woman in blue and the man he hated. Evelyn Lockwood had suddenly become the biggest burr in his side. Cade took it as a sign of Evie's fast paced city efficiency that she had accomplished to annoy him in just two days.

Kline. There is no way Cade could come up with enough cash to bid higher than Kline. He had till Monday. Hamerton had been financially depleted after buying out the loan; he would have to sell some horses. Damn her! He had sacrificed enough for the ranch. For Earl. For her.

Bethany Sampson slid into the pew beside him.

"Howdy, Cade you never replied to my letters. I was wondering what happened."

The chirpy and voluptuous brunette planted a hand on his upper thigh, sending sparks to his groin. More disturbing that her forthright nature, in church to say the least, had been Cade's inability to turn away from the sight of Evelyn. It was her image, her vivacious jade eyes, pert mouth and her hand on his thigh he had been thinking about. He sighed, and leaned close to the butcher's daughter, whispering in her ear,

"I have told you before Bethany, that my intentions were not honest, and nor were yours."

How he regretted one roll in the hay with this cheerful, yet vapid woman. Bethany Sampson had her appeal for fun, and he had not been the first and definitely not the last, yet for some reason since Earl had passed away, Bethany had set her sights on him. He knew that their next encounter, that he tried so hard to avoid, would land a trip down this very aisle quicker than her daddy could sharpen his knives.

For now, she wrote little love notes for him, describing in detail, what she wanted to do to him and how and when. Her creative writing had made even him blush at times, however as soon as he had caught sight of the peaches and cream of Evelyn Lockwood he had lost all taste for Bethany.

"But honey pie, don't you read them."

"I do and I think you need to redirect your talents elsewhere."

People's eyes were still locked on Evelyn and Kline at the front. Her stately Aunt Eustace sat on the other side nodding politely to condolences for her brother, for a moment Hamerton caught her eye. For reasons unknown to Cade, he tried to look as innocent as possible with Bethany.

"I will tell my Daddy what we did, sweetie."

Something snapped inside Cade.

"Do that honey pie, and I'll send all those letters you wrote me, and Taylor, and Shelly and Marcus to your father"

Her kitten mouth began to pout and then sulk before thinning out to a panicky grimace, "Well you have a good day won't you pumpkin,"

"And to you too, Bethany."

No one threatened Cade Hamerton.

Bethany swirled away in a ruffle of pink layers and Cade relaxed, trying to focus again on the blue dress to the far left of the room. His daydreaming ended when he thought back to her frigid conversation about Jorge and breeding. Despite her heavy lidded gazes and sultry pouts, Evelyn Lockwood was pure and virginal as the day she was born, he would bet on it. He should give up now, he wanted to bed her not wed her. Cade admonished himself for his sinful thoughts. Earl had raised him since he was 9 years old. Cade remembered Evie as a little blonde cherub causing trouble and always covered in dirt. It was hard to imagine the woman she had grown into. She had none of Earl's compassion, generosity or kindness. It would have helped if she had his crooked nose, flat face and hunching shoulders. The man had been the best father a kid could have hoped for. Well any father was an improvement on the one God had given him.

Levi Hamerton had been a poor excuse for a man, let alone a father. All of Dew Springs knew it, all of them regarded the apple had not fallen too far from the tree. He had never had to enforce one of his threats, the townsfolk, took it as a given that he would if he was pushed. He could thank Levi Hamerton for that temper. Yet it had been a lonely life. Until Earl had taken him in. He had regaled him with the stories, shared his cattleman's knowledge and taught him respect. He had let Cade make his own decisions, celebrating his victories and picking up after the fails. He had supported Cade when he bought his first breed stallion. He had agreed to rebuild the stables; he had even fronted up the capital, which Cade had paid back with the sale of his first geldings.

Cade had been there working hard on the ranch during the day and at the dinner table every night with Earl and Maybelle and eventually Pearl when she came along. It had felt like family. Damn the man for dying on him. Earl had talked about Evelyn on and off, most frequently after returning to the ranch from the Christmas visits. He loved her, definitely, yet there remained an unspoken failure in Earl with Evelyn. The closest Cade got to the truth had been one night after a few whiskeys. They had been sitting on the front porch listening to the evening crickets. Earl had suddenly started talking about New Orleans and all it had to offer Evelyn. Cade had filled in the blanks for himself.

Why then, did the man have to leave her the stock of the Angus Breed, or the homestead for that matter? Did he think he could try and coax her back, or did he trust in her business sense to sell it for a profit? Would it give her enough money for a proper income in the city? Maybe Cade was supposed to manage it and send her back to New Orleans.

Either way, while Cade had spent the entire sermon pondering Evelyn, she had spent her time more wisely. Rick the Tick, threw a crooked grin over his shoulder at Cade. Cade met his eyes and refused to waiver.

Chapter 5

Monday rolled around with dark grey thunder clouds threatening on the horizon. Evelyn had set the time for the meeting at midday, giving Hamerton time to get his finances sorted early. Aunt Eustace had demanded to accompany him for the ride to Dew Springs, no doubt another love letter needed to be sent to Jeffrey Willington Senior. Evelyn had the ranch to herself this morning and decided that her time would be best spent reading over the journals of last season, calculating the cost and profit of last year's sales. She would not be caught unprepared this time.

Nearing midday, Evie heard the front screen door bang open and rose to greet her Aunt storming inside with Hamerton not far behind.

"Evie," She barked and turned Evelyn by the elbow up the stairs and only spoke again once the bedroom door was shut, "I've had a letter from New Orleans," Her aunt started snatching at her belongings and tossing them into her suitcase,

"Aunt, whatever is the matter,…"

Her aunt paced backwards and forwards on the timber floor, the skirts of her ruby dress, ebbed and flowed as she passed,

"I can't believe it, the government…. The damn railway…. Jeffrey might not make it through with his heart as it is…."

Evelyn had to slam shut the suitcase to get Eustace's attention. Her Aunt handed her a hastily scrawled letter, signed and stamped by Willington. Her aunts words all came out in rush. So much so, that Evie had to hear it twice before she grasped the enormity of the situation.

"The money, Evie darling, Jay Cooke and Company is bust, half of the companies in New York have followed suit, the stock market stopped trading. New Orleans is next, some of the banks have foreclosed, there have been riots in the streets…..," tiny strands of silver wisped free of her bouffant adding to desperation in her voice, "I have to go back."

Evelyn got up like a firecracker had set her into motion, "So must I."

"No!" Eustace shouted, "Evie, Jay and Cooke is bust, it's gone, bankrupt. All the money.... all *your* money."

Evelyn's face went numb and a shiver of cold ran down her spine. Evelyn didn't even realise she had been screaming until Eustace slapped her face.

"All of it?"

"All of it, gone, except this," Eustace gestured to the ceiling and walls.

"Oh heavens!"

Gravity turned her stomach upside down and Evelyn had to lie down. The farmhouse and the unborn cattle and Jorge was the grand sum total of her fortune. And the damn chickens! How would she return to New Orleans, how would she marry Myers, how would she survive?

"No, I can't let you go by yourself," Evie tried to rise off the coverlet and almost lost her breakfast.

"You have to stay, you can't sell it and Hamerton's not going to work it for you and send you money either."

Aunt Eustace finished her frantic packing and kissed Evelyn on the head,

"Goodbye my darling."

"You're leaving now?"

"I have to Dear, the last Stage leaves this afternoon, and I've already bought my ticket. Don't worry I'll sort something out and send for you when the situation calms. This is all the money I have," Eustace handed her a wad of rolled up bank notes "Keep it safe."

"How am I...?"

Evie didn't get to finish the question as Eustace dashed out of the room.

"Stay strong my love," echoed down the stairs before the screen door slammed shut.

The shadows of noon and afternoon slid across the timber slat floor echoing Evie's mood. All her money gone, all her hopes, possibilities and dreams. She had counted on the dividends to double her fortune, not the opposite. The stock market stopped trading, what was happening? Hopefully Aunt Eustace would pull through, her latest Beau was quite wealthy, wasn't he? What of Myers, if the railroads had collapsed and "others followed suit" Myers would be taking losses too. Would he still want her, now that she was broke? She would be stuck out here in Texas, fighting the land and starving like her mother did. She read and reread Willington's' letter but the words never changed. At some point during the day, Evie heard Maybelle dismiss Kline with her no nonsense way of talking.

As the sun set, Evelyn had to dash away tears when she heard the stairs creak.

"Evelyn," Hamerton's gruff voice whispered through the door.

She couldn't stomach sitting up, how could she face him. She didn't have a choice as he opened the door and stepped in to crowd her pokey little room.

"You're Aunt got on the Stage alright."

Evie managed to hum in response.

"She told me you received some bad news."

Bad? The worst! Evelyn felt the edge of her bed dip with his weight.

"She also told me that you've changed your mind on selling for now."

"Yes." The word slipped out straining to escape her tight throat.

The last thing she wanted to do was talk about it, especially with Hamerton. The next minute Cade had scooped her up under the arms and into his embrace. As his strength flowed into her body, she felt a release of pressure. A flood of tears exploded and Evie sobbed into his wide solid chest. His clothes smelt of sweet moss and sage, fresh, wooded and safe.

"I'm sorry for your loss. So soon after your father."

Where did this empathy come from, Cade being so gentle and considerate with her? Evelyn expected a callous disregard or a pouncing on weakened prey. If he had offered her $1000 she might take it and be done with Texas. Yet this tiny sliver of cash flow was her last hope.

"Thank you, it's so sudden...."

"Most of the time it is,"

His deep timbre lulled her ears and she kept talking.

"It's unheard of, the stock market closed and all."

"I'm sorry," he pushed her back to arms' length.

Evie ungracefully wiped her tear stained cheeks, "The banks have foreclosed and who knows how the property market will be affected...."

"Begging your pardon, Evelyn...." His eyes narrowed.

Evie spluttered and sniffled onwards, "The money, the railroads, it's all gone. Didn't she tell you... my money...?" Her trailing words started a new wave of tears.

"No,"

Evelyn controlled her breathing with slow long breaths instead of desperate little gasps. Astonished Cade rose from the bed,

"This is about money?" His lips pulled back as his eyes brows arched.

"Yes," her last word peeped out.

Cade shook his head, "No one is dead?"

"No....no." Her voice returned and brought with it a rush of anger, "This stock market...." Exasperated at the look of bewilderment Hamerton threw her, she went on the attack, "Of course, what would you know?"

"What would I know?" Cade's jaw tightened and fists clenched. Waves of tension coiled up his meaty forearms, "Me?"

"Yeah you, the cowboy turned Ranch Owner. What would you understand?"

Cade's face fell flat, "I wonder, did you shed this many tears for your father?"

Something snapped. Loud, sharp and deliberate. Evelyn was screaming and without taking breath, she had the first tantrum, proper tantrum she had thrown since she was six. She heard herself screaming the words "Get out!" followed by picking up anything around her and throwing it at Cade. In disbelief, she watched the last item, her silver hand mirror smash against the closing door.

Cade tugged on his boots with extra effort and itched to be away from the homestead.

"Are you okay?"

Cade jerked his head up to catch sight of Pearl creeping around the porch to sit with him,

"Yeah, I'm fine,"

The heat fading from his tone as diminutive girl-child sat beside him.

"Did she just throw a hissy-fit?"

"Yes she did," Hamerton laughed.

Pearl's expression turned serious, "Was she awful to you?"

"No. Not exactly."

He pondered Evelyn's outburst and how cutting her words were. Money, money, money that's all she cares about.

"Well she shouldn't have come back here."

He sighed and turned to face the sweet Fourteen, no, time had cheated Cade another year, Pearl had turned Fifteen already. He flicked a lock of her straight black hair behind one ear exposing the scar to her jawline. A heavy weight sunk in his stomach whenever his eyes fell upon the mark.

"She's just different."

"I can see that with her flashy dresses and fancy shoes. She shouldn't be here."

Cade had inadvertently hit upon Pearls jealousy, "Don't you want pretty dresses like that some day?"

"No, I couldn't bear to think about all the people looking at me like they look at her."

Cade's heart warmed, "Don't ever change Pearl!"

She beamed back at his praise. Cade wondered if Pearl would every really fit in, with her mixed ancestry, that scar and his name.

"And by the way, the grand hissy fitting duchess Miss Evelyn Lockwood is staying on for now, so maybe stay out of her way for a bit."

That's exactly what Hamerton intended. Pearl giggled and threw her arms around his shoulder,

"Well if she is ever really horrible to you, you come and tell me and I'll sort her out."

"I can take care of myself, Pearl, don't you worry about that little lady."

"But you look after us, so I'll look after you."

Just like Earl, they relied on him and he relished it. He had his family right here.

"Ok, now off to bed before Maybelle starts hollering at me. I don't want her to stop making me those apple pies."

Tuesday morning greeted Evie with the noise of Hamerton lumbering around in his room. Each creaky floorboard seemed a deliberate attempt to annoy her. Without any hope of further sleep, Evie rose and washed ready to face whatever today could throw at her, including Hamerton. Plans had formulated overnight and Evie stole into her father's room for the first time since returning. She sat on the mismatched patchwork quilt, familiar odours of leather and sweet pepper dashed shivers across her skin. The bedside drawer loitered on four thin lopsided legs, tiny wooden figurines balanced daintily on its surface. She turned them over one by one, a horse, a cow, a wild cat, an eagle. Earl had brought one with him every visit to New Orleans, the last carving an elegant doe. Evie replaced the little statues and stole the cupboard. Guilt wormed through her gut, impending doom pendulum-like above her head. Nonetheless, she couldn't shirk away from what needed to be done.

Evie found a pair of well-worn denims, a blue checked shirt and her father's second oldest pair of boots before returning to the safety of her own room. The boots fit snuggly enough with only one extra pair of socks needed, the shirt tightened modestly across her front but the denims were another problem entirely. Her father had been bow legged and slender. Evie's bottom seemed to swell and stretch the tired fabric into indecency. She rolled the top which only compounded the issue. She could hear Hamerton heading to the stables, with a long inhale of breath, Evie settled the worms. Her hastened strides slipped on the wet dew, uncertainty dogging her heels as she marched out to meet the hangman.

By the time she reached the stables, Hamerton's hulking shadow could be seen sharing a morning coffee with the cowhands. The darkened shoulders moved out of sight, returning between the barn door gaps, the lantern light highlighting Hamerton's regal blue eyes that snaked across her body. He gathered a saddle blanket and disappeared from view.

A lump caught in Evie's throat. Pride was a disastrously bitter meal to swallow.

"I figured," Evie began as she pressed on the heavy wooden doors, "That I should take a look at this stock of mine."

"Of yours? Darling your stock ain't even born yet," Hamerton shouted over his shoulder.

Three, no four, brown faces turned to watch Evie as she followed Hamerton's large strides, to the second stall, a huge tawny Stallion waited, ears twitching, heavy lashes fluttered. Hamerton threw the blanket over a railing and Evie held her tongue until he returned a well-worn and sturdy saddle in his arms.

"Look, I know I owe you an apology, but if I'm going to make this work, I will need to inspect the cows, your cows."

Hamerton tossed the saddle over the Bay's back with ease, muscles bunched and rolled under the starched fabric. The horse nuzzled Cade's back pocket, generously filled and curved around his masculine frame. Evie followed Cade into the horse's bay,

"I was upset yesterday,"

Cade snorted and closed the strap into buckle,

"You have to understand what those events meant to someone like me." The energy in the stall bristled and Evie sighed, "I mean to say that my life in New Orleans is heavily dependent on money, securing my financial future with whomever,…"

A brief image of Lewis Myers formed before Evie's eyes until she realised Cade had stopped his fussing. He stood beside the horses' hind leg, one arm resting on its rump. The horse shifted on its feet closing the distance between Evie and Cade,

"I cannot rely on Aunt Eustace all of my life and no man in his… without …"

Cade seemed to swell in her vision and the stall suddenly became too small for all three of them. Her boot collided with the stall gate and she snatched at a strand of straw, twirling the twig between her fingers, concentrating intensely as her finger nail split the strand,

"What I mean to say is, when my last investment crashed so did any hope of a successful future for me. I didn't mean to take that out on you and I apologise."

Evie met his gaze, pitch black pupils swimming in indigo.

"That's has to be the worst apology I've ever heard."

Evie clicked her tongue, her heel disturbing a mound of straw as she drove it into the ground. The Stallion's neck raised, his ears twitched from side to side, pools of ebony widely regarding Evie, then Cade as if to evict the huffy female from his stall. Cade ran his long fingers up the animal's slender neck, scratching behind the ear. Evie selected another straw hostage,

"So?"

"So what?"

"You know what I mean Hamerton; you're riding out this morning so I'll come with you."

"What are you riding out on, Darling, hopes and dreams?"

Like a wildfire, heat surged through her veins,

"I'll take the roan over there then,"

"Ha!" Cade barked, "The roan, is my prize breeding mare and she's in foal. Dawnee is staying and so are you."

Cade tugged the stirrups. Evie swallowed hard, she hadn't counted on Hamerton refusing to let her go? *Nonsense, he can't tell me what to do!* She had apologised! Wait, Hamerton hadn't returned the gesture! Evie's jaw fell open, an argument ready to launch. She needed his help more than an apology. Evie ground her back teeth.

"What?"

"No," Hamerton ducked under the Stallion's chest to the other side.

"You can't refuse me!"

"Oh yes I can."

The stall gate banged and the Stallion pushed past, Evie isolated in the corner. Within moments, Cade had led the animal outside. Evie scrambled to follow; the remaining occupants snorted and whinnied, either in approval of Cade or mock support of Evie. The dawn broke over Hamerton's straight back and wide shoulders settling into the saddle. A sharp whistle split the frosty morning air as hooves beat down Evie's hope of cooperation.

Chapter 6

Hamerton let Maverick pick the pace through the house yards until they reached the open fields, then he let the majestic Bay stretch out, leaving the two Ranch hands trailing in his wake. The earthy odour of fresh trampled dew washed away any lingering scent of apricot and amber that thickened Hamerton's throat and tightened his denims. Evelyn Lockwood would be the largest liability ever to set foot on the Double E. Inspecting her stock? Hamerton half expected another tantrum, the blonde duchesses deep emerald eyes ablaze in the small morning light. Hamerton stretched his thighs, his hand on the saddle horn, and let the fresh Texas morning cool his temper. Evelyn could manage her shares and stocks or spend all day reviewing Earl's journals and counting beans, but out here, Cade had the world at his feet.

The broad southern sky paled as the sun rose, the harsh landscape softened with flecks of tangerine, saffron, ochre and jade, wildlife stirred in the underbrush or bedding down for the day. Cade inhaled deep, letting the flavours soak into his blood. Depending on the herd and the weather, he'd spend a night at the shack, before returning. A brief respite from Evie's self-centred sulking. If he'd let her join them this morning, he'd have to saddle her mount, listen to her whine about glorious New Orleans and watch every move she made so she didn't break her neck.

Evelyn Lockwood had lost her fortune and now had to slop about in backwater Dew Springs until she could sell her family home. Had she even grieved for her father? The stately Eustace had been keen to see Earl's final resting place yet Evie had pretended the fresh cross and barely settled earth been invisible. Cade resumed his seat in the saddle, his legs suddenly tired,

39

shoulder's heavy. He set his eyes on the escarpment to the south east, the mottled ruby and russet sliced with aqua and orange.

With Earls' death, Cade suddenly found himself knee deep in debt with a thousand plus acres of responsibility to manage. Most of the hands had been loyal to the Double E since Cade had been a boy, Earl had earned their respect and Cade had kept it. What Cade didn't have was a cash flow. If Evie had decided to stay, it bought Cade some time. With all her fussing and huffing, Evie would give up eventually. She'd spoken of the heat, the dust, the hunger; her memories of the Double E were not fond. Perhaps after a week of sweaty grime and manure, Evie would be begging Hamerton to buy the homestead. So long as it wasn't Rick the Tick. He needed more time.

Evie twirled the straw between her fingers. Four hands had ridden out with Cade. Two remained. Tomorrow, when Cade sauntered out to the stable, she'd be ready. The final two hands shuffled through the stalls, heavy lines decorated the dark circles under the eyes. Both dipped their hats in greeting, as Evie tiptoed forward.

One hand lifted his head as she approached, the silver mare's lashes blinked over black wet marbles and Evie's cheeks split into a grin.

"She's beautiful," Evie started.

"Ella es Hermosa," The older man said as he ran thick brown hands down the snowy foreleg.

"Ella es Hermosa?" Evie repeated.

The soft words whistled through chipped teeth, "Si Senorita,"

The mare snorted, her muzzle pressing against Evie's fingers, she stroked the flat long nose and inhaled.

"I'm Evie, and I need your help,"

Evie explained as only she could to Fernandez whose broken English was almost as bad as Evie's Spanish. Bit by bit the process unfolded. Fernandez shook his head and tugged the blanket up to the mare's withers. He coughed into his fist when Evie chose a child's saddle and rolled his eyes when she finally lugged the adult tack into the stall and sat it on the straw. He promptly scooped it up and waited till Evie's forearms stopped burning.

"Okay" She inhaled, stepping closer to the mare. She leaned back on her hips, the leather straps crumpled against her chest, "Nearly," she moaned. The mare retracted her neck her hooves stomping in the rear corner.

"Smooth," Fernandez smirked around his straw,

"You wait," Evie narrowed her eyes and puckered her lips.

Fernandez threw his hands in the air, eyebrows arched. When the saddle finally landed on the animal, Fernandez approached, tugging and wiggling until the saddle and blanket settled gently and evenly. He handed her a long thick strap with twin buckles at either end. He stole the straw from his cheek and pointed to the mare's belly. Fernandez held his round face in his hands as Evie walked up and down, the folds of the leather failing to reveal how and where this extra piece attached.

"I give up!" Evie said as she crossed her arms over her chest.

"Never give up, Senorita,"

Fernandez pulled down the girth strap buckles and with a string of Spanish instructions, Evie had it tied and latched to the even longer strap on the other side. Together they tightened the tack until it sat snug. Fernandez handed Evie the chest strap and she edged between the stall door and the horse, with the Vaquero's soft encouragement she had all buckles, clips and straps done. Fernandez clapped and nodded, grabbing his tobacco pouch to celebrate. Evie's hands came to rest on her hips, the mare's flat nose pressed against her shoulder.

"What's her name?"

"Nieve,"

"Nieve?" Evie repeated.

His fingers fluttered from above and he rubbed his shivering shoulders, "Nieve,"

"Rain?"

"No, no, Nieve" he repeated again.

Evie's finger tips trailed over the pristine coat of the mare, "Snow,"

Fernandez nodded wildly.

"Good. Shall we try again?" Evie said.

As the sun reached its zenith, Evie said farewell to the dainty little horse and promised Fernandez a tray of biscuits and an extra day off. She'd have to run that by Cade, but the biscuits she could handle. As she crossed to the homestead a thin trail of dust arose behind a single rider. A stocky Piebald trotted into the house yard, carrying the crisp gingham of Richard Kline.

"Do my eyes deceive me or is that Miss Evie-lyn?"

Evie's palms went to her hips like magnets, "Mr Kline,"

"Please call me Rick,"

"Rick," Evie answered

"It's going to take me a while to get used to the sight of you in those denim's Evie-lyn."

Rick's thumb tucked into his belt, with a flick of his knuckles sent the brim of his pale Stetson skyward. Evie rubbed her elbow, her shoulders hunched.

"What can I do for you Rick?" she said as she took the steps two at a time.

"Well, where's that southern hospitality Evie-lyn," Rick's boots thundered on the slats, "Don't you offer a man a drink when he's thirsty,"

Evie spun on her heels as Rick's almond gaze ran from head to toe and back again.

"Of course, make yourself comfortable," Evie said as she let the screen door slam.

"Whose it come to visit?" Maybelle piped up from the kitchen, her arms filled with yesterday's laundry.

"Mr Richard Kline is thirsty," Evie said.

"Rick the…" Maybelle placed the basket down, "Back again? You go out there girl, I'll bring something refreshments, off you go."

Maybelle's sturdy fingers twisted Evie's shoulders until she had no option but to march back out. Should she take a moment to freshen up? She tugged the shirt forward and stared at the grime covered checks and dusty boots. Her thighs coated in smears of dubbin and dirt. Evie decided against it and found herself facing Rick on the porch. He'd sat down in the single chair, boots on her father's footrest and all.

Evie snapped, heat suddenly bristled under her collar, "What do you want Rick?"

"I'll be honest with you Evie-lyn, I want the Double E. I'm a business man at heart and what I've seen, how this ranch has been run, well I won't speak ill of the dead…."

Evie's fists curled around the arm rests, splinters pricking her palm.

"I have a reputation for success and high profits. While my operation expands this Ranch has suffered, the stock, the Angus risks, Cade's damn horses, pardon my language, but the Double E stands in prime cattle land with bountiful pastures and a reliable water source that's being wasted on half breeds and fillies. Buying out the Double E is good business sense, an educated woman such as yourself couldn't argue with that."

Evie listened to the steady beats of her heart, Earl had made poor decisions and it had led to the brokering of his Ranch. How much of that had been influenced by Cade?

"I see."

"So with that in mind, Evie-lyn, I came to make my offer. I've heard you suffered unforeseen losses back in New Orleans."

The damn town gossips! "Unforeseen, but nonetheless I will recover," The words slammed into Evie's chest. Yes you will recover, you will thrive again. A thought lingered at the back of her mind, sending a pressure into her ribs. She pushed it away. A squeak drove rusted nails into Evie's spine as Maybelle arrival interrupted his bid. The tangy lemonade sizzled on Evie's tongue, the tart taste twisting her temper even more so. "What's your offer?"

"The homestead, the first calves and the Angus Breed, including the Bull."

Evie sipped again, "My apologies for disappointing you Mr Kline, but due to my unforeseen circumstances, I have decided to retain the homestead and my share of the Angus Breed, for now."

Rick leaned forward, his elbows on his knees, "Really."

Something about his tone made Evie's shoulders straighten, "Yes,"

"I figured you'd be tucking tail and returning to New Orleans than stay on here, with Hamerton and all his ……"

"All my what, Rick?"

The glass slipped from Evie's trembling fingers and landed on her thigh.

For reasons unknown to Cade, the herd had decided to graze within a two hour ride of the homestead, so they'd taken a break in the shade of grove of acacia trees. No calves on the ground as yet and no heifers missing or injured, so they'd set off for the Double E. Cade had recognised Rick the Tick's patchwork ride from a mile away and hadn't wasted any time unsaddling Maverick. Clearly the town's gossip had signalled the vultures. Cade had eavesdropped enough, when he finally spoke, Evie had jumped in her skin as Rick took his time getting to his feet.

"And here he is, the heir,"

Cade's gaze targeted Evie's lengthening spine, he registered the tremble in her words.

"How's the stock?"

"Oh you mean *his* stock?" Rick leant against the flaked railing, "Any calves on the ground yet, I'd be interested in seeing how Earl's *mix-breed* turns out,"

Before Cade realised, he stood face to face with the carrion-eater. With enough inches to spare, Cade towered over Dew Spring's most affluent Rancher.

"Easy Hamerton," Rick's palms upright, he slithered to the side, "Evie-lyn has told me the stock's not for purchase, yet."

Evie collected both glasses, her back still obscuring her profile.

"Not yet?" Cade's back teeth almost chipped.

"Not until I'm ready Hamerton," Evie snapped.

Rick hastily stepped forward, "And I respect that Evie-Lyn. Dew Springs doesn't have much to offer a lady such as yourself, but if you'd allow me, I'd be honoured to call on you again."

Evie just nodded.

"It's been a pleasure talking business with you Evie-Lyn," Rick tipped his brim, "And if you ever need a hand, I'm only a short call away. Good day,"

Evelyn turned on her heel and entered the homestead.

Cade advanced, "What are you playing at Rick? What are you going to do with an acre of land and a few calves?"

Rick tugged down his brim, the second day's growth shadowed his narrow chin, and his shirt reeked of three day old perfume. What Cade wouldn't pay to smack that smirk off Richard Kline's twisted lips.

"An acre and then some," Rick added.

Evie's footsteps could be heard pacing in the kitchen, for some reason she hollered for flour.

Cade pumped his fists together, "Suddenly the Double E is not all you want?"

"I didn't say that,"

"Bull shit."

Rick stepped down to the front yard, "I will have this ranch, Hamerton, piece by piece if I have to."

Cade's boots kept marching until Rick hastily climbed onto his ride, "You're planning on wedding Evie for her share? That's not going to happen," Cade's hand rested on the Piebald's reins.

"Oh Cade, I never said she's a long term investment, but I will have the Double E, starting with her share."

Cade let out a shallow chuckle, he'd seen Evie's rigid spine.

"You're not going to be able to *coax* anything out of Evelyn Lockwood,"

"Wanna bet on that?"

Rick tugged on his reins, the leather steadfast in Cade's grip. For a moment Cade considered Rick's proposition. He intended on bedding Evie or close to gain an acre and Jorge and the rest of the Angus Breed. Even with that narrow margin, Rick the Tick would hold on, sucking the life out of the Double E until he had it all.

Rick licked his lips, "I will have her share, one way or another."

"One way or another?" Cade murmured and released the leather.

Evie had enlisted Maybelle's help to drudge up an old cookbook, but that was as far as the matron would go. Cade entered the kitchen, a ring of his russet hair pressed neatly to his scalp like a soiled halo. Whatever had exchanged between Rick and Cade had been two boys fighting over old history; Evie had no interest in the subject of their contest, but more importantly how it could help her. Cade sheepishly ran his hand through his hair, the resulting tussles adding waves to his thick crown. Richard Kline had referred to Cade as the Heir, and rightly so.

Here he stood in her home, her kitchen with her inheritance and he dared to tell her what to do?

"You can't sell to Kline."

"I can do what I like with my share." Evie rolled her eyes and let her palms come slowly to rest on either side of her batter. You will need his help Evie! She cracked two eggs into the bowl and swallowed hard, "But not now, besides how is the stock, how are your ladies?" Evie cleared her throat.

"No calves, no injuries."

"That's good to know," Evie whisked the ingredients into a frenzy, "You'll need to give Fernandez an extra day off."

The bowl clattered across the bench as strong hands spun Evie about face. Cade filled Evie's field of vision, his dark brows knitted.

"Is he hurt? What happened?"

Evie let the fresh moss and well-oiled leather scent wash over her as she dropped her gaze to either hand that held her shoulders.

"He's fine."

Cade released his grip, "Is it his family?"

"No,"

"Then why?"

Cade's shy freckles crystalized in Evie's view, which mitigated Cade's rough edges. What could she tell him that wouldn't ruin her plans? Normally Evie would bat her eyelashes and add a coy smile, but something warned Evie, that empty promises and half-truths would be dangerous with a man like Hamerton.

"Because I told him, he could."

She put the tray of biscuits into the oven, the jam centres melting as she closed the door.

"That's not a good enough reason," Cade said, his tone softened.

She threw the bowl into the sink, "We'll you know as well as I do, that I don't have anything to bargain with Mr Hamerton,"

"You have plenty,"

Evie's heels squeaked. Cade's traced the back of the wooden spoon with his thumb, collecting the batter from the instrument, drawing his thump upwards to white teeth that nipped and full lips that squeaked. Tiny hairs across Evie's nape and forearms raised and she held his sapphire gaze.

"I'm not trading my share – "

"I was thinking something a little sweeter," Cade said with narrow eyes.

He drove his thumb through the creamy batter again. Evie watched his thumb roll inwards to his lips that snared the tiny delight. Cade's chest expanded in his dusty shirt, narrow hips supported by the bench, and thick thighs at recline. Evie's ribs compressed, her shirt suddenly too tight, flashes of colour blossomed on her cheeks.

A sharp smack brought Evie around to the back door, the screen retreated and the cowpoke puppy skidded inside followed closely by Pearl.

"Silly Chitto," Pearl scolded, without heat.

She eyed Cade, a bright smile and eyes like fireworks danced across her petite tanned face. Then Pearl turned, a thick scowl developed and even Evie's brows twitched.

"Chitto is a nice name," Evie said.

Pearl's heels thundered across the boards, Chitto's oversized paws slipping on the timber, Evie ran her hand down his sleek grey coat.

"It's Creek for Brave," Cade answered.

A door opened near the sitting room, mattress springs squeaked.

"Creek?"

"The Muskogee tribes from the Mississippi Valley," Cade said.

"Pearls' Indian?"

Cade's eyes targeted the floor, then the sink and finally Evie, "Maybe,"

"Should she take a bedroom upstairs?" Evie peered around the edge of the kitchen; she remembered her mother's small drawing room. The door firmly closed as long as Evie could remember, "It would be more comfortable?"

"She had, but moved down here to be close to Chitto,"

Evie shrugged her shoulders, Pearl was welcome to the room, her father had shut up any memory of her mother. A small warmth tickled Evie's ribs. She shook it off and closed the back door, plunging both arms elbow deep into the sink.

"Well I will trade you half a dozen biscuits for Fernandez's day off. That's my final offer."

Cade's laugh oozed down Evie's spine like melted caramel, "Deal".

Chapter 7

Evie returned from the Vaqueros huts with an empty tray and a lighter heart. Cade had conceded an extra day off for Fernandez, which had piqued the interest of the other Hands. If helping Earl's daughter could earn rewards, Evie would have less trouble next time she needed help. Maybelle had prepared a wonderful stew dinner and Evie piled an empty bowl full with left overs. She held her tongue when Pearl entered the kitchen. If Evie confused Chitto's loyalty, it would be the fastest way to loose Pearls trust. Evie made sure she held the young girls gaze when she stored the pups left overs under the sink while Maybelle's cleared the table. Cade had poured himself a coffee and retired to the porch, Evie took a deep breath. The screen alerted her presence with a shrill squeal yet Cade didn't move.

"How come you dislike Richard Kline so much?"

A steady tendril of steam disappeared slowly into the night air, a floral bouquet of evening primrose and jasmine tickled Evie's nose. Cade sipped his coffee, his boots flat on the floor. The single chair, Earl's chair, still empty.

"Old history,"

Evie clicked her tongue, one day she'd get more than a few curt words from this man; "Go on," She sat down on the top stairs, her back rested against the porch railing. She tugged a blade of grass and dug her fingernail into the middle, "I'm listening."

Cade sipped his coffee but didn't bite.

"Tell me about the Four Star Ranch?"

"What's there to tell?"

"The way Rick tells it, he's is quite profitable over there,"

"Don't believe all that you hear. They run their Hands into the ground, take huge risks with their lives and pay very little. They drive the cattle hard up the trails, harder than necessary.

When he gets his to market, what are left of his herd are nothing but skin and bones. He undercuts his competitors, because he has higher numbers and a faster turnaround. You're father's herds were never that large, we drove them straight and true, never missed a deadline, never lost a beast. In return, your father expected a higher price. Some would buy Four Star some would buy the Double E."

"He had higher profits."

"Sometimes ranching isn't all about profit."

Evie could hear the heat in his voice, but she pressed on, "The Ranch is a business. How do you run a business if there is no profit?"

"You keep reading Earl's ledgers and listening to Rick the Tick and see how far you get on the Double E."

Cade's cup tipped, the hot dark liquid splashing over the railing. He rose from the chair. A warning tickled Evie's ears, but she continued.

"My father didn't have the numbers to run the Double E like the Four Star Ranch, is that because of your horses?"

Cade halted in his tracks, the screen door ajar in his hand, veins thickened and twisted up his forearm.

"If you wanted a say in how the Double E runs, you could have come back from New Orleans any time, darling."

Evie watched the coffee drip slowly from the leaves of the weeds that sheltered near the porch, she'd picked a fight with the one person she'd need tomorrow. He was right. She couldn't harp on about decisions made between Hamerton and her father while she schemed her way through Society Balls and Chairman's dinners. Damn! She'd have to make another apology tomorrow.

Her mattress sagged and squeaked as Evie climbed in, she'd unwound her hair and finger braided it before turning in. Her silver hair brush that matched her now destroyed hand mirror had mysteriously grown legs. Never mind, there's always tomorrow Evie reminded herself.

Cade tossed from side to back and back again with the soft noises Evelyn stirred across the hall. She'd set his teeth on edge after dinner and yet his conversation with Rick the Tick had sparked the strange interaction over Evie's biscuits. Rick had been more than honest about his approach to gaining Evie's share and if she fell for his manipulations and false promises well good luck to her. A man like Rick had wealth, a good family name if not reputation and sickly charm that made woman bend to his will. Cade had ruins of ash and blood in his past, which had attracted only one type of woman. And Evie was definitely not that kind of woman. The only thing that worried Cade, if Evie bit at Rick, would be that Cade's future rested on the tastes and desires of the Duchess Evelyn Lockwood. The only thing, Cade reiterated. He faced the door again, he had to try.

As the sun whispered its first rays across the dewy grass, Evie strode into the stable. Hair tight, boots stuffed twice and the nicest smile she could manage before dawn, set on her cheeks.

"No," Hamerton barked, the softest chuckle in his tones.

Evie inhaled slowly, "Cade, yesterday you talked of ledgers and profit. You spoke as if the Ranch is more than just a source of income. Well, I'm here to learn, to see the Double E as you do. Show me and prove me wrong,"

Cade marched forward, a bridle in one hand, a rifle in the other, "No, Evie, thanks to giving Fernandez a day off, I'm already short one man,"

"Exactly, you need my help,"

Cade's head tossed back, his Adam's apple bobbed and chirped as a hearty roar escaped.

"I need your help?"

His eyes sparkled, the lantern light glistening off his blue iris's like a sunset of Lake Borgne. Evie flicking her palms down her thighs and stopped.

"Yes, that's how I see it."

"It's not safe out there; I'm not up for a day of babysitting,"

"You won't have to babysit and you said it yourself that the herd were close to home yesterday." The words twisted around her teeth, she pushed the thickening warmth away.

Cade sighed, "Fine,"

"Fine?"

"You passed the saddles on your way in. Hurry up Duchess; I'm not going to wait."

Evie set off to the saddles; she caught a round face peering at her from the far side of Nieve's stalls.

"You liked the biscuits,"

"Si Senorita," Fernandez dipped his head and pointed to the leather straps.

Evie hurried. Cade came over and Fernandez whispered a quick string of Spanish words at Cade. She recognised the word "Senorita" and Cade made a half-hearted backwards strike at the man before Fernandez left the stall, gesturing two thumbs up to Evie.

The sun had peaked over the horizon sending slashes of amber and gold over the rolling hills as the party of 5 rode out from the Double E. Cade issued some orders in Spanish and two of the Vaquero's rode off to the North while another Hand named Tomas dutifully followed Cade south-east.

Cade watched as his horses hooves stirred up colourful butterflies that took flight in the early morning sunshine. Evie had a point, he'd cast a few aspersions her way last night and it might do her good to see the Double E in all its glory. That and it kept Evie out of Rick's hands. One way or another Cade would win first option to buy Evie's share. He kept his eyes focused on the skyline surveying for his herd, with Evie safely behind him. After spying her climbing onto the white pony in those denims, Hamerton had cursed the Lord for not giving the woman the same lanky bean-pole shape of her father. Heifers. Calves. Grass.

"Beautiful, it's like an ocean," Evie murmured.

An old favourite of Earls perched on her crown, protecting that delicious peaches and cream complexion.

"See that over there," Cade pointed to the escarpment of burnished copper and aqua "Earl named it Edwina's Bluff,"

Evie's neck craned to the east, her eyes deep emerald against the bright Texan dawn, her lips thinned, she rested back in the saddle. For a city girl, she sat neat across the snowy mare's back, her hips soft, knees and hands relaxed. If he hadn't seen her in frills and lace, Cade wouldn't have believed her sophisticated upbringing. Evie's jaw twitched, her lips turned down. Cade held his tongue on what Earl had named the river that ran wild at the rear boundary.

"Tell me about New Orleans," Cade offered.

Evie's cheeks returned to full colour, her eyes scanned the foliage ahead. She chatted away about the multiple evolutions her adopted city had taken over time, including the war and Reconstruction, her life with Aunt Eustace, a place called Downtown, and the high society circles she'd mixed in until Cade heard Evie mention a name more than once.

"So this Myers is a suitor of yours?"

"Almost,"

Cade lifted the brim of his hat a touch, "Almost? How can a man – " Cade envisioned Bethany Sampson had similar ideas on how a man could almost be a suitor, "Never mind. Tell me what kind of a man could snare the Duchess Lockwood."

"Duchess Lockwood," Evie twisted in her saddle, her lips kinked to one side, "I like the sound of that," She flicked a strand of blonde hair behind her ear, "He owns a shipping company, and manufacturing warehouses in New Orleans, they've just expanded - ."

As Evie continued her rhetoric, Cade ran the reins lightly through his hands. Myers had a tornado heading his way if he ever made an honest offer for Evie's hand. Rick had no idea how short he fell of the mark.

"...And that's before he received the approval for additional warehouses."

"Well ain't he an interesting fellow,"

"Pardon?"

"I know everything about Myer's bottom line but I know nothing about the man himself."

Evie regarded her reins in her upturned palms, "But I just told you – "

"No Evie you told me about his business, his profit and loss, his future plans."

Her slender thighs twisted to face Cade, the pale mare inched closer to Maverick and the Stallion did nothing to prevent it.

"Well what did you want to know?"

"What are his strengths, his weaknesses? How does he treat his equals, his betters and his inferiors? How does the man handle pressure, how does he treat his women? You told me Evie, how you value a man, but not what makes Myer's a man, or more to the point, what make him your man, other than his bank balance."

Emerald pools narrowed to slits, Cade lightly kicked Maverick in the flanks.

At mid-morning they found the herd taking shelter in the trees beside the far bank of the river.

"Over there,"

Cade pointed to his companions and Evie gently urged Nieve forward, creeping into his view.

"Are there any calves?" Evie said as she craned her neck.

The tall grasses obscured her view, at the feet of the beasts. The whole herd milled about in close proximity to each other. Cade had been busy scanning the herd and hadn't noticed the snowy mare continue her approach. Tomas's harsh whistle shrilled and Cade envisioned a wilful Evelyn Lockwood trampled by a stampede of protective mothers.

"Hold it there,"

The dainty horse pulled up and danced on her foot locks.

"Why?"

"Just do as I say Darling and we'll both keep our necks." Damned if he could save her from a stampede.

"Don't you mean Duchess," Evie sneered.

Cade's comments had sliced through her cheery mood. The sun now had a healthy sting, sweat dampened her clothes and tiny insects buzzed and chewed around her face. Myers did have a healthy bank balance, but he had other charming qualities, that would surface eventually. She'd have some work to do when she finally did return to New Orleans.

They edged the horses around a rocky outcrop and Cade turned his attention to the herd. Their ears twitched, constant cud chewing, brown lashed baubles glaring at their onlookers. Evie inhaled as the meaty air clung to her throat, a bead of sweat dripped between her shoulders blades. Cade said a few words to Tomas here and there, a long finger tugged at his ear. Evie's stomach growled as loud as a prairie dog, and she shuffled numb cheeks into the leather. She eyed Cade's ladies, large hooked horns, mottled caramels, pales tans and rich coffee coloured coats. Evie turned her white mount to the rear of their position. Cade leant his hat towards Tomas who nodded.

The snowy mare picked over the uneven ground with delicate steps, carrying Evie forward through the low hanging brush, sweet crystalline trickles reached Nieves muzzle. At the edge of the narrow river, Evie stretched, the tiniest breeze whispered, sending dappled shadows on the tall grass. As Evie dismounted a thistle snagged behind her knee.

She released the reins and Nieve pawed the ground. Evie looked up.

"Who's the duchess now?"

"What do you think you're doing?" Cade barked over the neck of his tall Bay.

Nieve spun in a circle as the bay closed in, ear's twitching side to side, her teeth chipped against the bit. Evie ran her hand down her thigh until the tiny bard snagged her thumb.

"I got tired of your appraisal and needed some shade."

"Saddle up,"

As the words left Cade's throat, Nieve skited backwards, a flurry of hooves whistled past Evie's face, her shoulders stuck stone, the air rushed through her teeth. Cade shouted something, the sky waivered, blues and whites rolled into blacks and greys. Fingernails snagged in dirt, Evie spat a grass seed from her lips.

"Get down!"

"What? I just got up?" A half laugh chirped from Evie's throat, as her numb fingers prodded thumping skull, her hat absconded on the wind.

A rumble like muffled thunderclouds sent a splinter of ice through Evie's spine. Cade stood within a foot of the river, a cat, the size of a calf slunk into view, roped forearms tensed, and ears flat. Evie's vision blurred, her hand came to rest on the pommel of a saddle, her palms closed over wood grain and filigree, her gaze flooded down the double barrel. Like patting a kitten, she repeated and slowly crooked her finger.

Chips of gravel struck Cade's shin, the retort sent shudders through his chest, the pitchy smell of buck shot searing his nostrils. The tawny tail barely visible as 180 pounds of mountain lion disappeared into the undergrowth. Cade traced the shot; he inhaled sharply as the smoke cleared over Evie's frozen form.

Strands of honey blonde hair tugged by the soft Texan breeze, shot gun limp at her hip, her green eyes empty.

"Evie?" His boots found every divot and hollow before he reached out, his hands finding cold steel and plying it from even colder fingers, "Evie?" Nothing. He hit the hammer, the tall grasses flattened with the long arm. Gently he rocked Evie back and forth, her head lolled with the motion, her lips thin and pale, "Evie, come on Darling, come back to me," He swallowed hard, emerald gemstones dull against the clammy sheen of her cheeks. He couldn't slap Earl's daughter?

A voice had spoken from within the fog and Evie had followed it to somewhere dark and cold, suddenly the fog lifted to a landscape filled with Cade Hamerton. Heat infused into her compressed lips, through her chest and down to her hips, as leather tickled her nose and juniper whet her tastebuds. As if trapped, her palms refused to withdraw from the warmth that radiated from slabs of hidden muscle. Just who did he think he was! A ball of white hot lead formed in Evie's belly, Cade's hands shifted from her shoulders to her waist and the ball liquefied into traitorous surrender. His lips softened, Evie's thighs shuddered as she melted under the tender pressure of Cade's kiss.

Cade's veins writhed with lightening as he closed around Evie's slender waist, the stinging pleasure at odds with the sweet velvet of her lips. He retreated briefly, her delicious apricot sugar spurning him forward; he slanted his lips, and curled his fingers through her belt loops.

Evie withdrew, her fingers driving into his chest, "Let me go,"

Cade released a laugh but held tight, "You're injured." He pulled back her tasselled strands, tiny scratches behind her neck, one on her jawline.

"You will be if you don't get your hands off me, Hamerton."

"Oh really?" He crooked his finger, Evie stumbled onto his chest, the faintest sigh escaped her parted lips, the peaches and cream complexion flushed with pink, "I'd like to see that Darling?"

Suddenly, the ground quivered. Cade's arm hooked Evie's hips, her boots skipped from divot to rock and finally splashed ankle deep. Evie's joint rolled, her fingernails dug into tensed shoulders as frantic hooves beat a path north-west. God, they'd be trampled to death! Evie closed her eyes; she nuzzled into Cade's neck as panicked squeals neared.

As Cade drew Evie closer, her desperate clutching at his frame set barbs of wire to lash his body, when she burrowed even closer, he lost focus and twisted his hips. Evie followed and his veins ignited. One boot tripped the other and, entangled with Evie, Cade collected the river bank. He lifted his head as the herd steered away, Evie's hand slid up to his neck.

Evie's ears roared with the din of the stampede, the trembling earth echoed in her ribcage. Juniper and leather seared her blood, Cade's breath feather like across her temple. His bicep curled under her shoulders, the other arm tight around her waist. Evie leaned back, the sight of sunshine and freckles licked tendrils of warmth through her insides. Cade's heart shaped lips parted, and suddenly Evie wanted to draw herself upwards to meet his challenge.

Chapter 8

Evie watched Cade's lips kink with sinister anticipation, like a bucket of cold water, Evie wriggled against his bulk, his mocking laugh, and tempting masculinity, her words failed to register.

"Is this how you treat your women Hamerton, setting on them like a brute?"

Evie clawed to her feet, her ankle swelled against worn leather, she stumbled out of his reach. Hamerton's shoulders turned and in his absence a shower of ice cut through her bones.

Cade's empty chuckle sounded low and thin, "You aint my woman, Evie-lyn."

Evie's shoulders hugged her ears and she watched Cade's jaw twitch as he stalked passed and dug his rifle from the tall grass. From the river to his mount, Evie's feet hadn't stopped moving.

"Cade?"

A burst of hooves brought Cade's feet back on solid ground, the wicked pleasure of Evie's lithe frame in his embrace still lingered on his skin.

"Cade? Ms Lockwood?" Tomas called.

"We're fine," Cade answered, he cleared his throat in his fist, "See if you can't turn them away from the homestead."

Tomas tucked his hat down; standing in stirrups he led his mare south.

"If you see Nieve, send her back!" Cade hollered.

Evie's eyes scanned the tall grass flattened in odd places from her first tumble, to the next, encased in Cade's bulk. She whisked her trembling fingers down her thighs and inhaled slowly. It did no good, the whirlwind in her abdomen continued to spin. She winced at her cowardice, clinging to Cade like a leaf in a storm; her spine echoed the safe pressure of his embrace.

"Your mount has disappeared,"

Evie hummed agreeance, and swallowed hard. She spied Earl's second favourite hat in the brush. She grimaced as her heel hit another divot and she gathered her balance just as two more horses pulled up. Cade would have all the argument he needed to keep her back at the homestead. She'd disobeyed his instructions, set off a stampede, lost Fernandez's horse. Evie inhaled slowly and let her fingertips wick away the moisture.

The other Hands acknowledge her but spoke directly to Cade. Evie didn't mind as she limped towards Earl's faded Stenson. She plucked it from the long grass and picked specks from the brim, letting her ankle ease to a dull throb.

"We heard the shot, and saw the white pony running like a phantom!"

"Damn mountain lion. I sent Tomas on to turn them if he can, they're heavy and will blow off steam sooner rather than later. I want you two off North-West, to track that cat. It's hanging around for calves and after-birth, and I won't have it."

"Ci, Boss. You take the Lady Evie back, we catch him."

"Ci, Boss, we'll get a nice skin for the homestead. If Julius can shoot straight, did you bring the lady rifle with you or the Big Man gun?"

The two Hands continued to mock each other, as they took off over the creek.

"Will they be okay?" Evie said, her breath whistling through clenched teeth as she took another step.

"They'll be fine, Diego is a crack shot."

Not unlike you, Cade almost added. The heat wriggled under his skin, and Evie's laboured steps, compounded it. He'd warned her about the dangers, and she'd managed to land square in the middle of it. And to top it off, she'd called him a brute! Didn't matter that he'd probably saved her life! He whistled for Maverick who obediently trotted to Cade's shoulder.

"Okay," Evie bit her lip.

"Are you trying to impress me Darling? Cause you can save yourself the effort."

Evie's emerald stare warped waves of fury his direction. She had fired without hesitation and perhaps saved your skin Cade Hamerton.

Cade sighed, "Come on then," Without so much as a huff, let alone a warning, Evie fell against Cade's chest, and she clutched at his powerful shoulders, her fingers tickled by the russet curls behind his neck. Evie clicked her tongue as Maverick eased underneath her, "Let's get you and that ankle back to the house."

Evie dug her fingernails into the leather only relaxing her grip when Cade handed her Earl's well-worn hat. The leather dipped and creaked and suddenly Cade slid behind her. Evie's knuckles ached. So much for not being a burden! Maverick kicked out and Cade tugged on the reins.

"He's not used to a Duchess,"

A tiny laugh escaped Evie's lips, the smell of buck shot and juniper tangled with long lost memories. She had heard a voice before she pulled the trigger. She had stood facing a fence lined with cans, a delicate weapon in her small fingers. Evie fired and the memory vanished. Steady warmth seeped into Evie's clothes, a wall of muscle preventing her from tumbling. Something small and weak wanted to lean back. Evie shook her head.

"You okay Duchess?"

"I'm fine," Evie cleared her throat, "I'm sure it's nothing really. I feel…."

What? The sun bore down from above, the insects buzzed; somewhere a golden cheeked warbler chirped their sweet shrill call. Evie's throbbing ankle became distant with the gentle rocking of Maverick's gait. Tension fled from Evie's muscles, as if she'd been holding on for dear life, and now the reason for her terror had passed, safety arrived.

"I'm fine." Evie stammered.

"Good. That cat might have been following the herd for days, waiting for the calves."

"My calves?"

"Yes, Darling, you're calves. You didn't bump your head then?"

"No." Evie snorted and straightened her shoulders.

Hopefully her hair would hide the lump behind her ear. She needed to put an end to her self-pity or Cade would refuse to take her next time.

"You certainly scared him off, "Cade cleared his throat, "Otherwise he might have taken a swipe at me."

Evie eyed the horizon, the midday sun about to reach its zenith, "It'll cost you," she mumbled, watching the bright landscape simmer and squeak.

"Oh will it?"

The pressure of Cade's thighs at her own, and his chest colliding rhythmically with her ribs, brought Evie's attention back to the present. She glanced down at Cade's sun-kissed forearms enveloping her pale skin and Evie's shoulders relaxed. A few more paces, and Evie's spine softened, her buttocks collided with Cade's thick thighs. As if she'd touched a hot plate, Evie flinched, sending her breasts forward to be caressed by Hamerton's thick forearms with each stride. Evie's body responded in instinctive feminine betrayal, the hard centres puckering camisole and gingham alike. She heard Cade's breathe catch in his throat, and Evie retreated, Maverick stumbled, and the ground rushed upwards. Cade's palm flattened against Evie's middle, his little finger perched precariously at the edge of her belt. Evie's blood ignited with treacherous desire, Cade tugged back, and hard ridges found soft flesh.

"Cade!"

"Stop messing around!"

"Get your hands off me!"

"Sit still then." Cade snapped. Maverick snorted. "For both our sakes,"

"You need a bigger horse." Evie murmured.

"I need a bigger what?" Cade's grip retreated.

Evie blanched, "I said, what about the other horse? Will Nieve be alright?" she tugged her shirt from dampening skin.

Caramel tones slid down Evie's spine and into her boots as Cade spoke, his scent clung to her clothes, her hair and her lips. Evie tried to concentrate on the horizon, the homestead, a nice cool bath to scrub Hamerton from the memory of her skin.

"She'll find her way home, eventually." He said.

"How many trays of biscuits will it take to pay for a horse?" Evie joked.

She twisted her gaze left and right. Like she'd swallowed her own boots, Evie felt awful for spooking the herd, and now she worried about the dainty white horse running scared all on her own.

"If she's not back there already, I'll send out a search party for her." His tone had shallowed, the heat reduced, "Don't worry I'll find her."

"And if you don't?"

"It's cost you more than a tray of biscuits Darling,"

Cade ran his thumb and forefinger slowly down the reins, the leather felt stiff and unyielding unlike Evie's supple physique. His palm itched from her taunt stomach, his forearms burned from her arousal, and his desire had swelled too abruptly for his liking. Rick the Tick would try and bed her, Evie's herself had half a beau in New Orleans and she was after all, Earl's daughter. Even the notion of flirting with Evie, to gain an advantage over his competitor didn't sit right with Cade. If Kline was going try and woo Evie for her share of the Double E, he'd have to pry her out of Cades hands.

"And as I remember, you already owe me half a dozen."

"Do I?" Evie mumbled.

Cade hadn't bothered with courting, as ranching and horses had taken all his time and with good reason. The women he'd attracted knew what man they were getting, bad name, with worse intentions. He owed Earl a debt of gratitude and that included keeping Evie out of trouble.

As the tiny white fence of the Homestead came into view, Evie rolled her shoulders, the delicate nape of her neck drew Cade's attention and he regarded the horizon instead. The hardship of the land would wear Evie down eventually, he'd have to wait it out, and keep her from Kline's clutches. The chickens' squawked their indignation as his boots marched a line to the porch, Evie's fingers wound around his shoulder, her hip against his.

"I am fine, Hamerton." She repeated, the warn timbers creaked almost as loud as her wince.

"I'll send for the Doctor, Maybelle?" he called.

Evie spent the next few hours confined to the settee, listening to hollers of "I told you so," and "If you're daddy saw you," only subdued by the reassurance of Doctor Pointer that her ankle had sprained and nothing more sinister had occurred.

63

Cade had avoided the repeated admonishments with a promise of finding Fernandez's delicate horse; however the man had packed another two rifles when he mounted up. Evie found her jaw tensed for the rest of the afternoon, ears straining for a gun shot that never came.

As the sun dribbled the last light of the day across the canvas of golden cherries and violet blues, Evie found Maybelle suitably distracted by Chitto's latest delivery of prey to rise from the front room. Evie shuffled to the back door as the hound and Pearl received Maybelle's latest bout of irritation, the carcass of a small brown hare unappreciated. Evie swallowed her laugh and scooped up the pail, the distance to the water pump taking twice as long. Evie bent to the handle and lifted the iron weightless, the spout dry. Evie tried again. The pail remained empty. Evie regarded the fresh cross in her peripherals.

"Well how do I fix this?"

The soft grass caught her knees, as she spied the mechanism that failed to collect to the pump handle. She moved the action again. Evie's back heated, certain a pair of eyes spied her from the Homesteads eastern side. Evie's fingers trailed through the fluffy greenery, a bolt stabbed under her fingernail. The rusted metal flaking in her hands as she drove it back into place.

Evie dusted off her hands as she rose, exclaiming louder than necessary, "Would you look at that,"

The handle squeaked, a splutter of liquid into steel, music to Evie's ears.

"And what do you think you're doing?"

Evie's eyes rolled, "Having a bath, Maybelle,"

"You go on, I'll fix it. Don't need no more injuries for the likes of you, your Daddy would be …"Maybelle cut off her own words, "You get on inside, girl," the buxom woman leaned on the pump, and inhaled sharply, "Pearl, get on out here!"

A small smile slid across Evie's lips, as the dark haired beauty slipped into sight. Evie gave her a wink as she limped towards the Homestead. Serves her right! Evie wondered, although if she had intended remaining in Cade's good books she should try to mend some bridges with the young woman. Pearl's lanky frame, stalked past, a sheet of black strands over one shoulder, eyes burning like coals in last night's fire. Evie would have her work cut out for her.

As the water rose above her shoulders Evie's muscles relaxed, the lumps on her ankle failing to register, as the heat deliciously scorched her skin. She unwound her hair and let her neck rest against the chipped edge. Evie's lids became heavy. The screen door squeaked and Cade's voice penetrated the thin timber door. Evie jolted upright, a wave of water cascaded over the edge. Cade's words died as the liquid rushed to betray her sanctuary. Evie clutched the washcloth to her chest; a delicate chill had entered the water. The timber rattled in its hinges.

"I found Nieve."

"Thank you,"

Evie tried to slink under the water, another splash decorated the floorboards. The light shifted under the door sill,

"Is there any room left in that tub?"

Evie's tongue cleaved to the roof of her mouth. Did he insinuate she had room to share? Or did his tone spark an argument about waste?

Evie stuttered, an octave too high, "It's full the brim, and I don't care, I've been covered with enough country filth today," She tugged a strand of grass from the blonde, and scooped up her oils.

"I suppose you have Evelyn," Cade snapped.

Evie bit her bottom lip. Well he had man-handled her, but she meant the landscape not the man. She'd disappeared into a world of shock, and thankfully Cade hadn't slapped the silliness clean out of her. She traced her mouth, the gentle yet definite kiss of Cade Hamerton ghosted across her lips. Evie wriggled her toes. Cade Hamerton was not the man to tempt or tease.

By the time Evie vacated the bathroom, Cade had settled Nieve back in the stable. Julius had returned to collect supplies; they'd tracked the cat heading to the rear boundary before losing it over rocky ground. They'd camp out overnight and see if they could pick up the trail the next day. He regarded the stables; Dawnee was so close to foaling. He regarded the homestead, the delicious flavours of Maybelle's beef pot roast stirred a rumbling in his stomach, and the sweet apricot flavours of Evie's freshly washed skin awoke a very different hunger. He saddled Maverick.

Chapter 9

Evie had managed to make it through dinner without asking a single question of Maybelle as to Cade's whereabouts, primarily due to her lips being filled with Maybelle's salted roast beef. The day's activities had left her famished, and now with a full belly she rose slowly from the table. Maybelle took her plate and disappeared into the kitchen, by the time she reached the sink, a line of bubbles decorated the woman's thick forearms.

"Will they be safe out there?"

"Cade ain't never miss a shot. Don't you worry 'bout him, Miss Evie-lyn."

Yet the normal forthright nature of Maybelle had dimmed around the edges.

"And Fernandez?"

Evie couldn't even imagine how distraught the man had been when Nieve had run off. Thankfully the dainty white horse was now safe and sound in the stable.

"Of course, all them boys have been hunting big cats since they was knee high to a grasshopper," Maybelle grabbed Evie's cup and added it to the sink, "They'll be fine."

Evie sighed, a small part of her felt relief that she could avoid Cade; the other half seemed on edge. More than once, she found herself glancing out into the darkness, her ears straining for the sound of hooves or boots or both. Evie picked up a cloth and plate only to have the fabric whisked from her hands,

"You rest,"

Her fingers curled around the navy stripe as she retrieved her weapon, "I can manage."

"I know you can Ms Evie-lyn. But if your ankle is no better tomorrow, you will be resting. Here. With me."

"I'll be fine tomorrow," Evie mumbled. "He can't make me,"

The large woman smiled and retrieved the cloth, "Go on and rest. Tomorrow we'll see,"

Evie limped in retreat, and grabbed a journal of her fathers on her way to the front porch. Her father's chair still vacant, she sat down in the spare to the right. No sooner had she turned the first page, Maybelle appeared, wafts of steam rising from the mug between her hands.

"Night Miss Evie,"

"Thank you, Maybelle. Rest easy,"

Evie accepted the gift, the chipped ceramic stinging her palms. She inhaled the sweet evening flavours that danced across her palette as she sipped the dark hot liquid. Evie pondered Hamerton. She needed his cooperation, to work her share of the inheritance while she worked out the exact value and how to wrangle the biggest profit from it. How would she get her beasts to market? The scent of sage mixed with evening primrose curdled her thoughts, "How do I tame the beast?"

Had Cade Hamerton been any other man from her society circles in New Orleans' she could swivel her hips, and pout her lips and the man would trip over his own feet offering assistance. Even Myers, if Evie had the heart to face him broke and destitute. But Cade was not any other man, and he was definitely not from New Orleans. If she swivelled anything, she'd be compromising more than just her stake in the ranch. And she had Richard Kline to deal with as well. She needed profit, before she could consider trading anything with Kline.

Evie let the coffee work its way through her system before she rose to bed. Pearl sauntered into the kitchen, Chitto bundled under one arm. Evie peeled off the layers of frills and petticoats, her nightgown cotton soft against her tender skin, the pillow caught her head, and her eye's closed the moment her shoulder's relaxed.

The springs squeaked Evie's last defiant stretch as she rose for the day. She looked down, the swelling abated, she rolled her joint. The floor boards heated with the late morning sunshine as she dashed to her cupboard. Empty. Every linen skirt, every boned corset gone. She entered the hallway in her nightgown. Hamerton's door remained closed. Evie pressed her ear forward, her heart thumping in her chest. He wouldn't have risked his horses travelling through the darkness. Evie spied Earl's room. After careful consideration she selected a red gingham shirt and faded denims before being satisfied. She paused at the night stand, the tiny wooden animals begging for attention. She selected an owl, roughly hewn around the edges, the eyes tacked black. Evie set it down on her own night stand before traversing the stairs. The screen door clanged in its hinges as Evie regarded the washing tub, filled to the brim with emerald satin, aqua silk and burgundy lace. Evie's cheeks heated, her neck stung. The screen door collided with her buttocks.

"How's the ankle?" Maybelle chirped.

"Fine," Evie spat.

The larger woman turned, eyebrows skyward, and Evie exhaled slowly. If she tattled on Pearl, who knew what the girls punishment would be. Evie need a plan.

"Just a pinch here and there, although much better, thank you,"

Evie let the heat run out with her words until Maybelle's lips stopped pouting.

After breakfast, Evie plonked Earl's second best Stetson over here blonde strands and wrung out her clothes. Pearl noticeably absent, yet more than likely enjoying Evie's toiling. By the time Evie had finished the old three lined wire sagged with the weight. She tried to hang her more delicate items out of sight to no avail. Hopefully by the time Cade returned home, the Texan sun would have done its work.

Evie took a spell around the grounds, absentmindedly checking the stables, her eyes on the horizon. If something had happened to her calves, she'd be ruined. At least that's what she told herself. She watched the dainty white horse snort and shuffle from stable and paddock and resolved to bake Fernandez another batch of biscuits for her irresponsible treatment of Nieve. She owed Hamerton half a dozen too. By the time she returned to the Homestead, the Texan heat had infused her veins with energy. She riffled through the straw and collected her treasures, the eggshells still warm, before heading inside.

She whipped the batter back and forth as toenails scraped across the floor, something grey and soft nipped her ankle and Evie retrieved her leg.

"Hello Chitto,"

A flurry of huffy heels clicked into earshot, the dog yipped, tail thundering against kitchen doors. Pearl strode into the kitchen, just as Evie's fingers stroked the back of the pups joyful head. The girls jaw dropped. Dark chips of fury burning a hole through Evie where she crouched.

"That's a good pup," Evie continued. Damn it if the girl didn't bring out the worst in Evie!

"Chitto come!" Pearl barked.

"You're a good boy!" Evie added her voice an octave higher.

The poor cowpoke pup didn't understand but appreciated the fuss all the same.

A splat landed in front of Evie's boots, the gloop of batter a declaration on the floor boards. The tendons in Evie's neck strained as she rose, her fingers coating in batter as she withdrew her shoulder. A blob splattered into a sheet of ebony. Pearl gasped. A spoon became a catapult armed with raspberry jam, clouds of flour burst in the air like cannon fire, Evie squealed as butter became Pearl's weapon of choice in hand to hand to combat. Evie snatched the bag of sugar, crystals falling like empty shells. The younger girl improved her aim as shell shattered against Evie's chest, her thigh, her chin. A rumble burst from Evie's chest, hiccupping into a hearty chuckle, Pearl's squeal revolved into giggles as Chitto barked and yelped catching misfires and licking the spoils of war. Evie tossed her last grenade, the yolk dribbled down Pearl's pinafore. Evie threw her arms together, as Pearl's last egg left her hand; the resulting splash breaking across her elbows.

"What in the devil!" Maybelle boomed.

The windows rattled in their sills. Chitto barked in retreat as both girls sprinted out the back door, the low walled vegetable garden the last trench.

Cade rolled his shoulders as Maverick topped the last ridge before home. It was strange how the word had twisted on his tongue since Evie's return. She owned the Homestead. He owned the rest. But he still thought of the Double E as his home. Luckily his heifers hadn't done an injury during the stampede. Lucky for him and for Evelyn, when she sold her wieners, she could return to New Orleans, marry her beau, the unprepared Myers, and Cade would be left with what? He'd sell Dawnee's foal, and a few more, he'd have his bull service the heifers but that all took time. Time he didn't have to buy out Evie's share. Would he have to pick up work on another ranch? Who would hire Levi Hamerton's son? Worries piled on top of mountains. Maverick's hoof set off a shale slide, and Cade snatched the pommel. He cracked a yawn. The night had been hard, good for his bones difficult. His back had found every sharp pebble, his denim caught every thistle.

The lionesses tracks disappeared over the hard ground, headed north to the Four Star. He'd send someone over to warn them while he caught a few hours. The midday sun plastered his shirt to his skin; he wiped his brow and squinted. Instead of coming back south, they'd circled to the East and for a moment Cade thought they'd lost their way. Like a dozen rainbow flags, the washing line sagged under the weight of a plethora of shiny dresses. Cade replaced his hat and tugged the reins. Fernandez whistled through his teeth but Cade didn't turn.

"*Esta leona es vibrante hoy*"

"She is more day old kitten than lioness" Cade replied.

The screen door suddenly swung wide, and from Cade's slightly elevated position he could watch as two figures sprinted across the lawn, Pearl's ebony locks billowing in the wind, Evie's blonde locks bobbing free of her tight bun. They cowered behind the vegetable garden.

Instinctively Cade flattened against Maverick's neck. Fernandez soft chuckle crept under Cade's skin until Maybelle's hollering echoed off the embankment. The Hand's chortle died in his throat as he took cover. Maybelle paused at the door, arms on hips, cheeks huffing and puffing. Cade's gaze returned to Evie. She'd chosen Earls red gingham shirt and another pair of obscene denims that stretched as she kneeled behind the narrow barrier. Evie whispered something to Pearl who slunk down lower, Chitto doing nothing to conceal their location. Both girls turned onto their backsides. Evie stood. Pearl's hand clutched

Evie's wrist, but she gestured softly. The younger girl rotated to watch as Evie surrendered. Cade kicked Maverick's flanks and ignored Fernandez's whistling.

"In all my time here.... Not once, not even close .... I should tan your hide girl, from sun up to sun down."

Evie thinned her lips and shrunk into her shoulders, it did no good. A giggle rolled into the space between Maybelle's wide eyed battlefront. Her brows rose even higher,

"I'm sorry Maybelle; I'll clean it up straight away,"

Evie's palm clapped her lips, something sticky remained. She licked the jam from her fingers, a new wave of giggles erupted.

"You're damn right girl!" Maybelle's arms crossed under here weighty chest, "What am I supposed to cook for dinner, that's all today's eggs gone, lucky I've already done tomorrow's bread or you'd be more than sorry missy."

"I'm sorry, you rest, I'll put on a pot of coffee by the time you finish your cup, and I'll be done. I promise,"

"Why," The wind blew straight out of Maybelle's sails, "I think I'll do exactly that, Miss Evie. Thank you,"

"You're welcome," Evie picked up the coffee pot.

Maybelle turned and paused, "What the devil were you doing?"

Evie regarded the debris splattered from one end of the kitchen to the other, the sugar that crunched under foot, the liquid that congealed with dust on bench, doors and floor.

"Trying a new recipe," Evie swallowed her laugh.

Evie delivered Maybelle's coffee without delay and set about her task. The bubbles fizzed and hissed as she wiped. The ingredients on the floor had solidified in the Texan heat so Evie sunk down to her knees. Boot steps vibrated the timber, Evie clicked her tongue.

"I'm not done yet Maybelle,"

"So I see,"

Evie's chest skipped a beat as the thick devious tones of Cade Hamerton echoed off the ceramic. Evie pushed back the strands that tickled her nose.

"You're back," She said as she stood a little too quick for her liking, and regarded his suntanned features. Tiny lines decorated the sides of his sapphire eyes, his lips kinked to one side, "How's the stock?"

The kink disappeared, sapphires dulled, "They're fine. Lost the cat's track heading north," Cade ran his finger across the bench, "You were always covered in muck and full of trouble," Cade mumbled.

Evie pivoted to the sink. That girl is gone, "Pardon, Hamerton?"

"Ah, what happened here?" Cade said.

"I'm …. I was trying a new recipe," Evie put cloth to work.

"Looks like another tantrum to me,"

Evie's neck heated, "Yes, that's it Hamerton. I set about making your batch of biscuits and lost my temper when I remembered your lack of manners."

"Lack of manners?" Cade's tone sharpened.

"I would think a simple thank you would suffice for saving your life, and an apology for – " Evie swallowed hard, "Otherwise, I'll have no option but to –"

Cade stepped forward, "You'll do what?"

Evie met his steely stare, his chest rose and fell in even breaths, but the set of his shoulders, the tendons that pulsed in his neck, the tightening of his jaw told Evie otherwise. The man who held her father in such high esteem, the man her father trusted with the Double E, now attempted to bully her?! Full of Trouble! Evie concentrated on the uneven ridges of his nose.

"Put you to work!" she snapped.

The cloth left her fingers, the wet projectile landing in the middle of his chest. Evie swished to the side and cleared the gap the sudd filled sink suddenly safe.

"Aren't you already?" Cade said.

A spray of dishwater erupted, the liquid trickling down Evie's chin, the remainder soaking through the layers to her camisole. She glared at the washcloth missile and then at her new foe, Cade's eyes widened, his brows dipped, his full lips twisted.

"Evie, I didn't mean for it to –"

Evie didn't hear the rest as her hands cupped together, Cade turned but Evie's onslaught landed true. He shook his dampened curls flicking droplets in every direction. Sapphire gemstones sparkled.

"Pardon, Cade I didn't hear you," Evie taunted.

"I meant to say –"

Evie let another round loose.

"That's it!" Cade stormed forward and to Evie's shock she squealed in retreat. His hands dove into the sink and she caught a barrage down her back, "Looks like you need to wash another layer of Texan filth off, Duchess Lockwood"

"There's so much of it around, Hamerton. It must have been awfully dusty on top of that high horse of yours!" A cup became her catapult. A laugh escaped her throat as the splash landed across his cheek.

Cade dramatically dug a finger into his ear, "I can't hear for y'all whining Duchess!"

Evie closed her eyes at Cade's returning fire. A deep chuckle added to her misery as another splash dribbled down her neck. Her fingers snagged wash cloth, her back struck the bench.

"I wouldn't be complaining if you'd quit being so insolent and hard-headed,"

With a twirl of her fingers, the cloth whipped forward narrowly missing Hamerton's forearm. Cade's brows raised, dimples softened his hard features, his blue checked shirt, trail smeared and damp clung to his broad chest, Evie kept her eyes trained on his mocking gaze.

"Are you threatening me, Evelyn Lockwood?"

The kitchen filled, any exit now obscured by Cade's bulk and Evie wrinkled her nose as his moss and sage musk infiltrated her defences.

"So what if I am, Cade Hamerton?" Evie jeered, the cloth twirled through the air.

Cade advanced his fingers winding around her weapon, he tugged. Evie retreated, her palms and hips coming up short against the bench. The cloth splattered on the floor as Cade's hands seized Evie's waist. Cade's lips snared hers and her backbone melted. A spike of energy clawed through her wriggling abdomen to heat her chest. Strong fingers curled around the nape of her neck, callus's tickled her jawline and reverberated through her thighs. Cade withdrew his thumb smearing tender pressure across Evie's mouth, Cade dipped his head; moisture slicked her bottom lip.

74

"Is that Raspberry?"

She opened her mouth for a rebuttal, but Cade's tongue glided over the threshold to the soft corners of her mouth. Evie's veins coiled in on each other, as her hands sought to be filled with the rough bulk of this man.

76

Chapter 10

Cade inhaled sharply, as Evie's delicate lips had offered no defence when he advanced. Her breathe warm and light, as he slanted his lips. Sweet nectar ensnared a fog around his senses, his arms begged to be filled with plush curves. Cade checked himself, until Evie's palm grabbed his wrist, the fingers on her other hand twirled in the wet fabric at his waist. Restraint fled, his blood pumped like the first rains after the drought. All the other women, retreated, happy for Cade to pillage and plunder at will, the damsel subdued. However, Evie's naïve hunger called him forward, like a seductress unaware of her power. Cade closed the distance, her supple breasts catching his tensed chest, her hips provoking his desire. The screen door banged, Cade retreated.

"You're back!" Pearl squealed,

Cade coughed, "Yeah, just now."

Evie pushed passed to neutral space.

"It should be me who is helping," Pearl began, "But it looks like you two made an even bigger mess!"

Cade's fingers trembled as he collected the dish cloth, "Miss Evelyn Lockwood can start an argument in an empty house." Evie clicked her tongue and Cade sighed. He'd definitely made a mess of it now. Weren't you supposed to be protecting her from Rick the Tick, not your own lecherous ways? "You should be training that puppy of yours," Cade added.

"Maybe teach him some manners," Evie's cheeks suddenly ruby red.

"I tried sit and stay" Pearl grumbled.

Cade eyes snagged jade green; Evie squared her shoulders, her delicious lips, thin and serious.

"I was thinking more like heel,"

Cade shook his head, he deserved to be put in his place, but Evie's words sliced deeper.

"You mean, roll over, and beg," Cade's spine ratcheted tighter.

A sinister curl crept across Evie's sultry pout, she spoke, "Every good hound needs to know how to be courteous and play well with others,"

Cade exhaled, and wiped his hands on his thighs, "And I suppose you think you're capable of training any dog, be he a mongrel or prize winning pup?"

Evie spun to face Hamerton, her knuckles white, strands of blonde framing her furious glare.

"Yes,"

"Just because a chicken has wings don't mean it can fly, Evelyn Lockwood."

Cade snatched Evie's slender hand, the wash cloth plopped into her open palm. Sleep. He needed to sleep to reset his defences. The woman made his blood boil and his thighs itch.

Evie let the rhythm of her cleaning consume her; thoughts collided with memories as she tried to untangle Cade's fluctuating moods and her own. One moment she wanted to slap the dimples from his snarky cheeks, prove worthy of his respect. The next moment.... Evie returned to her smeared circles. She rinsed the cloth. Pearl had seemingly ignored Cade's boots that strummed defiant chords above their heads.

"Well Chitto is learning. I helped make this mess so I'll help clean it up, besides Maybelle is snoring so loud, I think Jorge will be back soon."

Evie snorted the shallow clefts of Maybelle's nose ripped through the afternoon air.

"Thank you Pearl, but I shouldn't have started it."

"I started it Miss Evie, I just, well. Your pa was always nice to me, did all he could for everyone, I guess I miss him. And when you came, I realised...," The girls words caught in her throat.

Evie swallowed hard, "I know," but Evie couldn't continue, "So where did you get Chitto from?"

"Cade bought him for my birthday," Pearl swept up the crumbled shells and sugar, her voice even, "From the Lacy brothers over in Burnett,"

"He's a nice present," Evie's ear strained for any sound above. The man looked like chewed twine; hopefully he locked himself away to catch a few hours, "Well happy belated birthday, from me Pearl. I suppose a nice silver hairbrush should do as my present?"

Pearl chin dipped. Evie smirked and changed the topic.

"Were you born here, at the Double E?" Evie queried, as she wiped batter and flour into concentric smears.

"No. After my mother took off, we came back here. I was born somewhere south or so my father used to tell me."

Evie stumbled over her words, "Oh Pearl I'm sorry,"

"Sorry for what Evie?" The dark haired girl chirped along as she worked, "You couldn't have stopped my ma from running."

"But your father too -,"

Pearl snorted, "Oh he's not dead he's just –"

"Gone," Cade interjected, his bare feet left a trail of wide foot prints to the back patio.

Damn! Evie's elbows raced to scratch off splatter from the cupboard doors.

"Right well, I hope Maybelle made you a cake to celebrate, I suppose I could have tried, if someone hadn't thrown all this flour around the place,"

"Thank you but she did make me a small one," Pearl giggled, "How was she when you came back in?"

"How was I what?" Maybelle boomed and Pearl ducked to the floor, "Oh Cade I didn't see you there boy, did they rope you in to helping as well. Why are you all wet?"

Cade looked down at his shirt and back at Evie's damp gingham, the impression of his body outlined on supple feminie physique.

"Cade needed a bath," Pearl added.

"Well he does now, and you!" Maybelle hollered, a smile crept across her plump cheeks, "Look at what you're doing, trampling muck from one end to the other, all of you go on get out and get clean." Maybelle chased them from the kitchen. Evie paused near the stairs, as Maybelle spoke, "Cade, after this I'm going to need supplies." The older woman's tone deepened, "The Mercantile's accounts will need to be settled before they'll let me purchase any more,"

"I'll have a word to them tomorrow," Cade replied.

The screen door banged and Evie raced up the stairs.

As she tucked her now clean strands into her bun, Evie wrestled herself into the last pair of Earl's denims that would fit. The stairs squeaked under her steps as she returned to the kitchen. She'd counted Aunt Eustace's emergency notes and decided to have a word with the Mercantile herself. After all, it was Evie's quick temper that had wasted the supplies. Maybelle finished the benches and Evie picked up the broom. The muck shifted under the thick bristles, and Evie tried to forget her conversation with Pearl. She couldn't.

"So Pearl's father has moved on?"

"Yes Miss Evie, when she was only a little 'un," Maybelle's top lip quivered.

Evie smelt a rat, her eyes narrowed, "What happened?"

"Well Cade sent him on his way Miss Evie and so he should – "

"Really?"

"Uh, if you want to ask more, you ask that boy himself, " Maybelle's voice mumbled back from inside the storeroom.

"I might,"

Evie opened the screen door, the last of the debris flicked past the stoop. Her eyes snagged the water pump. Strips of checked cotton peeled back from slabs that buckled and rippled across Cade's shoulders. He dipped to the pump, the water sluicing across his frame, the sunlight catching the drips that loitered near his narrow waist. The man twisted as he bathed, ropes and cords furrowed to rivets that lined his abdomen. Evie drew her gaze upwards, the tip of her tongue gelling to the roof of her mouth. A light dusting of russet decorated his wide chest, his curls, now dark clung to the side of his neck. Sapphire pips met her appraisal. She flicked the broom rapidly, hoping the movement would drive away the lingering curiosity that turned to viscous longing in her veins. She raised her eyes, snagging generous thighs that fought dusty denim. Evie let the screen door slam.

"Maybe later Miss Evie?" Maybelle added.

Evie didn't answer. Not only had Hamerton insulted her, and tried to bully her again, more than that he'd managed to manhandle her into knots. For some reason he'd sent another Hand away from the Double E? Had Pearl's father been more competent? Did Earl have another contender to take over the reins? If she could manage to navigate Hamerton's boorish attitude and try harder to avoid his clutches, she might get to the bottom of it. For now she had made amends with Pearl, she had to take each little victory as it came.

By the time the man had resumed common decency, Evie saw Cade swagger into the stables. Didn't the man sleep? Evie spent the rest of her afternoon straightening precious silks and satins. Tomorrow she would make her way into town. It might do her good to dress like the Lady she had become and see how Earl's other accounts faired. Hopefully the Mercantile account didn't exceed Aunt Eustace's reserves.

At dusk Evie ushered a basket of corn husks to Jorge who snorted and slobbered when the dairy cow received her share. Cade resurfaced just as Maybelle set down plates of corn bread and brisket. Evie bided her time as Pearl peppered Cade with questions of his cat hunt. She chose her moment well, as the man lifted his last full fork to curved lips.

"What time should I expect to be ready tomorrow?"

"Huh?"

"Please don't talk with your mouth full Hamerton." Evie turned to Maybelle, "I need to purchase some things from town tomorrow and I figured the pantry needs restocking."

Cade coughed, and gulped back water.

"You could say that Miss Evie. Cade do you think you could find the time to provide an escort into Dew Springs for a few ladies?"

Hamerton's jaw cinched, as he worked his attitude around the remaining morsels. One eyebrow arched at Evie and the other at Maybelle. Cade ran his hand upwards through his curls and slowly rested it beside his plate as he tried to swallow. Evie rose in one swift movement, the chipped ceramic whisked out of sight.

"Half past 8 sounds reasonable," Evie shouted as she entered the kitchen.

Maybelle snatched a cloth and set the kettle to boil. Evie sighed. Her fingers trembled as the spoon clinked back and forth. She ground her teeth as she neared the porch. Hamerton reclined in the chair to the right, one boot up on the stool. Evie squared her shoulders.

Cade took one cup and shifted his boot, "Thank you,"

Evie stood at the rail, her fingers seethed as she blew into her mug, "You're welcome, Hamerton."

"Is this what you call training?"

Evie took a sip, "Would you prefer a tantrum?"

A thick rumble shook the man's chest, "At least the tantrums are honest,"

"What is that supposed to mean?"

"You're very good at," Cade paused, "Getting your own way, Evie."

He wanted to say that Evelyn Lockwood was well versed in wrangling every last drop of sweat from a man and then some, but he took a sip from his mug instead.

"For once, that's not a total insult Hamerton," Evie said.

Cade watched the woman's silhouette, the high cheeks bones that accentuated her heart shaped face, the wide eyes that reflected tonight's peachy glow. Cade tried to ignore the apricot flavours that danced across the breeze as he sipped his coffee. His gaze returned to the curves that seemed at ease in Earl's denims. Evie leaned forward, her forearms resting on the rail. A low growl began in Cade's throat and he coughed when Evie faced him.

"Well I'm trying to not be so - what did you call me?"

"Insolent,"

"That's it," Cade softened his voice. In all fairness he had set upon her in the kitchen.

"So how were the … um your ladies. None of them were injured,"

"They were fine, although try not to set off another stampede," Cade reflected on Evie's aim with the rifle, "Where did you learn to shoot like that?"

Evie's narrow brows dipped sharply, "I don't know,"

Cade lowered his boots slowly to the porch, "You don't know?"

Her voice thinned, "I mean… I remember standing in a field shooting tins…."

Cade rose to her side, "On the Double E?"

"I'm not sure…." Her white teeth dug into luscious bottom lip, "You said you remembered me covered in muck?"

Emerald swum in a sea of blue, timber splinters snagged in Cade's forearms.

"Back then you were. A little blonde whelp climbing trees, running around frog hunting, and causing more trouble for Ruth than the boys,"

Her lip curled but only slightly, "Doesn't sound like me at all,"

"Well, that's what I remember,"

Evie shook her head, memories of a shadow stricken boy scowling from stable to barn popped into her head.

"I can't imagine I would have been more trouble than you Hamerton,"

Cade exhaled and tilted his cup, "Maybe you're right."

He had always been in trouble, but whether he caused it or not was another matter.

"Still he never sent you away," she mumbled.

A weight swelled in Cade's throat and slid uncomfortably down to his chest, "No,"

"In fact, he gave you everything,"

"Not everything Evelyn,"

"Let's not split hairs Hamerton," The heat returned to her words, a flash of colour spiked in each cheek. The liquid that had threatened to drown emerald gemstones, now glistened like poison in the half-light, "He gave you 15,000 acres,"

"I didn't ask for this Evie," Cade spine straightened, "I was content with my horses until " Cade cleared his throat, "I never wanted this Evie. "

"Then give it me," She pouted.

"So you can sell it?"

"Yes!" Evie snapped.

"No deal Darling, nothing good can come from selling the Double E."

"But it makes sense if Kline is willing to pay –"

"Kline knows more ways to take your money than a roomful of lawyers. If you believe you're getting a fair price, you've got your head in the clouds,"

"He's a shrewd business man, that's all. I can handle him." Evie started.

Cade turned on his heel and dug his hands under his arms. If he didn't, he'd end up trying to shake some sense into her, or worse. Cade tried to soften his tone.

"He'll turn this land to ashes, and while you're sitting in your silks in New Orleans, where will everyone else be?"

"Well I – " Evie spluttered.

"You might not care Evelyn, about your father's legacy but I do. Do you want everything he worked for, all the sacrifices he made to turn the Double E into what it is today to mean nothing?"

Evie's gaze turned back to the now blackened horizon, "His sacrifices?" crystals droplets splashed across her cheek.

Cade snorted, "Don't tell me the Duchess didn't have enough sugar cubes in her tea in ole N'Orleans?"

Cade strode down the steps. How could she rankle his temper so quickly?

"That's not fair!" Evie spat

"None of this is fair Darling,"

The grass crumpled under his heels. If Cade had his way he'd still be working shoulder to shoulder with Earl, he'd still have eight of his first blood-line, supper surrounded by family, his nights filled with warm sheets coated with apricot and amber. Wait. Cade cleared his thoughts. Evelyn Lockwood would be far from home and out of his life.

"You're colder than a winter-chamber pot Hamerton and twice as pleasant!"

Cade faulted a step at Evie's curse words. He almost turned but figured another war with words would end in a bigger disaster. He could refuse to take her to town tomorrow, but that would only make everyone else suffer. Perhaps he could dim the sparkle and fury with another Hand. Fernandez seemed enamoured with her so therefore the man was no good. Cade inhaled the salted manure scents of the stable and regarded his fawn mare. Polished ebony whirled under thick lashes as the heavily pregnant horse greeted her master. He stroked her nose as she nibbled into his hands. He should have brought Dawnee a sugar cube! The woman had her father's way with words, if not his patience. Cade retracted his hand and the mare nosed forward for more strokes. Perhaps he needed a defter hand to wrangle the other Duchess.

Chapter 11

The sun peaked over the horizon spilling peach beauty across the rolling hills, as if a paint brush had left wide strokes, the blush-coloured clouds highlighted the paling blue from north to south. Evie selected her dress to match. Adorned in burnt cherry she descended the stairs, one squeak at a time. She hadn't heard Cade retire last night or him rising this morning. She entered the kitchen with wide eyes, checking the corners as she advanced. It seemed she couldn't spend five minutes in his company without stirring his deep seated loathing or vice versa. Well it probably would do some good, if Cade disliked her, so long as they could still work together. Evie set the coffee pot on the stove and blew softly into the embers. As the coals reignited, Evie jostled with her corset. A few days without the constriction had been sinister bliss. A soft scratching disturbed her ministrations. Evie opened the back door to the prancing and tail-whipping hound that carried another present.

"Oh Chitto!" Evie hushed.

The pup squeaked around a lump of slated fluff, Evie inhaled, her hand came to her nose to ease the sour odour.

"Chitto, what have you got now," Evie coughed.

If it was a skunk Maybelle would be merciless, a Coon and Cade would put the dog down. Pearl would be inconsolable.

"Drop it!"

The pup dropped the carcass at Evie's rounded toe-boots, the pointed face blizzard white, two half opened pips of black stared blankly.

"Is that a possum?"

Evie sighed relief as she blinked away the tears that welled from the stinging odour. The silly mongrel will not answer you, Evie laughed to herself. She pushed her toe forward and Chitto retreated. A thunder of steps on the timber pushed Evie into action. She snatched a wash cloth and bent down, the wiry tail still warm between thumb and forefinger. Evie sprinted across the yard. Where the hell could she hide a stinking Opossum?

"Chitto stay!" Evie barked.

Chitto did his best at looking ashamed, his offering accepted, as he plopped onto his hind legs. If only Evie had enough courage to toss it in Cade's bed. He deserved it after the constant dressing downs he gave her, the heartless seemingly endless insults he tossed her way. She spied the stable. What if she could get it into his saddle bags? The stable doors budged ajar, and Evie spied her target within reach. The possum stink didn't stir the horses, so Evie proceeded.

"And what have you got there?"

Evie jumped, the mammal launched, its fluffy corpse spiralling through the air. Cade dipped his shoulder as the carcass breezed past his elbow, narrowly missing his crisp cream shirt.

"Is that some sort of N'Orlins curse Evie?" Hamerton's syrupy chuckle slithered under Evie's silks.

"What, no I …"Evie stuttered, "…it's just that…. I mean of course not, it was Chitto he…"

"That damn dog!" Cade's boots stirred the straw, he bent down and retrieved the rodent, "It's just a Possum."

"I know that Cade!" Evie snapped, "I was worried it was a danger. To the pup, I mean," In the name of the Lord she'd dropped the dog right in the middle of it. Cade would shoot him! "Pearl would be distraught, Maybelle furious – "

The man reached to the shelf above, and brought down a long wire contraption.

"I've never seen a possum go rabid, but I'll keep an eye on him."

He tossed the animal inside and closed the door.

"An eye on him?" Evie sniggered.

"He's not dead, Darling. Just playing, see,"

Evie took a timid step closer; the darkened interior of the stable coupled with her proximity to Cade took focus from her thoughts. She tried to sift the odour of freshly washed juniper and Oak moss from her tastebuds. The animal stunk and she'd do well to remember Cade's attitude did too, yet his scent still permeated her senses.

"See," Cade whispered.

His breaths shifted strands of her hair across her cheek and Evie shivered. The rodent's side rose gently before falling, his nose twitched in miniscule increments. Evie's eyes flew wide. She carried a live possum in her hands! Suddenly a laugh tickled her ribs; she rolled her lips inwards, her shoulders twitched.

"What's so funny Evie?"

The giggle would not be suppressed, and her laugh broke the cool morning air.

"You weren't expecting to find me, were you?" Cade's blue eyes refocused razor sharp.

Evie clamped her lips together as Cade; cage still in hand retraced Evie's first steps. He spied his saddle bags, his gaze, almost navy blue in the dim light blazed at Evie's hiccupping frame. Evie straightened her shoulders as the image of a Cade finding a live possum amongst his belongings faded from her mind.

"Good morning Hamerton."

She marched past at lightning speed. Cades voice echoed as her boots slipped on the dewy grass.

"Careful what you start Evie-lyn,"

By the time, breakfast had been had and cleaned, restlessness had spirited through Evie's limbs, her heels eager to be away from the homestead. Tomas brought the Homesteads wagon around, a long timber contraption with a double seat at the front, a bench along the side and no shade. A single chestnut gelding pulled it forward. Tomas levered himself into the driver position as Cade lead Maverick by the reins. He'd thrown a tan coloured leather vest over his pale cream shirt that accentuated his sundrenched colourings. A pistol clung to one side, his cream Stetson hung low over his brow.

"Expecting trouble Hamerton?" Evie queried.

"After this morning, who knows," He replied.

Evie stood at the step, for a moment regretting her choice of bustle and skirt. Cade circled behind, and Evie's hands shot out, her narrow boot slipping off steel. She scrambled, her heel finding purchase, just as Cade's hands closed over her waist.

Evie squeaked as the ground disappeared, Cade's strength effortlessly propelling her upwards. Her heel caught her hemline, her palm slammed onto the rail. Standing upright, Evie tugged on her corset as Pearl climbed up next. Cade's smirk seemed to stretch from sunrise to sunset and Evie exhaled slowly.

"Is the Duchess Lockwood ready?"

"Just about –"

Cade's palm came down with a crack on the gelding's rump and Evie's elbow collided with Pearl.

"And we're off!" the girl shouted.

"Wait what about Maybelle?" Evie said, the ribbons of her bonnet tearing through her fingers.

"She says she wants peace and quiet with everyone gone, so she gave me the list,"

Pearl jiggled a thick piece of paper at Evie. Pearl had dressed suitably drab, a dress a size too big for her narrow frame, the pale beige colours, perhaps used to be blue or even green. Evie wriggled in her corset, her Aunt's wad of bank notes had better be sufficient. She'd add a new dress to the girls' wardrobe if she could. She stuffed her curls into her bonnet and tied the ribbons. Damn Hamerton would get more than he bargained for if he thought threatening Evelyn Lockwood would bring him peace!

The sky opened up to perfect blues, azure, turquoise and cobalt, dainty silver clouds buffeted along at the same leisurely pace Tomas took. Cade and Maverick took off, across the fields as if both horse and rider had been begging for release. As they crossed the tiny bridge Maverick danced on heavy foot locks, Hamerton's cheeks flushed, his eyes sparkled with life.

"Show off!" Chirped Pearl, "I want a go,"

"On Maverick?" Cade replied, "I thought he scared you, besides you're not dressed for it today Pearl,"

"If you sit side-saddle and hold on," Evie added just to watch Cade's brows twitch.

"Yes, come on Cade!"

Cade resettled his hat, "Alright come on,"

Tomas whispered, "Whoa Pluma" the gelding and the wagon jilted to a stop.

Cade put out his arm as Pearl clambered over the wagon rail, with ease Hamerton lifted the slender girl the rest of the way, until she sat neatly on the saddle.

"I'm fine on my own!" Pearl added.

Hamerton sighed loudly, his boot dipped low into the stirrup, the wagon shook as he came aboard.

"Not too far and not too fast!"

As soon as Tomas restarted *Pluma*, Pearl hooked her thigh over the pommel and tapped her heels into the stallion's flanks. The dark horse set off at a bolt and Pearl squealed in delight.

"Perhaps you should be training her," Cade muttered.

Evie cricked her neck to watch ebony stream through the early morning breeze, "Perhaps. She mentioned her mother ran off."

Cade brushed back his russet curls and adjusted his Stetson. Something about his long pause unsettled Evie.

"She did."

"Was this before or after you ran off her father?"

A soft whistle bled through Tomas's teeth and Evie checked herself. She could hit low when she wanted to. Cade's head shook slowly from side to side.

"Before. Maybe if I'd done it sooner, the woman would still be around."

Evie's words caught in her throat. She judged quick but not fair. Evie watched as the outline of a slender rider atop the gigantic horse closed in on the wagon. Evie tried to soften her tone.

"And what of your family, were you close to your mother?"

Cade scoffed as he stood to rein in the delinquent rider, "Nope."

He struck two fingers between his lips, the shrill call pipped Maverick's ears and the stallion obeyed. Pearl's cheeks plastered with windswept tears of joy, her dark strands tangled in enthusiastic nightmare. You couldn't wipe the grin off her cheeks, one side marred from hairline to jawline. Cade brought Pearl back aboard the wagon and took his rightful place on Maverick.

"Not at all?" Evie implored.

Foggy scenes of her mother blurred in her vision, but refused to focus.

"I knew more of your mother than I did my own Evelyn."

And with that Cade trotted Maverick out of earshot of the wagon and remained there for the rest of the journey. Although Evie's rump stiffened, it was nothing compared to the ache that riveted through her heart. Cade Hamerton had more of her father than she had. And now her mother! Evie whisked away tears with her fingertips, as Pearl tried to braid her hair into neatness. Evie unwound her bonnet ribbon and offered it over.

"Riding in skirts is not very lady-like," Evie added.

"Nor is starting a food fight."

Evie snorted, "I suppose not."

"Or starting a water fight,"

"Alright, thank you Pearl,"

"Nor carrying a possum, Miss Evie." Tomas interjected.

"And thank you, Tomas." Evie raised her voice slightly.

"Carrying a what?"

"Don't mind, Pearl." Evie rushed. Tomas's chortle piqued the young girl's eyebrows, "Now how would you like a few more ribbons for your hair, what about a new dress?"

They closed in on Dew Springs as Evie had talked Pearl into at least looking at bolts of material that, if the girl really wanted, Evie would convince the seamstress to sew into a split riding skirt. Evie called it a draw as the wagon came to a halt outside the mercantile hitching post. Evie stepped backwards, only to have Hamerton's hands close around her waist. She wriggled her distaste, only to slip further, Hamerton's palms sliding upwards, her corset cinched, her chest swelled.

"If you don't stop manhandling me – " Evie hissed.

"You'll what?" Cade's whisper sent diamonds down her spine and thunder into her veins.

Evie's wits abandoned her, "You'll find out soon enough, don't you worry about that!" She snapped.

Cade's laugh brought her surroundings into focus, "Careful, that's sounds like something I might enjoy."

"I'll tan your hide, like your ma and pa should of!" She bit back, the unavoidable twang coating her words. Cade's smirk vanished as he turned on his heel to the mercantile. Evie ruffled in her silks, as she stomped up the three wide stairs, to the shopfront, "If you don't mind Hamerton, I will not have you lurking over my shoulder, while I purchase my personal requirements." She threw her chin into the air for emphasis. His brows furrowed, his bottom lip thinned, jaw tense.

"Fine. Be back here by 1 or I'll leave without you, and if you can't tell Duchess, that's a fact, not a threat."

Cade stormed back to the wagon to have a few words with Tomas, "Pearl?"

"Don't worry I'll keep her out of trouble," The girl whispered, the fifteen year old, had more insight than Evelyn had in her little finger.

"Okay. Keep an eye on them Tomas," Cade added before he crossed the street.

Evie could have all the time she needed without his company. He had loose ends to chase up. He found all three of them in the darkened interior of the Nine Lives Saloon.

"Hamerton! Sit down, we'll deal you in."

"No thanks Taylor."

The small time Rancher pulled back a chair for Hamerton, his auburn hair the same colour as his weary eyes, a three day growth crawled across his chin.

"You never know, you might just win yourself enough to buy that old sour nag out of her share."

"Sour nag ain't quite the description I got,"

Shelton 'Shelly' Murphy threw down his cards. The man stood on height with Cade and shook his hand. His sandy hair in dire need of a trim as it scuffed his dust colour collar.

"Really, well that might just get me out of my seat." Marcus Kearby, fourth son of his family line had more spare time than a broken watch, pushed more chips into the centre. His hazel eyes wide as he watched Taylor match his bid. Marcus ran a thick finger across a jaw that looked too wide for his stout height, "Well if you're not playing you could at least sit, you're making my neck hurt."

Cade took the spare seat, "Did your pa at least think it over, Marcus?"

He hated asking for favours, yet he'd sold Marcus' father good stock and the man had been impressed. The shorter man turned over his cards and hissed.

"Sorry Cade, he won't even give me the time of day let alone a loan for you. Wish I could do more. Hey are you competing in the cutting competition at the First Day Festival? First prize is twenty five dollars. I might drop a dollar or two on your name"

"Yeah might as well,"

Twenty dollars would do him well, every penny counted. Cade had better see the Farrier, Maverick needed a new pair of shoes if had even half a shot at the prize.

"You can have these Cade but something tells me it won't be enough to outbid the Tick." Taylor scooped up the centre pot.

"I doubt it, but thanks."

A painted girl circled the table, a tray full of drinks; Cade bypassed the liquor and selected a sweet tea.

"If only there was some way you could guarantee her share as yours," Taylor's grizzled cheeks split into a grin.

"Don't even say it. She's Earl's daughter," Cade clicked his tongue,

"And if she wasn't?" Marcus added.

Cade's shook his head as he rose, "Thanks for the effort boys."

"Come on, he's just joshing you Hamerton. Stay, one round." Taylor flicked over a handful of chips, "You know you won't be walking away with it, so come on,"

Cade rose from his chair, "Thanks Taylor, but I hear Bethany is looking for you. And I don't want to be anywhere near you when she finds ya!" Cade added.

Taylor shrunk down in his chair as the other boys light up with laughter. Cade tipped his hat in farewell. He needed to sort out the mercantile debt and then head over to the farrier.

"Take it easy boys,"

"I need some fresh air, Cade wait up." Shelton grabbed his Stetson and plopped in on his head as they walked out into the sunlight. Shelly lit up a cheroot as they leaned against the saloon railing. "My pa said he could loan you a third. That's all."

Cade straightened his shoulders, "Why didn't you say that before?"

"Because Cade," Shelly ran a long finger up the side of his crooked nose, "If you didn't pay it back within the three months, even though I know you'd break your back to do it, and you would too, if something happened and you couldn't well..." his eyes darted behind one shoulder and then the next, "We'd be under."

Cade shook his head. He wouldn't risk another Ranch to bankruptcy, like a vulture on a carcass Rick the Tick would swoop in and gobble them up.

"Thanks but no thanks Shelley, tell your old man I appreciate his generosity."

"I will. It's a rough position Earl put you in, but if you're there, I have no doubt the Double E will survive," Cade didn't know what to say in the face of his friend's confidence. He wished he felt the same. The Duchess emerged from the Mercantile. Shelley's gaze followed her hip swaggering sashay down the boardwalk, "Oh yeah he definitely put you in a rough spot there, buddy! I don't see what you're so upset about,"

Cade snorted, "You're welcome to her,"

Shelly whistled softly through his teeth, "Really?"

Cade's gaze tracked back to the burnt ruby satin, and then to his dusty comrade. He regarded Shelly's voracious observations of Evie.

Shelly met his eyes, "You going to ask her to the First day of Fall Dance then?"

Cade didn't answer. The whole town celebrated the first day of Fall with a day of shooting and cutting competitions, rodeo displays, the Tex-Mex chilli bake off, designed to bring the Ranchers together, discuss payments and agreements for the upcoming branding and the eventual drive to market. But he'd forgotten about the damn end of Festival Dance! Cade ground his teeth.

"You won't mind if I do then," Shelly took a step forward, Cade caught his elbow. Shelly smirked, "Yeah I didn't think so Hamerton,"

Chapter 12

Cade passed Evie on the street, the corner of her eyes kicked up in strange apprehension. The interior of the mercantile twisted his nose, the herbs and spices that usually overwhelmed his senses had been coated in a thin dusting of amber apricot.

"How much do I owe you Percy?"

"Oh Mr Hamerton," The weedy man chirped, a narrow grin crinkled his small features, he shoved his wire framed glasses higher on his narrow nose, "Miss Lockwood was just in here,"

"Yeah so I see," And smell and taste and – "So what's the damage? I'll head down and see Virgil and be back."

"There's no need."

"Percy, I know the account hasn't been settled since Earl passed,"

"Its fine Hamerton, surely she told you?"

"Evie?"

"Miss Lockwood settled the debt just now. Francis will have it all loaded by the time you're ready to leave."

"All of it? Today as well?" A measure of irritation infected his veins; it coursed through his limbs and itched his insides. Although it was directly Evie's fault that Maybelle had no flour, the last months account had been his responsibility. He turned on his heel and paused, "Thanks Percy,"

By the time he reached the street, the woman was a phantom. How could she disappear in such gaudy fabric in this drab town? He headed east and west to no avail and decided to see Virgil instead. He owned the Double E now without debt. Perhaps the bank would loan him the remainder to buy her out? Dew Springs Bank lending a Hamerton money? He almost laughed out loud. He should save his breath, yet he had to try.

Evie wandered across the boardwalk arm in arm with Pearl as they stopped outside the seamstress. She had more than enough to buy a dress for the girl and herself if she wanted to. A group of youths sauntered down the boardwalk and Pearls arm tensed.

"There she is," one of them whispered, just old enough a ball of fuzz had started sprouting on his chin.

Evie's eyes narrowed as she tracked the boy's annoyance to Pearl and not herself. One boy, shorter than the rest checked the narrow street for signs of someone.

"He's not here," he mumbled to the others.

"She can't help being what she is, but she could stay home." Another mumbled.

"I beg your pardon," Evie barked. "You look like you have to sneak up on a glass of water, boy"

The youths stopped.

"And you smell like you sort skunks for a living," Evie added.

Pearl gasped before a wave of giggles erupted.

"Listen lady, doesn't matter where you come from, she ain't welcome here."

"Least she could do is cover up, my eyes are watering." The boys broke out into sniggers.

Evie's jaw dropped, "It will be in a minute!" Her fist curled, and her shoulder pulled back.

Pearl clenched onto her elbow, "Evie its fine," she whispered.

"Francis!" A boy shouted, his voice breaking as he hollered, "You apologize now!" The older boy stepped into the laneway, rolling his shirt sleeves up as he went.

"Come on Jesse, you know - ,"

Francis didn't get to finish as the older boy grabbed his shirt collar and threw the scrubby faced youth down. Francis threw a handful of dust into Jesse's face; his boot collided with the older boys' ankle. Jesse went down onto his knees, his grip unrelenting as his fist landed true. He dragged himself and Francis to his feet.

"Apologize,"

Francis wiped the back of his hands across his cheeks, smearing the dust with tears, "I'm sorry Miss Pearl."

Jesse dragged the boy in closer and let go, Francis feet tangled, over one another and his body slammed into his comrades. Evie's jaw had remained open and now she snapped it shut when the boy dusted himself clean.

"Sorry Miss Pearl and Miss…?"

"This is Miss Evie, I mean Miss Evelyn Lockwood." Pearl's eyes targeted her boots, the sheet of ebony across one cheek, "This is Jesse Kline."

"Kline?" Evie straightened her skirts, "Are you kin to Richard."

"I'm his cousin Miss, but don't hold that against me." He snorted.

Evie's ears prickled at Pearls hushed laugh. The girl had practically folded in on herself. Evie ran her gaze over Master Jesse Kline. He ruffled the dirt from his pale brown hair, as he stood, on height with Evie and a foot taller than Pearl. His generous green eyes, slanted at the corners invited honesty, his jaw line slightly thicker than Richard's sharp vulpine lines.

"Cousins, really?"

"Yes, Ma'am,"

"Well thank you Jesse, I appreciate your assistance, for a moment there I thought – "

"I saw your crooked elbow Miss Evie and I think you would have surprised him, a lady like yourself, if you socked Francis on the chin."

"Next time then, thank you Jesse," Her cheeks colored, she could blame the Texan heat, or her morning arguments with Cade, but deep down, she knew her temper was getting the better of her. Her R's had even slowed down. Evie cleared her throat, "Well good day to you Mr Kline."

"Ah yes," Jesse shuffled his boots and bit his lip. He shoved his hands in his pockets.

"Unless there is something else,"

Pearl shivered on Evie's elbow.

"Um, no I don't think so; um we're you going to see Missus Devlin for a spell?"

Evie titled her head, "For a bit Jesse. Although, I believe I owe you lunch, my treat, for your gallantry."

"Oh there's no need."

"Rubbish Mr Kline, every good deed deserves to be rewarded. If you're happy to wait, we'll see Missus Devlin and then retire to the café?"

"Sounds great."

A cheeky grin slid into place, his green eyes fluttered over Pearls shrinking frame.

"Wonderful,"

Evie clapped her hands together as Jesse opened the seamstress's door.

Cade should have saved his time at the bank, a trail of sweat dribbled down his spine as he finished at the farriers. Poor Henry had to deal with his bad temper as he stocked up on steel. Damn Dew Springs. Damn Levi Hamerton. Damn them all.

"No need to get wild about it Hamerton,"

"I'm not."

"Alright, stop making so much noise then!" Henry counted out the lengths of iron for his client, "It would save you some time, if you bought them pre-made."

"And you'd charge me for it too Henry." Cade re-counted the lengths before he paid.

"You know if it was anyone else I wouldn't let 'em! It's undercutting my business, boy."

"Henry," Cade counted out his payment, "Sometimes you're a decent man."

"Ha!" Henry barked, "No I'm not, but I've seen your work, you're pretty handy with the hammer." Henry laughed at his own joke, "With calving season almost 'ere, I'll 'ave plenty of work for someone who can swing one and not lose 'is thumbs."

Cade stewed over the idea as he made his way back to the cart. Did he have enough hours in the day for his horses, Evie's cattle and the anvil? How bitter would his pride taste? If only Evie wouldn't sell until his horses were ready.

Cade buried the metal strands in his already loaded wagon and turned Pluma around to the main street. He spied the empty boardwalk outside the Mercantile, forming a string of expletives ready if he had to wait a minute past one. A flash of ruby caught his eye, as Evie and Pearl exited the Café in company with sixteen year old Jesse Kline, or all people. Cade's instincts had been on high alert for weeks after he'd caught Jesse's trailing after her at Earl's funeral. The boy had been sniffing around Pearl for almost two months now. Although Cade didn't hate the boy, he certainly hadn't appealed himself to Cade either Movement at the far end of the street raised Cade's hackles as Rick the Tick spotted his prey. By the time Cade unhitched Pluma, the Tick had attached to Evie's elbow. A wave of mercury sped down Cade's back. He pumped his fists, his thighs already moving.

"Afternoon, Hamerton," Richard Kline, "Didn't catch that big cat yet?" He winked.

"Afternoon Rick, not yet"

"Don't worry, I'll send you the tail."

"If you get her Rick,"

Emerald gems flittered from Kline to Hamerton and back again.

Kline broadened his chest, "We'll see, Hamerton. I here you're entering the cutting competition?"

"And yourself?"

"Of course Hamerton, can't have the Double E without any proper competition. I reckon Miss Evie-lyn should enter the shooting completion."

"I don't think so,"

"First prize is twenty dollars,"

"Sounds tempting."

Cade sighed, if Evie won a twenty dollar prize that would set them even.

"Ready Evelyn," Cade bit.

Rick interrupted, "Wait on a minute, I want to know why Miss Evie-lyn has been spoiling my cousin with cakes all afternoon"

"He helped us with some –"

Pearl and Jesse chirped together, "Errands."

Jesse's gaze met Pearls, a sly grin on both cheeks, as Cade's brows dipped.

As Evie watched the exchange unfold, she couldn't be sure if it was Richards close proximity or the scowl on Hamerton's face that brought the hairs on her neck to attention.

"Yes thank you Jesse, I suppose it is time we get back to the Double E, Pearl."

"About time," Hamerton snapped.

"Ah, um – " Jesse coughed into his hand, his boot scuffed the dusty timbers, "Mr Hamerton...,"

The color of Pearls coppery cheeks began to darken, her eyes alight at the lanky youth that quivered under Hamerton's glare.

"Yes," Cade hissed.

Evie clicked her tongue. The man was a bully.

"The First day Festival is only a week away, and I'd like to ask your permission – " Jesse's voice ran out of steam. Rick took a step back, Cade advanced. To Jesse's credit, he cleared his throat and continued, "To allow you for me to take Pearl, I mean for Pearl to accompany me to the Dance. The Fall's dance. Next Saturday."

For Evie, Pearl's frozen frame gave it all away, as if she moved an inch, Cade would launch and Jesse would be scared away. No wonder she didn't want him knowing about the boys in the alley, he'd probably skin them alive in the street. Kline tugged his thumbs into his belt line.

"Well, if you have a problem with it Hamerton, I'm sure you won't object to Evie-lyn as a chaperone,"

"Pardon?" Evie focused on Kline again,

"Well Miss Lockwood if you'd do me the pleasure of accompanying me, as Chaperone, for these two, to the Falls Dance."

A vein as thick as a wasp began to throb at Cade's neck, his lips kinked to the side. Evie straightened her spine. If he found her predicament uncomfortable then it suited Evie's purpose.

"I'd be delighted to Mr Kline," the words turned sour before they'd passed her lips, "That is if Miss Pearl accepts Master Jesse's invitation."

Pearl nodded vigorously. The vein pulsated in rapid beats as Cade cracked his neck from side to side.

"Fine."

Evie strode between the two parties and eventually shook Kline from her elbow. Cade's boots stood fast until Pearl chastely bade farewell to Jesse. As Evie reached the wagon, she hoisted her dusted hemline, and scrambled only to have Cade's palms encapsulate her waist. Her spine pressed against his chest, a rush of butterflies crashed into her abdomen, only to be shooed away by Cade's grunt of annoyance.

"I'm fine Hamerton!"

"You should be lucky I don't throw you up there, Duchess"

"You already did," She snarled back.

The ride back to the Double E remained punctured with hushed conversations of dresses and etiquette with Pearl and heated sulking glares to Hamerton. He had said that Pearl needed guidance on more ladylike behavior. As the wagon labored over the tiny bridge, the tall stallion took off across the field.

"A tantrum if I've ever seen one," Evie mumbled.

"He's mad at me," Pearl began.

"I'm not so sure,"

"I told him I wasn't interested in dresses or the like. It's Rick the Tick's cousin for goodness sakes." A gloom took over Pearls features, "I'll send a message over and cancel, he's probably only stirring for fun, so they can all look at me and my – "

Evie clutched her hands to her chest. She stretched one arm around the girl and pulled her in gently.

"Trust me Pearl, he only had eyes for you and it had nothing to do with that mark." Pearl threw her hands to her face. "You are more beautiful than sunshine, inside and out. That's what Jesse sees. Cade is just a thick headed bully who is sulking because no-one asked him to dance."

Pearl's shoulders shuddered in half-hearted giggles.

"I'd be pleased if you'd let me fix your hair, if you know where I can borrow a brush?"

Pearl chortled.

"So long as you stop doing my laundry."

Pearl lifted her head, "Thank you Miss Evie,"

"Just Evie is fine Pearl. And Cade Hamerton should know by now that girls can manage just about anything, whether they are wearing skirts or not, don't you worry about him."

Pearl scrubbed the back of her hand across her cheek, "I do worry about Cade."

"Leave me to worry about him," Evie grumbled.

"Whoa, *Pluma*"

Tomas brought the horse to a halt amongst familiar faces willing to lend a hand to unload. Hamerton resurfaced, a scowl set thick and hard as he shouldered a pound of rice and a pound of corn meal into the homestead. Tomas aided Evie to the ground, and she lifted tins of syrup and coffee from the wagon.

"Don't worry Miss Evie," Tomas said as he snatched the items from her hands.

"I want to help,"

"Ci, I know," The cowboy shooed her away with his free hand, "If you worry about Cade, you already have your hands full."

Evie clicked her tongue, "I suppose you heard it all,"

"Ci," the brown faced Hand nodded vigorously, "You two very alike. Prickly pears,"

Evie's brows rose, "Are you calling me a Cactus?"

A wide grin split Tomas's wide cheeks, his narrow moustache twitched, "Ci, rough on the outside, not so, on the inside."

Evie ambled inside and upstairs to her bedroom. Her bonnet landed neatly on top of a pile of washed denims and checks. Maybelle, a God send. Evie changed into the more relaxed attire while she pondered Tomas's words about Cade. The man was certainly full of spikes, yet he cared deeply for Pearl, Maybelle, his workers, more like family. He respected her father, who in turn chose Hamerton worthy enough to take over the Double E. Why did she constantly butt heads with the man? She spied the tiny timber statues that Earl had carved over the years. Patience. Her father had cautioned Evie about her temper many times. Evie put down the tiny wooden armadillo and returned down stairs. The walls seemed wider, the afternoon sun warm on the timbers. Evie spied the stable doors open. She turned on her heels and entered the kitchen.

"You did well Miss Evie," Maybelle praised.

"I hope so, I bought some pecans for a pie, if you don't mind showing me sometime?"

A tin dropped onto the floor and rolled to Evie's booted heel.

"Sure thing Ms Evie," Maybelle replied.

Evie bent down to retrieve the tin as it made its way past the benches and to Pearl's door. The door pealed inwards, and the girl scooped up the wayward grocery. She handed it to Evie. They shared a smile, until Evie spied the interior of the younger girl's room. On the far wall hung frames of pressed flowers and leaves, Pearls bed square against the wall. On the closest side, a faded oak writing desk loitered, the lid jammed half open, a pile of frayed journals stacked to one side. Saffron curtains wafted through open window, small wooden animal statues littered the sill.

Chapter 13

"Something wrong Evie?"

"Um," Evie tore her eyes away from the window sill and to the writing desk, "It's been a while since I've seen my mother's desk. It caught me by surprise," Evie cleared her throat, it wasn't Pearl's fault Earl had given her the statues too.

"Oh, it's a bit wobbly now a days, I don't try and write on it, it's mainly storage for her journals. You're welcome to take it out back and - ."

Evie's ears strained.

"Beg your pardon Pearl, did you say her journals?"

Pearl's lips thinned, her eyes darted over Evie's shoulder and back again. She turned to the writing desk.

"Your Pa never mentioned them, and I never asked, I thought you'd read them already," the three thread-bare journals landed softly in Evie's open palms, "I'm sorry."

"No need to apologize," Evie's thumb scratched across the cover, "Thank you,"

As if guided by Divine force, Evie wandered to the front porch, the rocking chair catching her frame. She pealed open the first dusty cover. Her mothers' flowery letters slanted across the pages.

Today I am in love.

Evie scanned the dated top corner, she quickly did the maths, and Edwina would have been 19 years old.

Today I am in love. I have never seen my father so displeased, my mother is cautiously optimistic, however Earl Lockwood has stolen my heart.

Evie clutched the journal to her chest, her cheeks became rivulets of too many silent years. The sun crept towards the horizon as Evie immersed herself in her mother's early life. Edwina had married Earl within days of his purchase of the

107

Double E, the excitement her mother felt at the prospect of Ranch life bled through the pages. Evie's ears registered boots meandering along the timber, a waft of spicy beef lingered in the air.

"Supper,"

Evie glanced up, the lamp light engorged Hamerton's already bulky frame. Evie's eyes returned to the page, the almost invisible delicate script now illuminated.

"Thank you,"

She took the plate of beans and beef with vegetables and flat bread. Hamerton vanished in the shadows. By the time Evie finished the first journal, Hamerton had returned with a cup of coffee.

"I should apologize for today in Town,"

Evie chose her words carefully, Pearl shouldn't shoulder the blame for Cade's wrath. Hamerton paused his retreat.

"It wasn't your right to pay the Mercantile account,"

Evie twisted her lips, what did Pearl have to do with the Mercantile? The pieces then fell into place, "By rights, it was my father's flour I tossed around the kitchen,"

"The Double E debts are my responsibility,"

Evie's energy reserves had depleted, "Think of it as an investment Cade,"

Juniper and moss, dallied a little longer than expected, before the screen door creaked. As the crickets finished their nighttime song, Evie climbed the stairs. Her bones trail ride sore, her soul weary.

The next day Evie descended the stairs later than expected, Cade had already hitched another horse, this time a stocky tan and brown to the front of the wagon.

"Don't you make me late girl!" Maybelle blustered as she jammed a plate of bacon and eggs into Evie's hand.

"Sunday?"

"Yes!" The larger woman returned digging pins and bonnet into her slick hair.

Evie inhaled the fluffy yellow morsels and carried a rasher of bacon upstairs. Evie selected a pale golden dress, the dark chocolate lace billowed around her throat and hips. She slithered into her stockings, eyeing the tiny wooden creatures that mocked her youth. Patience. Earl had oodles of it to deal with her high spirited mother, fending off his in-laws and starting the Double E from thistles to a thriving ranch. Evie twisted her hair behind her neck, unable to make it neat before Maybelle's voice boomed through the floor boards. At the sight of the rustic wagon, Evie's palm instinctively rubbed her rump.

"Need a hand."

Cade's rich tones slide overs Evie's skin like a ribbon unwinding; Evie's palm swung wide and collided with Cade's shoulder. The man didn't budge.

"Manners!" She snapped.

"I was offering you a lift up, Evie,"

Cade's freckles danced across his nose, sapphires shone in the shade of his Stetson.

"For heaven's sake," Evie grumbled before her feet left the ground.

Hamerton's hand warmed her skin, his scent now mixed with fresh soap tickled her nose. Pearl sat silently along one bench, her cheeks flat, lips straight, until Cade threw the young girl a wink. As if a rope loosened in Evie's chest, she plonked down next to Pearl. Evie watched Cade mount Maverick, dark blue denims sprinkled with soft dust, a neatly pressed white shirt tied at the collar with a thong, the non-descript leather belt around his narrow waist, matched the neatest pair of boots the man must own. The pale Stetson perched atop a crown of damp brown curls, the man looked good. He smelled good. Evie turned away. Tomas and Fernandez assisted Maybelle into the wagon, her bright purple floral illuminating her dark skin.

"What are we waiting for, I'm here now, go on."

She flicked her wrist and Tomas kicked the solid horse into action.

As Evie stepped over the church threshold she cleared her thoughts. The entire journey from the Double E to Dew Springs had been filled with daydreams of crisp white linen and thick forearms.

"Morning Evie-lyn," Richard Kline appeared at her side.

"Good Morning Mr Kline,"

"Please Evie, call me Richard."

"Don't you mean Rick," A man, tall with scruffy blonde hair and a crooked nose, chewed a toothpick and winked at Cade.

"It rhymes so well," added another man, slightly taller than Kline, with darker coloring and a stockier build, wearing the proudest jaw Evie had seen in all of Texas.

"Morning Murphy, Morning Kearbey" Kline snapped.

Cade raised an eyebrow, his full lips kinked to one side, "Miss Evelyn Lockwood this is Mr Shelton Murphy, Blue Crow Ranch,"

The scruffy blonde took Evie's hand and dipped his hat, "Pleasure to finally meet you,"

Evie risked a glance at Hamerton, who suddenly regarded his other companion.

"And this is Marcus Kearbey, Crooked K Ranch."

"Pleasure Evie. I'm sorry for your loss, Earl was one of kind around these parts." The short man's immense jaw cracked, his eyebrow raised at Kline.

Evie smiled, her voice calm, "Thank you Mr Kearbey, do you own the Crooked K Ranch?"

"His father had too many sons, so he's gonna be a Ranger," Another cowboy, sandy haired, with deep brown eyes, emphasized the last syllable and Kearbey cringed.

"Taylor Stone, Windy Hill Ranch." Hamerton added.

"How is old George handling Windy Hill these days?" Richard Kline asked.

"Fit as a fiddle Kline," Stone answered.

"So he'll make another drive then?"

Evie sensed the tension shift, "Do you own the Windy Hill?" Evie asked.

A crowd milled about the interior of the church watching the interaction between Kline herself and the four men. Kline snorted, and Taylor continued without pause.

"No ma'am thinking about mining."

"You need land for that," Kline sneered.

Evie's ears bristled with Richard Kline's tone, "Well I am pleased to meet you, and I wish you well in your endeavors."

"And you too, Miss Lockwood."

Cade's palm collided with Kearbey's chest, the pressure on Evie's elbow increased and she turned with the weight to follow

Kline. He threw out his arm, and Evie took her place on the pew beside Maybelle and Pearl, Jesse Kline on the other side of the dark haired beauty. Rustles and sniggers chirped behind Evie and she spied Hamerton still loitering uneasy at the door, while his three comrades filed into the pew behind Evie and Kline. The Four Star rancher sighed, and tugged at his collar. Evie inhaled the scent of bruised perfume and tried to focus. She fidgeted with her fingers as she tasted a thin layer of juniper and Oak moss creep into the air. Evie's hands curled in her lap.

Rick leaned into whisper, and someone, perhaps Kearbey, cleared his throat. Rick's eyes narrowed. The pastor took his place and began his sermon. Rick's shoulder dipped to Evie's, Shelton's cough barked. Another ten minutes into the rhetoric and Kline dipped his head towards Evie. A boot collided with Kline's and his knee flew forward. Evie rolled her lips inwards. Kline sat upright. The sermon carried on past any decent hour, the church air stifled, the heat of so many bodies warped the morning flavors into a frenzy of sweat and crumpled flowers. Evie gently inhaled, Hamerton's juniper scent still lingered over her shoulder. Kline twisted his neck to Evie and someone sneezed.

This time Kline ignored them, "After this – "

Kearbey leaned forward, and tapped Kline on the shoulder, a finger to his lips. Kline clicked his tongue and someone shushed. Evie's tried to remain still, a wave of giggles threatened to breach her resolve. Eventually the session ended and Evie's knees bounced, her legs demanding to be stretched. Kline's fingers like a snare on her elbow, as he led her from the Church. The sunlight streamed over Evie's frame and she tugged her elbow backwards, relieving the suppression of the stifled church. Within five steps she made it to the shade of the large oak tree and wiped her forearm.

"I thought, after this Evie-lyn, you might like to take a ride out to the Four Star for some lunch, take a look around."

Evie tensed, Hamerton and his pack of cowboys exited the church, all four eyes tracked to Evie's position.

"Right now Richard, I'd like something cool to drink."

"Of course; how remiss of me."

Kline turned on his heel and headed to the refreshments, half-way across, he spied Hamerton and the shorter rancher missed a step. Hamerton had been imposing on his own, now surrounded by his rough-neck friends, the man appeared even more menacing. Evie continued to observe Hamerton as he conversed with his comrades. All three smiled and jeered at Cade who dug his hands into his denim pockets as he watched Rick's journey across the lawn. Polished sapphire snagged Evie's gaze, and the space between seemed to vanish. Crickets chirped over the hubbub of the church goers, a gentle breeze stirred Evie's golden skirts. A desire to be near him struck Evie in the chest like a wayward bird at a glass window. She sucked in a shallow breath. Across the divide Cade's chin lifted, his brows knitted. When his hands reappeared from his pockets, Evie began to pace. Her mother had perished in the Texan heat over a man. If she'd listened to her parents, Edwina might still be alive. And where would Evie be? A figment of parchment; a story never written. If Edwina knew her fate, would she change it? Would she wish the same for her only daughter?

"Here you go Evie-lyn,"

"Thank you Richard."

Evie drank the sweet tea until her courage had returned. Hamerton leaned against the Church wall, one heel kicked up, arms across his broad chest. Evie's knees quaked.

"Are you alright Evie-lyn?" Kline queried as he grabbed her elbow.

She closed her eyes and inhaled, if he called her Evie-lyn one more time, if his fingers touched her skin again. Evie exhaled and opened her eyes.

"I will have to postpone the afternoon at the Four Star for another day, I'm afraid."

"Are you sure?"

Evie bit her lip, "I am a little under the weather today, the heat, my ankle – please accept my apologies."

"Of course,"

Kline's fingers grabbed vacant air as Evie paced towards the crowd. She spotted the lilac magnificence of Maybelle and changed direction. Hamerton stepped off the wall and then paused. A chirpy brunette filled Evie's vision.

"Miss Lockwood, please accept my condolences about your Pa,"

Evie ran her unforgiving gaze over the apricot lace ensemble that barely restrained the curvaceous woman, a flurry of dark curls encroached her round porcelain face, brown eyes filled with anticipation.

"Thank you, Miss?"

"Bethany Sampson,"

"Pleasure to meet you Miss Sampson,"

The girl hooked arms with Evie and walked towards the refreshments table.

"I have been meaning to say howdy, it's taken me a while on account of – "

"Bethany," Taylor Stone crept forward, his lips thin, eyes downcast,

"Taylor!" Bethany squeaked.

"Ah yes, Bethany I wanted to talk to you for a moment, if you could spare the time."

Evie's arm plopped by her side as the woman hooked arms with the lanky want-to-be miner. The brown haired, cowboy threw Hamerton a dark reproachful look. Cade's usual suntanned cheeks, bleached white, eyes wide, his full lips pursed. Evie tracked Bethany and Taylor's stroll before she flicked back to Cade. Her eyes narrowed, fingers curled into fists. Hamerton's shoulders shrunk.

The wagon skirted over the tiny bridge, the only noise Evie acknowledged as they approached the Homestead. Maybelle lulled into a post –hunger nap. Pearl rested one arm on the railing, her mind wandering no doubt on thoughts of Jesse Kline. Cade had silently scowled when Richard Kline had assisted Evie into the cart, and had ridden Maverick a subdued distance behind the entire journey home. Evie didn't have the energy to unravel the mixture of emotions that tore through her gut. Cade had sent his friend, to intercept Bethany, possible one of many *ladies* that Hamerton spent his time with. That in itself didn't add up to the irritation that weaseled through Evie's veins. Was it Hamerton's gutless unspoken admission, or her disappointment at something intangible but almost grasped, now shattered.

Evie retired the golden satin and climbed into gingham and denim. The sound of axe on wood ricocheted off the surrounding hills. Evie listened intently as Maybelle took her step by step through a pecan pie. Pearl meandered through her chores, her mind miles away from the task at hand, every now and then her gaze would wander towards the stable. While waiting for the pie to cool, Evie grabbed the third journal and retired to Earl's rocking chair. As the pages turned, Edwina's hand grew bolder with each stroke. The years that had passed between Edwina and Earl had been filled with love and adventure. A line of her mother's writings caught Evie by surprise,

Earl has spoken to Hamerton again about the intolerable nature of his actions and the consequences.

So Hamerton's father was a womanizer too?

Edwina wrote about a household filled with the noise of numerous children at roundup time, including the trouble and stickiness they brought with them. An image of Cade flashed in Evie's mind and she pushed it away. Edwina wrote openly about her longing to be surrounded by many of her own as soon as possible. And then her wish came true, swollen with child, Edwina remained at the homestead. The imminent ending approached unbeknownst to the author. Evie turned the page, a new flurry of tears swept down her cheeks.

Today I have fallen in love all over again. Today I met my daughter, Evelyn.

Whether her mother told the truth or her eyes had been coated with those of a new mother, Evie's infant life had been pleasant and unperturbed. Life now adjusted to the homestead walls, her mother regaled watching Earl introduce Evelyn to day old chicks, her squeals at her first horse ride, while Edwina took to daydreaming of the future. Throughout her journal writings, Evie regarded a change in her mother's fervour for Ranch life.

Life for Evelyn will be stilted in Dew. Earl is not convinced.

Eustace has visited again, a bevy of trinkets in her trunk, promises of prosperity in her bouffant.

It is our nature to wish for better tidings for our children and our right as parents to provide them.

And then;

Earl is over the moon, another child. Pray it is a son! My apprehension of another daughter, another flower left to wilt in the heat, threatens to overwhelm me. Eustace has promised to take Evelyn, despite Earl's reservations, to New Orleans when she is old enough. By that time, Earl will come around and see my arrangement is the most suitable, the best for Evelyn.

Evie flicked the pages until she reached blank parchment. She worked backwards until she found the last entry. Evelyn read her mother's description of a perfect Texas day, the blue sky stretching without a cloud to disturb its brilliance, the slight afternoon chill that cooled her feverish skin. Her father returned from the Ranch, Ruth fixed supper as Edwina charted her emotions. The last line snagged a hook in Evie's heart.

Evelyn put her ear to my belly and once again asked me, "When will she be done?" This time it feels different, I am almost certain he will be with us soon. I squeeze her tight until she squirms off my lap and I tell her, "When he is ready." She is not satisfied and pouts very much like Earl when I eat his last slice, "Then we can ride?"

"Yes, Evie, then we can ride."

Waves of sorrow crashed over Evelyn so fierce she stood upright, her thighs pumped until no strength remained, the earth inclined, she fought for breath. Her palms caught the tuffs of soft grass and she clung to each strand as the sound strangled in her throat.

Cade's eyes caught sight of Evie tearing through the fields, she ran like the devil chased her shadow until she collapsed. The axe haft left his hands before he realised what he was doing. Cade brought his steps up short and waited. Evie slumped there, curled over her knees, back to the sky and shuddered. The wind brought a whisper of her despair and he couldn't bring himself to intrude. The woman grieved. He waited. Slowly her shuddering subsided and Evie leaned back on her haunches. She rose to her feet and he crouched low, a blade of grass twirled between thumb and forefinger as he watched Evie turn to her father's grave. A weight collided with Cade's chest and he rolled his shoulders to shift it. Evie sat beside the pine cross, her lips moved slowly, the words lost on the breeze. Cade blinked rapidly, his ribs ached, but he had firewood to finish.

Chapter 14

Cade tossed in his sheets. Damn Bethany Sampson. No, Cade your immoral lecherous ways have come back to bite you. The image of Evie's narrow eyed stare at Bethany and then Cade had lashed him with an invisible whip. The duchess once again thought him worthless. Cade jammed his fist into his pillow. What did it matter? The woman would see through to weaning and branding and be on her way, cashing in her "investment".

At least she had made peace with Earl. A sliver of hope that Evie would hold onto the Double E for loyalty to Earl had vanished, but he knew it was good for her soul. Perhaps he needed to offer Evie the chance to run it for her, send her back to Miller or Myers or whatever, just to keep the Ranch whole. Would she let him? Would that earn you her respect? Cade groaned and rolled onto his back, he'd have to swallow his pride and earn a few bucks with the farrier. Cade's lids finally closed, only to have them snap open as the Cockerel crowed. He rose slowly, had he slept at all? The early morning chill evaporated as the furnace glowered; the coals stung Cade's bare skin as he pulled on a leather jerkin. The horses snuffled in their stalls as the first hammer strike rent the air.

Evie rose to the soft chink clink of metal on metal. Maybelle offered hot bread, bacon and fried potatoes. Evie pushed the fried potatoes around her plate; something about Cade's early morning absence had her unnerved. Did he sulk, or rebuke her for her silent accusation? The Double E had worn her thin, Dew Springs frayed her edges and now Cade's silence became the breaking point. She spent the rest of the morning helping Pearl with her chores and studying Earl's accounts. Evie needed an out. The stalemate she had intended had revolved into a game of catch-and-kiss and Evie wasn't even sure who the players were anymore.

Just before noon, Maybelle interrupted her calculations.

"That boy'd be dying of thirst by now,"

A pitcher of sarsaparilla splashed into Evie's lap together with two slices of pecan pie on a plate. As Evie opened her mouth to argue, Maybelle swivelled on her heel, leaving a wake of flour behind.

Evie grit her teeth as she marched down the three porch stairs. With both hands full, Evie pressed her backside to the timber, the stables double doors eased. The hammer fell silent. Evie walked past the stalls, some empty, their occupants enjoying the adjourning paddocks. Dawnee entered from her stable yard, her neck craning to reach the sweet treat Evie balanced.

"Cheeky girl," Evie mumbled and walked further.

A second side opened up on the right, the sun streamed down around a small shanty, the furnace heat warped the air around the man that rose from the stool. Cade plunged the long tongs into a barrel; the resulting hiss caused Evie to jump.

Cade spied Evie over his shoulder and retracted his arm, the tiny item twanged on top of its mirror images, followed by the heavy leather glove. Evie waited in the shade of the stable, as Cade sauntered past without a word. Evie put the bottles down one by one, ready with another scalding of manners and ignorance, when Cade suddenly shucked the leather jerkin. Muscles bunched and heaved as he tenderly dragged his shirt over his thick shoulders.

The hammers energy ghosted through Cade's fingers as he struggled with the little buttons on the fabric. He gave up and tucked it into his belt line. Jade green coursed over the triangle of bare skin. Well the Duchess would have to deal with it, for now. He rolled his shoulders. What the hell could he say? He reached for the plate,

"Manners Hamerton!"

Great, the Duchess returned to calling him by his surname. Cade crammed the whole sliver into his mouth as he cracked the tops off the Sars.

He took a swig, and grumbled, "Maybelle's a good cook," You're being a Boor and you know it, he scaled himself!

"Be kind that is my handy work!"

Cade coughed and swallowed, "So you can cook Duchess."

She popped the top off the second bottle and tipped it to her lips.

"I told you I was trying a new recipe," Evie flicked a strand back from her forehead, yet Cade registered her wince. A squeak interrupted the dead air, "How is the possum?"

Cade wandered over to the caged animal.

"Still fine, I'll give him one more day to be sure and then…"

"Send him on his way?"

Cade watched Evie break off the crumbs of her pie crust and flick it to the poor creature.

"Um,"

"You can't kill him!"

"What do you want me to do with him?"

"Set him free!"

Cade scrubbed his cramped hand across his eyes.

"Maybe you should keep him as a pet, you seem quite good at wrangling rodents"

Evie clicked her tongue, "I was going to apologise for putting you in that position with Pearl and Jesse, but if you'd rather go with Richard, you're welcome to him,"

Cade snorted, "So it's Richard now?"

"Don't be so obtuse, I'm trying to apologise. Besides I know what you're worried about with Pearl and Jesse and I'm going to -"

"No you don't, Evie, she's treated as an outcast in this town, with her mixed heritage, her scar and her fam-,…her…. What's to say Jessie isn't going to humiliate her in front of the whole town, his cousin - "

Evie pointed a finger at Cade's chest.

"Not everyone sees the worst in people like you do, Cade. Jesse Kline is enamoured with Pearl, besides I'm sure he knows he'd have to deal with the town tyrant if he even thinks of putting a toe out of line!"

"Damn right he will!"

Evie dropped her finger from Cade's bare skin, and crossed her arms under her breasts instead, "I didn't come here for a fight Hamerton,"

Cade took a step back and raised his palms. She should be running from the Double E by now, instead she tapped her boot in the straw, and pouted.

"Fine,"

He chugged back the final dregs of the bottle and retrieved the itching leather jerkin. He had at least another dozen to go as well as shoe Maverick before he could rest. He peeled back his damp shirt, just as Evie's voice quivered through the air.

"I want to inspect the stock,"

The hairs on the back of Cade's neck stood to attention, his denim suddenly tighter than comfortable. He revolved slowly to find Evie's attention drawn to the Opossum.

"Do you now?"

Evie narrowed her eyes, "The heifers Hamerton. Tomorrow,"

"And if I say no?"

"I'll go anyway,"

Cade jostled into the leather fabric, the material scratched his weary muscles. She'll do it too!

"Fine. If Fernandez lets you take *Nieve*."

Evie nodded and retreated to the house yard. She marched over to the cowpoke huts and promised the olive skinned man another tray of biscuits before he relented. Evie spent the rest of her afternoon sitting with Pearl, listening to her regale stories of Earl while they tried to train Chitto. The lanky pup unaware his possum friend might seal his fate. Something told Evie that if Cade wasn't worried, then she shouldn't either.

With a full stocked pantry again, Maybelle laid on a heavy dinner of chilli beef and beans with butter milk biscuits and apple pie. Cade snatched a plate, and Maybelle hollered that he eat at the table or go hungry for the next month.

Evie and Pearl both sniggered into their chilli, while Cade subduedly took his place at the far end of the table. At each mouthful the man paused, his lips pursed, the freckles across his nose twitched. Instead of commenting he jammed forkful after forkful past his white teeth. Evie cleared her plate and waited, as Cade's chipped ceramic dipped into the suds. He stifled a yawn as he retreated.

"Did you talk to him about Jesse and the dance?"

Evie rolled her lips inwards, "Of a fashion, yes. It will be fine."

Pearl beamed and grabbed a cloth, "Will you be entering the shooting competition?"

"Oh no!" Evie groaned, and together they laughed.

"Well we'll all be there to watch the cutting completion. All the Ranch's compete,"

"Has the Double E ever won?"

"Many times, your Daddy even won a few!" Maybelle interjected, "As soon as I'm done with my Chilli, I'm there. I wouldn't miss this one for all the ribbons in the world."

"Will you be there to watch it, Miss Evie?"

"Sure,"

Evie wasn't even sure why she doubted it. Surely cutting the herd was a regular activity on the Ranch. It might do well for the Double E Brand if she could say they won awards for their ranching. Would any buyer care that a cowpoke won first prize in a Dew Springs competition? Evie snorted to herself. She slung the damp cloth over the bench and filled two cups with coffee. The hinge squeaked as Evie's backside pressed against it.

"Here," She said before pausing mid step.

Cade slumped in the chair to the right, his hand propping up his chin, his hat low over his eyes. Evie left the cups to steam on the porch as Jorge lulled for his corn husks. The Angus stomped his hoof and rolled his eyes at Evie's tardiness as she approached the fence. With a tentative hand, Evie offered the treats. As his tongue sort the greenery, Evie's palm came down gentle on his nose. The bull snorted, the ground shook. Evie retracted her arm.

"Come on Jorge," She lulled. The bull advanced, his thick neck strained, Evie's fingers traced the coarse bridge hair. She released his reward, "Good boy." Evie repeated the gesture until all the husks had been inhaled, "One beast down." She mumbled.

Wait a moment, Evie; you don't want to tame the other one. Do you? Her mother's writings echoed in her mind. Aunt Eustace would scold her for her choice of *investment*. As the last light warped purple hues into navy skies, Evie returned to the porch. The homestead interior darkened and still Cade slumbered on the porch. She tipped the cool coffees onto the fauna wondering how the plants ever grew, before tiptoeing towards the man.

"Hamerton," Evie whispered. Nothing, "Cade," Evie said. Nothing.

She took a step closer, she gently raised the brim. Cade inhaled, a pressure gripped the back of Evie's calf and ascended to her hip. The man moaned, his lids creased.

"Yeah,"

Evie froze as his palm circumnavigated her buttock and halted behind her knee.

"Cade," She whispered.

His head lifted, his knees collided with hers, his hand dropped to the armrests, "Evie?"

She stepped back, her heart leaping into her throat.

"You fell asleep, it's late you should probably go to bed,"

"Bed?"

He ran his palm down his red rimmed eyes, his legs heaved. Evie waited for him to turn, ducking as he stretched his arms. His shoulders rolled one and then the other, his boots dragging across the timber as a yawn cracked his jaw. Evie snatched a lamp and pushed the small of his back as he ambled up the stairs. At the entrance to his door he paused.

"Night."

"Night, Cade."

Evie heard the soft collision of timber in jam and opened her own door, a tiny click teased Evie's curiosity. She raised the lamp higher, to see Cade's door widen. She peered through the narrow crack. The man twisted one boot off then the other, before tugging his shirt over his head in one swift movement. The dim light flickered, disturbed by Evie's heavy breaths. Her teeth sunk into her bottom lip as metal jangled on clasp. The man shucked his denims in the same speed as his shirt. Evie averted her eyes, as heat infused into her cheeks. Like an itch that had to be scratched, Evie wrestled with her sinful thoughts, a thud broke her resolve and she peered through, Cade lay prone, bare from top to toe, he wrapped his arms around his pillow.

"Duchess of possums,"

Evie tumbled into her own bed; images of suntanned skin with smooth creamy ridges penetrated her dreams. Her legs tangled in the bed sheets, the night's temperature either too hot or too cold for restful sleep. Evie stirred. Colours of slate, ash and snow streamed through Evie's window, her arms lengthened above her head in the pre-dawn light. A rustle piqued her ears. She turned over and pulled the sheet up to her neck. Her pillow itched against her hair, something rattled. Evie opened her eyes. The faded paint of her window sill came into focus. Something squeaked. Evie rolled over. On her floor, still caged, Evie met two terrified black pips in a face of fluffy snow.

Cade tiptoed around the kitchen, missing every timber boarded that creaked. He'd already been awake for over an hour before he'd lost his patience and decided on how to wake Evie. He placed the pot on the stove, within moments; the bitter odours had woken the matriarch resident who waddled out of her kitchen side bedroom.

"Don't you go without my food Boy?"

"Food? Maybelle, we're going to inspect the stock, not have a picnic."

"Sure Cade," Maybelle twisted her dark hair into a sash on top of her head.

"Maybelle, when the calves are done, Evelyn will be heading back to New Orleans and nothing about your chicken, chilli's or pies isn't going to stop that."

"I didn't say my food is going to stop her Boy,"

Cade clicked his tongue. Maybelle paused her fussing.

"I know this year has been hard for you Boy. I know what you need best, a balm for your soul and solace for your heart. Since Earl passed, your burdens have grown, and none of us; not from trying mind you, have been able to alleviate them, until now."

"Maybelle – "

"I see what I see Boy!"

A shout of his name thundered overhead

"I wouldn't get your hopes up Maybelle." Cade chuckled.

"What are hopes for if not for raising them?"

Cade shook his head and snatched a slice of dried beef; Maybelle's reprimand stung the back of his hand.

"And I hear what I hear Boy!"

Cade pondered Maybelle's words as he slipped out the back door. His responsibilities had grown, including looking after the grand Duchess Evelyn Lockwood. Earl's death had been the final straw in a year of trouble. He'd battled through. Evie didn't ease his worries at all, she added to them. Instead of concentrating on his horses he had to manage her and her unborn stock. How could Maybelle think Evie had changed a thing about Cade? He was still Levi Hamerton's son, and Dew Springs treated him as such. He still couldn't find two pennies to rub together, and his family's future hung in the balance. He had Maverick and Nieve saddled by the time Evie ventured outside, her friend caged in one hand.

"You could have just knocked on the door!"

A smile crept across his lips and he cleared his throat, "You want to set him free, then he's your responsibility."

"You're intolerable sometimes Hamerton."

Just sometimes? Cade pondered, "Mount up."

Chapter 15

Julius and Diego headed over from the homestead, as Evie mounted up. Just as she considered stuffing the creature in a saddle bag, Tomas filled it with a parcel of savoury smelling delights. Evie held the cage upright, by the time they crossed the first hill, and she rested the box on her lap. Every now and then Hamerton turned around, his lips kinked to one side. Evie pushed away thoughts of Hamerton sneaking into her bedroom when she slept. Gritting her teeth she tried to take in the magnificent scenery.

Dusty pinks revolved into hues of tangerine and lemon, tiny wildflowers sprouted pockets of colour, amongst a sea of green. The air carried with it the early morning chill that seized Evie's lungs and ignited her veins. The little rodent cowered in one corner, his lips sucking on his claws.

"You'll be free soon," Evie mumbled as Nieve walked forward into the halted horses.

"Are you talking to him now?" Cade asked as Maverick pawed the ground.

The other Hands spread out in either direction, leaving Evie alone with Hamerton.

"Where are they going?"

"Scouting for the herd, same as us. Come on,"

The tall chestnut strode forward and Nieve followed. Silence soothed Evie's confusion until she reflected on her mother's writings.

"You said you knew my mother."

"I remember her," Cade's voice softened.

He trailed a hand along the long grass and twisted it between his fingers.

"Tell me about it."

"Well," Cade sighed, "I remember her hair, thick and yellow as corn silk, she smelt of roses and cinnamon."

Evie blinked away the welling liquid, "Go on,"

"I don't remember much else,"

In truth Cade remember her shepherding the kids around from the roundup onto the porch of the Double E, there she sat with a blonde cherub on her knee and read, her audience transfixed by her animated retelling. He remembered the bitterness, the yearning. He shook his head.

"And my father?"

"He was a stand up man," Cade said, "Dew Springs respected him, loved him dearly," Cade cleared his throat, "He took the time to stop and talk to everyone, hardly said a cross word about anyone. Came to my aid more times than I can count,"

"I can imagine," Evie said with brows raised.

"This one time, Taylor and I snuck a bag of manure into Virgil's cart instead of apples."

"You thief!"

"They were tasty apples," Cade replied, "Another time, Kearby, Shelton and I snuck into the Saloon storage, had to carry Shelley's drunken rump all the way home and explain to his Ma."

"Boys," Evie jeered.

She let the rhythm of Cade's words sink into her soul as Nieve picked her way gently over the ground. Images of a freckled faced youth causing trouble for Dew Springs danced through Evie's mind. Including Cade's confessions of moving wagons from hitching posts while their owners shopped and running from a stack of fireworks prematurely igniting during Church.

"Well we figured, no-one would look in the Church, we didn't count on Old Bill nipping out for a smoke halfway through the sermon."

Evie laughed out loud.

"Don't tell me you didn't get into trouble in New Orleans, Darling."

Evie hummed, "Maybe. I never lit anything on fire mind you; there was a time when we almost sent our French teacher mad."

"Not very ladylike,"

"The woman was ghastly! She was as friendly as a bramble bush!"

"So?"

"Every time she left the room we changed something. It started with small things, from the ruler on her desk to the apple in her drawer. We'd convince her that was how she left it. Then as she got more irate we got bolder. In the end we changed entire classrooms. There she was standing blankly across the hall, eyes bulging in disbelief through the glass panes."

Cade laughed and shook his head.

"A while back, maybe 5 years ago, Earl got a letter that sent him red in the face."

"Aunt Eustace the rat!" Evie cursed, "Did he take it well?"

"As well as any father, whose teenager daughter had run about town with a bunch of conscripts, could. You're lucky to be alive,"

"They were perfect gentleman, Ivy eventually married one," Evie mumbled.

"Perfect gentleman, if it had of been me -," Cade's words died in his throat.

Evie ignored Cade's words and scanned the horizon, a row of trees snaked to the south, in the middle a grove of acacia trees huddled in the centre.

"And what about you, Cade, I don't believe the great Church firework racketeer settled down in his adolescence,"

Cade scratches his twice broken nose, "No,"

"I'm listening."

"It's not a story worth listening too. I'm not proud of what I did or who I was back then,"

"Go on Cade, I told."

"Fighting. Shelly and Taylor would get into all sorts of trouble, calling out card cheats, running out on wo-, um all sorts, knowing I was there, just one cross word away from swinging. For a while there I couldn't go ten steps without ending up wrestling in the dirt. Earl had to bail me out a few times,"

That explains why the whole town seemed terrified of Cade, unpredictable and violent, with size and anger on his side he probably never lost.

"What happened?"

127

Cade ran a blade of grass through his thick fingers and cleared his throat.

"I nearly killed a man,"

Evie let the sentence hang for a moment, "What changed?"

"Earl. Set me straight as only he could, a few harsh words spoken softly, and time to realize he was right,"

Evie didn't want to intrude on Cade's misery but she had to know, "What did he say?"

"He asked me if this was the man I wanted to be."

Evie nodded gently, he'd told her in just the same manner that she needed patience to find happiness.

"Sounds like him,"

They enjoyed the silence for a moment, letting the horses pick their way over the uneven ground, before Cade spoke again.

"So Earl's long horns are usually branded with the Double E, but your calves are going to be a new breed."

"What does that mean?"

"You can either stamp them with the Double E or other, or have a new one registered by Mr Franklin,"

"What do you brand your horses?"

"A slanted hammer, I suppose the heifers are mine so officially -"

"What? No!"

"Fairs fair Evie, they're currently in my stock,"

Evie regarded the approaching grove and halted Nieve.

"Looks a good a place as any," Cade said as he dismounted.

Evie slid her thigh over the pommel, Cade extended his palm. Evie handed over the cage, a waft of dust kicked up as she landed.

"You're not a real lady are you, Duchess?"

Evie winked, "You're only just figuring that out Cade?"

Cade lifted the cage up to his line of sight, the nervous mammal squeaked.

"And she has the gall to lecture me on manners,"

Evie retrieved her captive and walked into the cooling shade; she gently placed the cage down on the grass and popped the pin. Cade walked Maverick and Nieve under the branches of the grove and waited. Eventually Evie toed the rear edge and squealed as the rodent dashed into the underbrush.

"Real brave," Cade sniggered.

"I didn't see you over here coaxing him out."

"I don't coax honey," Cade's words slid down into Evie's boots and made her toes wriggle. She had to keep herself in check. Think of Bethany Sampson! "Come on, let's go. Diego and Julius will have my hide if they think I'm shirking."

"Alright," Evie's lips turned down.

Cade walked back to the horses his thumbs tucked into his belt in case he reached for her, a thought struck his foggy brain.

"Did Earl ever take you to Edwina's Bluff?"

"No,"

"On a day like today, we could probably see the herd from up there."

Evie's voice rose, "Really?"

Cade nodded. Something warm tingled underneath his ribs, and he tried to shift it. What the hell was he doing?

"Yeah, but it'll cost you,"

"I'm not branding the calves with a wicked hammer or whatever you called it."

"Slanted, but I like that better."

Evie spied the outline of the bluff and then her opponent before her lips kinked, "I'll race you for it."

Cade regarded the distance to the base of the cliff face, "Deal," Suddenly his hair shifted, and the sun beat down on his forehead as Evie, on tiptoes, launched his Stetson across the grass. "Oh you want to play it that way huh?" He grabbed the reins of Nieve and led the dainty horse to the weeds. He released a sharp three beat whistle and Evie growled from somewhere behind him. Cade took his time tucking his curls under his brim, as he turned to see the woman in Mavericks saddle, "Guess you didn't bet on the fact that I broke both these horses?"

"A gentleman would give a lady a head start"

Cade threw his head back, a deep chortle rumbled across the field.

"I ain't a gentleman and you ain't a real lady,"

Emerald and saffron wildflowers sprouted between boulders of burnt cherry and russet, as the cliff face loomed. Cade inhaled the scent of pines and mountain laurel; a faint amber scent itched his thighs.

"Ready?" Cade extended his hand, Evie tossed back a strand of blonde and sauntered ahead, "Have it your way, Duchess"

Evie wandered around the northern side, a path way edged by washouts now over grown. As it ascended Evie's energy flagged, Cades palm pushed in the small of her back. She bit her cheek instead of reminding him how he got to bed last night. The image of Cade buck naked jolted her brain, her boot slipped.

"I'm fine."

Evie continued until an aged trunk blocked the path.

"Hang on," Cade tried to shoulder past but Evie lifted her boot, her hand dug into the dry bark, she scrambled over the obstacle and waited. Cade swung his arms upward and vaulted upward. He landed inches behind Evie, "I think a broken crown would go nice, maybe a rat?"

"You wouldn't?"

"I won Evie,"

Evie's lips kinked, as her hips sashayed from side to side in the sticky underbrush, thorns and vines clawed to reach her soft features.

"Not yet,"

Her heels slipped on the thin stones, her thighs pumped, dirt snagged in her nails, until the noon day sun beat down on her upturned face, a cautious westerly dusted strands to tickle her cheeks. Her hands came to rest on her hips as she took in the summit view. A line of rocks peaked to her right, held together by a scrappy Madrone tree that wound its roots around the structure for purchase. In front, the Double E's patchwork sea of meadows undulated below her boots. The white homestead roof sparkled like a diamond nestled in an oyster of viridian. To the West, a snake of trees slithered towards the North, a hidden necklace of turquoise glistened between the ashes. Evie wandered to the Madrone, the reddy-brown bark coming away in her fingers, Evie sat down, her boots to one side, in the shade below the gnarled twin trunks. Cade crouched down, and handed her a canteen. She sipped sparingly, until Cade pushed it back into her hands, he rotated until his back rested against the stone work, his knees raised.

"Alright you win,"

"I should think so," Evie removed Earl's second best hat and wiped a hand across her sweaty brow. Cade laughed and Evie joined him. She picked up a handful of stones and flicked them over the edge, one by one, "It's beautiful isn't it?"

"Yep. From the river to the bridge and all across here," He pointed out the west and eastern boundaries, "Then another full day's ride to reach the Four Star."

Evie's followed the line Cade indicated, "All yours,"

She tossed another stone over the edge. It doesn't have to be, Cade wanted to say. His lips wouldn't form the words.

"For now. If Rick gets his hands on the homestead, he'll probably move in a hundred head of cattle into the house yard on the first day."

"He wouldn't?"

"Evie, the man is – " Cade bit his tongue anything he said now, would sound like sulking.

"Influential."

Cade snorted, "In this town, yes."

"Well it might bode well for Pearl to have such an influential interest in her welfare,"

Cade tossed a pebble over the edge, "She's only just turned 15," Thank the Lord.

In every direction, sand poured through an hour glass Cade couldn't see. Any minute now, the grains would run out.

"She won't be forever."

An argument began to form on his lips and he didn't want it to blossom, "I can try," Cade rose to his feet, "I supposed I should be looking for this herd."

"Yes,"

Evie peered over the edge just as Cade's voice tightened in his throat.

"Evie, get away from the edge."

Evie regarded his freckles now strained across his ridged nose, sapphire gemstones wild. He loitered at least two arm lengths back. Evie took a step closer to the precipice. Cade's jaw cinched.

"Cade Troy Hamerton, are you afraid of heights?"

"No. Just of falling. Darling."

131

Evie pirouetted, "I thought you'd be used to heights up there on your high horse, oh wait, I've heard enough today that says otherwise," she smiled.

"Funny Duchess, now step back,"

Evie took another step forward.

"You shouldn't have followed me up here, if you were afraid."

"I had a bet to win."

"So you'd risk it all to win a silly bet hey, Hamerton?" Evie pushed her hands skyward and rolled her shoulders, "I don't know why you're so afraid, it's so nice over here, the breeze is cooler, the scenery delightful,"

Ropes of muscles bunched around her waist, her feet left the ground, only to stumble on rocks under the Madrone. Her vision filled with Cade's solid chest. His hands pushed back on her hips and she lifted her chin. His full bottom lip peeled away, and she mirrored the action. A tornado of butterflies erupted in her belly as she ran her hands down his ropey forearms. Cade snatched a stray strand that blew across her cheek and gently placed it behind her ear. His thumb caressed her neck, Evie's ribs ached.

"Cade, we can't keep –"

In an instant, the man withdrew.

"I know, come on. Race you down."

As they mounted, Evie watched Cade's mood darken as the clouds provided some relief over the Texan sun. She scalded herself for the decision to be isolated with him again. She'd made her decision, why did it seem so damn hard to stick to! Cade halted. His gaze tore up to the northern sky and back to Evie.

"What is it?"

Cade pointed to the numerous divots in the flattened grass.

"You're ladies!"

"And a follower,"

Evie traced the arc of Cade's extended arm, a single feline paw print visible in the melee.

Chapter 16

"I don't like it either Evie," Cade spat. The woman refused to budge an inch, "Your investment is under threat and there is a thunderhead looming on the horizon." Evie's brows furrowed, her lips pouted, "If you ride straight south, you should come across the others,"

"If I find the others, I don't like it Cade,"

"Go now, before you get your precious skin drenched or a hiding from me or both!"

He grabbed Nieve's bridle and turned her around, Maverick snorted his agreeance.

"Fine, but take this," Evie tugged a parcel from her saddle bag, "its Maybelle's lunch,"

He took the bundle of food, "Thank you." Their knees touched as the horses jostled and his palm twitched to touch her thigh, to pull her into him and kiss those sulking satin lips, "You'll be fine."

"I know I will be Cade, it's you – " Evie exhaled and kicked Nieve in the flanks.

Cade said a silent prayer that the woman had enough sense to follow his instructions. He didn't like leaving her to ride back alone, just as much as he didn't like the thought of some cat stalking day old calves. He returned to the feline print to start his track.

Evie let Nieve trot at her own pace, at twenty step intervals she stood up in her saddle and scanned the horizon. After a dozen or so she began to whistle, her parched lips wrestling with the high pitched sound. A faint squeal relayed her last. She booted Nieve in the flanks and headed west. Diego and Julius slowed their rides as Evie came in ear shot.

"He's tracking the cat north, he sent me back to find you."

"As well you did, Miss Evie, now head on home."

"Diego?"

"Don't worry Miss; we both brought the big guns today,"

Diego slapped Nieve on the rump just as Evie wound her fingers around the leather. The horse trotted to a reasonable pace and Evie relaxed. She spied the homestead ahead and turned in her saddle. The sky had darkened the ashen clouds now thick slate. Lightening brought fire. Evie dismounted at the stable and lead Nieve into her stall. Dawnee slung her neck over the railing and sniffed.

"No pie for you little Miss," She stroked the caramel nose, Dawnee's swollen belly brushed the sides of the stall, "Look at you, you little strumpet. Ate supper before you said Grace didn't you."

Dawnee's nose pushed into her palm, another question begged to be asked, yet Evie already knew the mare's answer.

"You're back early!" Maybelle hollered as she rose from the lounge, her feet resting on the side table.

"Cade went on; he spied the cat's track following the herd."

"Oh!" Maybelle rose, "Well don't worry about him for now; I have a mind to fix a new chilli recipe. You wanna help? Last year I came second and I'm itching for a blue ribbon,"

Evie nodded her head, the inside of the homestead shadowed in the approaching storm. Evie half listened as first Maybelle and then Pearl regaled her with recipes and stories of the homestead. The busy-bodies in Dew Springs had talked and how Widow Garcia had started to bring pies around for Earl last winter. Evie replied with the correct sighs and giggles but her eyes kept rising to the horizon. As Maybelle served up her second batch for testing, thunder cracked overhead and Evie jumped.

"I hate storms too; I think it's the noise."

Evie smile faded as the second clap broke. The noise only made it harder to listen for hooves. Evie kept it to herself and let the chilli burn her tongue.

"It's nice. A bit sharp," Evie coughed, "A lot of heat!" She chugged back a glass full of water and then the second.

"So it's a goodun?"

Evie wiped away the tears, "Good, yes," She coughed.

Pearl snorted water out of her nose and Evie fanned her face with the tea towel.

"Here comes that blue ribbon."

Maybelle turned to the sink. Evie snatched her cup as Pearl poured milk over the brim. She swallowed it in one long gulp. Finally the heat eased.

"What in the name of Beelzebub did she put in it?"

"Cascabel's, baby Red Bells and Jalapeño's," Pearl hissed.

She took another sip and poured another glass. Evie did the same.

"I'm thinking of adding a cup of brown sugar, sweeten it up a bit?" Maybelle hollered from the kitchen, "The sweetness should take away some of the sting, don't you think?" Evie coughed and spluttered in agreeance, "It's a good recipe for life I suppose," Maybelle nattered to no-one in particular, "I'll get another batch on and holler when it's ready."

Pearl downed the rest of her milk, "We're going to need more of this!"

Evie followed Pearl out to the dairy cow and watched as the girl instructed Evie step by step on the process. Evie managed three splashes in the pail before the clouds opened up, both girls having to dash to the homestead to avoid a drenching. Evie loitered on the patio for a moment longer, until Maybelle hollered for more taste testers.

The premature darkness eclipsed the homestead, as the deluge continued well past supper. Evie wished Maybelle and Pearl a good night as she took a cup of coffee to the patio. The droplets eased slightly, and Evie sat down in Earl's rocking chair, her mothers' journal unopened on her lap. Her eyes stared blankly through the darkness, the screen door squeaked, Maybelle tiptoed with blanket in hand.

"On nights like this your daddy and Cade would stay out at the Shack, they'd ride on in the next morning, looking like they'd been chewed up and spat out, wearing a grin from ear to ear."

Evie nodded, "Hope there's room for Julius and Diego as well."

"Them boys will be fine," Maybelle handed over the blanket, "Don't stay up too late Miss Evie,"

Evie stretched in the grey light of the next day, the pitter-patter of rain still drummed the homestead roof and into Evie's chest. She managed a spoonful of eggs and a bite of bacon, after passing Cade's empty room, a knot tightened in her belly. As she helped Pearl with the day's milk, she spied Fernandez heading out. He dipped his hat in farewell. Evie bit her lip.

Dawnee whickered as Evie approached, "I know." Immense glistening black baubles sought reassurance, Evie sighed, and "He'll be back soon."

Pearl sniggered, "He better be, I can't stand another one of Maybelle's recipes!"

"Does Cade like chilli?"

"No but he tries," Pearl chuckled.

Another squall of rain hit the homestead just on dinner; Evie's fork tumbled between her fingers. Even Maybelle and Pearl seemed subdued as the lamps quivered in the grizzly dark. Evie offered Chitto more than half her serve and finished by doing the dishes before Maybelle could argue. Then she scooped up the blanket and carried her cup of coffee to the porch. The bitter liquid scalded her tongue as the rain slowed to a sprinkle. A sharp whinny split the air. Evie's threw the blanket over her head and dashed to the stable, the occupants swivelled their long noses at Evie's intrusion. All but one. Evie rushed to Dawnee's stall, the pretty little roan on her side, a dribble of saliva leaking from her muzzle.

"Oh Honey!"

Evie dashed to the homestead, Maybelle sent Pearl to rustle up a hand, with Cade, Julio and Diego still absent and Fernandez riding out this morning, Tomas hurried into the stable.

"We'll help her Senorita."

Pearl climbed on top of a nearby barrel, and sat one arm over the rail, eyes wide.

"Should I ride over to the Four Star?"

Tomas whistled between his teeth, "No, no she just has to work for it."

Tomas began to hum a lullaby as he opened the stall door, Dawnee snorted and backed away. Her muzzle went to her flanks.

Evie paced near the door, Dawnee's nose rubbed into her palm. A thick sheen of sweat came away in Evie's hands.

"Is she okay?"

"Ci, ci, I see the *potro*. Sing to her."

A gush of liquid splashed onto the floor, a sickly sweet odour thickened the air as Evie began the chorus to Spanish ladies and she stroked Dawnee's nose. After an hour or more of Dawnee resting and rising, Tomas's brow began to sweat.

"Is it supposed to take this long?" Nobody spoke. Evie swallowed hard, "Come on girl!"

"Miss," Tomas beckoned, "Come,"

With trembling fingers Evie opened the stall door, and entered, Dawnee stomped and whinnied her irritation, "I know Honey, come on,"

"She needs to be down," He pulsed his hand in swift movements, *"El potro no está en la posición correcta."*

Evie nodded and began to stroke the horses neck as Tomas pressed her hindquarters, Dawnee balked at first, her knees shook before she rolled to the ground. Dawnee's head came to rest in Evie's lap as Tomas delivered another long instruction in Spanish.

"Tomas?"

The olive skin man put both arms forward his head tucked between his shoulders, then he pointed to Dawnee's belly and repeated the gesture, just this time with one arm bent at the elbow.

"Oh okay, the foal's leg is that right? Needs to be repositioned?" Evie said.

Dawnee's teeth gnashed out, pinching Evie's thighs, the denim damp with saliva.

"Miss Pearl, Miss May" Tomas clicked the fingers on his free hand,

"Oh no way you'll get me around the back end of a labouring horse Tommy," Maybelle wrung her fingers together.

Pearl entered the stall and Evie wiped a hand across the back of her brow.

"Well she can kick me if she likes, I'm sure he would prefer me broke than one of her legs or this damn foal!"

Pearl slid her hands under Dawnee's neck as Evie made her way to Tomas's side.

"I wouldn't be too sure on that Miss Evie." Maybelle mumbled.

Tomas found his charge, and Dawnee's leg straightened, her hoof clipping Evie's upper arm. Her hand caught the straw before her buttocks did and Evie scrambled to the Hand's side.

"Hold here,"

Evie did as instructed, Dawnee's struggles slicing through Evie's chest. Come on girl! She willed every last drop of energy into the mare to deliver safely. Once Tomas finished his straining, Dawnee's flanks relaxed. Her sweat slicked sides, convulsed as the contractions continued. A marble coloured sac became visible; Evie shifted as Dawnee's legs kicked out again the stall struck her back. Tomas snatched his hat and stepped back as far as the stall could accommodate.

"Stay put. Stay still," Tomas cautioned on the other side of Dawnee's belly.

Evie nodded. Within moments, tiny hoofs and a muzzle appeared, partially hidden in the semi-transparent bag. Evie's knees came up to her chest, her hands splayed against the rough walls. Dawnee's legs lashed out, the space between Evie's head and hoof narrowed.

"Tomas?"

"Wait. When she stands, you run to me," he whispered back.

Between rests and contractions, the foal emerged in a slippery heap in front of Evie, turning silent prayers into tears of relief. Evie's heels tangled in the straw. Dawnee needed to stand. In the sac, the foal twitched,

"Oh Lord!" Evie's fingers snagged in the thick membrane and stretched, the gelatinous substance gave way, and four chocolate spindles tried to stand, the foal's broad nose snorted and huffed, knobbly knees struggled in the straw. Dawnee's head lifted.

"Evie!" Pearl cautioned.

The mare's neck craned to reach her offspring, her leg's gnashed. Evie darted to the far side, Tomas snatched her wrist, and her boot clipped her heel. Her straw scratched down her chest as Tomas dragged her clear.

"Well done Miss Evie, and Miss Pearl. Maybe next time Miss May?" Tomas jeered.

He closed the stall gate behind him. Evie took a moment to stare at the miracle of life as Dawnee met her newborn.

"No one is traipsing that muck over my floors!" Maybelle chirped as the others cleared out.

"You go Miss, *Esperare por el parto*"

Evie nodded to the riddle of Spanish. A rush of energy coursed through Evie's system, a tingle rode her spine and liquid began to pool. She scrubbed it away with the clean back of her hand and smiled. Pearls eyes glistened too and they laughed out loud as the crossed the soggy house lawn.

Evie ran herself a short bath; the scalding hot water barely covered her hips, as she studied, the thin welt that lined the top of her thigh. Dawnee's bite, she sighed. Evie ran the soap over her arms and winced at her swollen upper arm. Her heart still lightened by the event she witnessed. Dawnee's hoof didn't matter a lick, as the tiny life had been brought into the world.

As Evie dressed, she heard Maybelle's fussing, and Tomas's boasting, the flavours of bitter coffee rushed Evie's ministrations. She buttoned up her red gingham and chucked on clean denims. She pushed her heels into Earl's second best pair of boots and wondered if she should order a pair that actually fitted her. She shook her head, you're not staying Evie. Maybelle had already brewed two cups of coffee and offered them to Evie.

"After all that, that man deserves a cup,"

"Yes definitely, Tomas did wonderful,"

"Ah yes, Tomas," Maybelle hummed.

Evie carried the steaming drinks out to the stable. She put one down on the barrel outside Dawnee's stall and edged closer. The roan mare now stood, her offspring trembled behind her chestnut flanks.

"Well done you cheeky girl!" Evie whispered.

Dawnee whinnied.

"I should say the same to you,"

"Cade!"

Evie jumped, she scanned the stable with more attention this time, the stalls buzzed with exhausted horses, wet leather and tack lay across the beams.

"Tomas tells me I only just missed it."

The wave of relief ebbed and Evie resisted throwing her arms around his neck.

"Yes, Tomas was a God send thankfully, I'm not sure how we would have managed."

"Something tells me you would have,"

His voice resonated through the damp air, heating Evie's insides. She tucked a strand behind her ear.

"I might have to bake him a batch of cookies. How are your stock... *the* stock I mean?"

"No calves still, they will sleep a little safer tonight."

We all will, Evie thought until she registered Cade's words.

"You caught her?"

Cade's shucked his ankle length oil skin and removed his saturated Stetson, the felt curved deep at the brim. Yesterday's shirt clung to his frame.

"It's better for the stock,"

"I know," she hiccupped.

"It was a clean shot."

Evie sniffled into her coffee and turned back to the sticky foal being licked clean by Dawnee. This is what she remembered; the unexpected joys peppered the harsh truths of rural life.

"Well then it's done,"

Evie heard the scrape of ceramic lift from timber, the stall door dipped as Cade leaned his forearms over the edge.

"You'll have to name her you know,"

"Really? I didn't do that much work, if anything Tomas should name her,"

"Tomas named Dawnee,"

Evie regarded the little treasure, legs gaining strength, chocolate eyes blinking under heavy lashes that focused in the low light. If Evie sold up and left, this might be her last mark on the Double E. If it had of been male she'd name it Earl. Her mother already had a monument to her name. Evie smiled thinly.

"I supposed Bethany is out of the question?"

Chapter 17

Cade ran weary fingers across his brow.

"Yes, definitely out of the question, and has been for at least six months."

He didn't have the energy to bicker. Evie had enough sense to figure things out without Taylor's awkward fumbling. Cade inhaled, he needed a hot bath and fresh clothes, his mind had turned to mud like the meadows and his self-control waned. The dim lamps turning Evie's haphazard bundle of locks into a ball of spun gold, a few delicate tendrils drifted down to caress her pale neck. Cade studied Evie's backlit profile, prominent cheek bones that dimpled the corners of her mouth. Lashes that curled to meet her brow surrounded her wide emerald stare. His fingers itched to turn her delicate chin, to kiss her lips that seemed to pout even at rest. The woman's beauty compounded when not layered in shiny silks and satins. Cade tried to ignore, the cherry red checks that puckered around her ample breasts or the fabric that tucked into back of stretched denim. His body failed to heed his warning. His chest compressed, his thighs quivered as he registered the significance of Evie's question.

"Why do you bring it up?"

"Perhaps um… you should um, make her an honest woman?"

"Is that what you want?"

Evie's throat bobbed, "Pardon?" her tongue licked her lips.

Cade's restraint slipped. His palms trapped her waist, plush feminine curves spun into his arms. His mouth snared hers, heat transferred from her moist tongue to his. A moan escaped Evie's throat as Cade tasted sweet apricot flavours. His desire spiked, denim stretched to its limits. An urgency filled Evie's movements, sending lightening ricocheting through Cade's veins. He'd travelled into dangerous territory and he didn't have the strength to fight it. He massaged her narrow waist, until her arms curled behind his neck. Cade's hands filled with tensed flesh as he lifted Evie from the ground. Her knees pressed against his hips and he drove forward, timber struck his shin, ceramic shattered on the floor, Evie leaned back.

"Cade," his name strangled from her throat.

He rested her on the water barrel; his fingers kneaded her upper thigh. Golden strands tickled the back of his other hand as he kissed a line down her jaw.

"Yes Darling?" Cade suckled the tender flesh of her throat, her veins thundering under his tongue. It felt so good to be so bad with this woman! "Tell me what you want Honey,"

"Cade – "

His grip tightened on her buttocks and he dragged her off balance until she clung to his neck, his arousal pressed between her heated thighs, her supple femininity teasing, nurturing, and demanding. Evie gasped and Cade returned to plunder the soft corners of her mouth, cherry gingham ran through his fingers, satin chemise next, until pure velvet met callused skin. Cade shuddered, as his long strokes coveted her creamy plateaus, Evie's ribs shivered as Cade ventured higher. A growl escaped his throat as Cade encapsulated Evie's pert breast.

Evie opened her eyes only to have them close over in pleasure as Cade's lips sunk to her throat, her shirt tugged and dipped; his lips scorched her shoulder. She couldn't form words. Her fingers dove into the moist fabric that clung to his frame, his muscles twitched under her caress.

Evie melted against Cade's hard arousal; her ankles encircled his buttocks, as he gently rolled his prize between thumb and forefinger. A shower of sensations ran rampant through her nerve endings. Every touch awakened another chord begging to be strummed by his caress. Evie stroked the feathering of hair across his chest, Cade's groan dampened by her tongue. She needed to halt, but years of insipid flirtations and Luke-warm kisses demanded satisfaction. Nothing about Cade was Luke-warm. His desire collided between her thighs and she rocked against him.

Evie's moist heat magnified Cade's carnal thirst. He wanted her, if only her hands across his chest didn't feel too warm, her kisses too delicious or her kitten purrs too adoring. He needed to have Evie with pure primal desire, like any man needed a woman. Just a woman, not your woman! He reminded himself. A flash of irritation leaked into his muscles, his lips soured. Her palm raked his chest again and he winced. His fingers fumbled with tiny buttons; if she could keep her hands to herself he could concentrate on the task, and not the shadow of disappointment of the temporary future. He rolled red checks off slender shoulders, Evie's wandering hands subdued, her position now accentuated her taunt nipples that dimpled satin and demanded Cade's attention. Cade's lips seized his treasures; Evie moaned and wound fingers lovingly through his hair.

Evie fought for breath, Cade's tongue flickered against her hard centre, she needed release, from the pleasure he threatened and the strength of his embrace. An awareness of Cade as a man, lingered in Evie's peripherals, his heart, his desires, what made him whole and what would break him. As if she'd opened a window just a crack. A spell of affection came over Evie; she needed to think clearly to push passed the intensity. Yet oak moss and sage coated her tastebuds, sculptured honey filled her hands, finally she lengthened her arms, her palms on bulging shoulders.

"Cade, stop,"

Cade kissed between her breasts, his lips suckling his way up her throat, "Are you sure?"

Evie contemplated saying nothing, inside and out Evie couldn't stand under the onslaught of pleasure her offered, her voice caught in her throat, "I can't defend myself."

Cade stepped back.

Evie dragged her shirt upwards, the buttons failing to comply with her trembling fingers. She wished her body would cease its indecent display. She regarded her surroundings, half undressed, surrounded by watchful equine eyes; anyone could walk in, "This is not me, … not here.. .not with…..someone … -"

"Yeah I know," Cade stepped back, his bowed lips caught between a grimace and a smirk. Something about his tone had sent river stones into her stomach, "Believe me I know, Evelyn,"

What had she said now? Without warning liquid populated her lower lids, Evie turned away,

"I need to go,"

"Yeah you do," Cade cleared his throat.

Evie tore from the stable, droplets of rain splattered her cheeks blending with the liquid that already streamed down. As she closed her bedroom door, Evie threw herself face down, the pillows capturing her cry. For a moment she'd been under Cade's guard and cherished in his kisses. The magnificence of that moment gnarled into dark shadows of regret and stupidity. Evie hadn't realised she'd cultivated a vision of Cade as something, a possession? No, that didn't sound right. A reason to stay? You don't want to stay remember. An immature, idealistic view of the man, an alternative future, now shattered. And good riddance! Evie tried to rally, but the tears kept coming.

Cade paused at the bottom of the steps. He rolled his shoulders and pocketed his hands in case he stormed in and demand what Evie would never give, to someone like him. He knew he'd handled the situation wrong, his exhaustion and thirst getting the better of him. Evie had felt too close, too warm, too much like she'd melded to his frame. And then she'd realised Cade Hamerton was a bad investment that paid no dividends. He paused again as her door came into view. Evie needed to leave before he made a mistake that would cost them both. New Orleans, Myers, Rick the Tick, Aunt Eustace, Earl. Cade repeated his litany in his mind until sleep eventually found him.

Cade woke with the slate dawn, the scent of apricot seeped into his room and roused his senses. He resolved to avoid Evie as best he could within the bounds of the Double E. He grabbed a clean set of clothes, and once half –dressed wandered to the water pump. The chilly water sluiced over his body, the early morning breeze dampening his nerves. He checked on Dawnee and her foal before returning for breakfast. Maybelle had a pot on the stove, the scent of bacon and fried potatoes, caused his stomach to moan.

"Sure glad to see you back, Boy"

"Maybelle, you'd be the only one,"

"No I'm not,"

"Pearl," Cade said before he stuffed a roll of bacon and hash into his mouth.

"Don't play me for a fool Boy. I'm serious you should have seen her, pacing around the patio, didn't think she could sit still for ten minutes!"

"She's impatient," Cade managed after he swallowed. And determined.

"Barely ate my chilli,"

"Inconsiderate," Even Cade could only manage so much of Maybelle's chill. He grabbed another two bacon rolls for the journey to the stable.

"It took all our energy to hold her attention,"

"Immature,"

A floor board squeaked. Cade closed his eyes afraid to turn around, flavours of apricot and amber seared his lungs.

"Morning Miss Evie," Maybelle's deep voice quivered.

Cade shoved a bacon roll past his lips, the grease spilled down his chin. He turned to regard Evie in hickory blue, brown denim, her gaze like twin daggers dipped in emerald poison. Cade grunted. Evie straightened her spine, and reached for a ceramic cup.

"What an insolent, conceited, and thoughtless morning to you too,"

Cade nodded his head, he deserved it. The space between Cade and Evie's svelte form shrunk and he strode out to the dining room. He needed to get clear of Evie until his chest didn't burn, his loins didn't harden and his heart didn't sing when she called his name.

"Oh Hamerton, I want to go into town to collect a few things," Evie called after him.

Perfect. Diego will want to boast about his kill.

"Every spare man is bone tired after the last two nights. The last any of us want to do is...." He softened his tone, "I'll go myself and be back before lunch."

"Fine, there'll be two parcels at Ms Devlin's."

"Right,"

Evie bit her tongue, there was no way she was going to say thank you! Impatient, inconsiderate, immature. She wanted to slap the smirk right off his cheek. Who did Cade think he was fooling? His ego had been bruised and rejection stung. Well he

145

better get used to it! She spent the morning finishing chores with Pearl and trying to teach Chitto to stay.

Evie listened to Maybelle waffle on about sugar saving tea from turning sour and clicked her tongue. She'd been sweet. If she was any sweeter she would have turned into a donut. She still had to name the foal, perhaps if Cade saw her being sweet, his demeanour would change? Unlikely. And why do you care anyway Evie? Deep down a whisper of acknowledgement gained a voice. Evie tried to push it away, tried to shake the emotions that tangled in her gut. Earl had said she needed patience. How could she treat Cade with patience if she wanted to stomp on his foot and push him over! The screen door squawked and Pearl ran to relieve Cade of the two brown paper wrapped parcels in his thick arms. Evie rolled her lips inwards and followed Pearl upstairs. Evie took possession of the parcels, two white envelopes rested on top. As she rested the items on her bed, Pearl rushed to open them, tears of paper revealed ruffles of pale blue and navy ribbon, in the second, pink, and lemon clashed in glorious fashion.

"Oh Evie how can I ever thank you,"

Evie pushed the torn wrappings onto the floor and sat beside the girl.

"By having the time of your life Pearl,"

"I will," Pearl wrapped her arms around her neck, and squeezed, "I didn't know he made them for you're too?"

"Huh?" Evie pulled away,

"The animals," Pearl pointed to the tiny row of wood carvings.

"Ever since I can remember," She picked up a small lion, the mane and tail carved into little cedar triangles, black pips seemed to wink at her.

"That's sweet Evie,"

She put the lion back on the bureau and scooped up Pearl's dress, "Shall we hang them in here?"

Cade watched Diego boast about his handiwork while he crossed the street to the post office. Cade regretted not shaking one of his drunken comrades from the Saloon as a shield, as he spied the eager Bethany behind the desk.

146

"There's a few here for the Double E,"

She handed over two envelopes addressed to Evie and a telegram with his name on it. His gut clenched like a boot had sunk into his flesh.

"Something wrong there Cade,"

His name slithered over her tongue like a demand.

"He's just sore I'm taking Evie-lyn to the Festival Dance, and Bethany I believe you also have an escort for the night?"

"True Rick, Taylor Stone has been a right gentleman,"

"He better be, for a young lady like you."

Cade almost swallowed his tongue as Rick winked at Bethany,

"Well I'm off to the Blue Bell secure a few rooms for me and my guests,"

A second imaginary boot landed in Cade's abdomen, "Oh really Rick,"

"Yeah all the affluent Ranchers are booking a room so they don't have to camp with the rabble."

Cade's neck heated. He knew exactly what ploy Rick had up his sleeve,

"Won't worry me none, Rick. I expect I'll be bunking in somewhere warm by the end of the night."

A cloud of dust circled his boots as he strode across to Maverick, with one foul swoop Rick the Tick had stepped between him and his family.

Cade climbed the homestead porch and sat down in the chair to the right and opened the telegram. He read and re-read the single line of writing. A tip tap of tentative boots headed his way.

"I should say thank you," Evie started.

A weight slammed into his chest so heavy, he didn't realise he hadn't replied. He knew this day was coming, but it didn't hurt any less.

Evie continued, "I was thinking about naming her Duchess,"

"Why cause she's stroppy and self-centred," Cade snorted.

The pressure in his chest released, out of instinct his palm turned to reach behind Evie's knee, the air empty as the screen door slammed. His boots stumbled over the threshold into the homestead, a waft of beef pie lingered in the air. He heard Pearl

147

reprimanding Chitto in the back yard. He should apologise to Evie.

"You can be as mean as a rattlesnake sometimes, Cade,"

He handed Maybelle the telegram. She read the scrap of paper twice and sighed.

"On any other day, I'd spank you myself," The large brown woman stood by Cade's shoulder as they stared out to Evie sitting in the garden, Chitto and Pearl doing their best to cheer her up. "When are you going to tell her?"

"After the Dance,"

Maybelle nodded and returned to her pie.

"Rick has booked rooms for Evie and Pearl at the Blue Bell Inn,"

"Now why would you be telling me that Boy?"

Cade picked up his Stetson and marched himself to the wood pile. He shucked his shirt, the axe haft sliding into his palms. By the time his forearms stung, and blisters covered his hands, the ache in his chest had shifted an inch. The weight upon his shoulders seemed doubled. He watched Evie and Pearl carry in washing, Chitto tugged down the linen until reproached. The Hands milled about the stable re-shoeing their own horses with Cade's handiwork. For a split second, Cade sensed peace settling over the Double E. He shook his head, a Hamerton didn't deserve happiness. Another blister popped as the axe swung.

Evie sat down to supper. Waiting, she cut through the beef pie, pushing the pastry around her plate until Maybelle threw her a dark glare. The pastry disintegrated on her tongue, the salt gravy divine. Cade shovelled in his serving, without so much as a sideways glance. Evie held her tongue. She wouldn't speak to the man or in his company until he apologised. Judging by his lack of manners, she'd be learning a lesson in patience.

"Good pie Maybelle," Cade pushed his plate forward an inch.

"Thank you, Cade." Maybelle rose, "I'm making another batch of chilli and -"

"Oh I um –"

Evie dared a glimpse of Pearl whose cheeks churned cherry.

"I really couldn't fit anymore –"

"Nonsense Boy,"

Maybelle returned with a pile of minced beef decorated with black beans. Cade's fingers trembled as he scooped up the spoon. Evie caught a glimpse of immense blisters on his palms. He rushed the spicy meat over his tongue, in the time it took Evie to blink. Evie focused on Pearl, a mistake as the girl began to jitter.

"Mmm, delicious," Cade coughed, "Although," Cade's eyes began to water.

Evie closed her eyes and tried to count to ten. Pearl giggled.

"Yeah, it's ummm" Cade wheezed, "I think I like it with a bit more sweetness in it," Cade chugged back his glass of water and sniffed, "Yeah, some sugar Maybelle and it would be just right," He cleared his throat and snatched Pearls glass of water.

"Sweetness fixes everything,"

Maybelle picked up the plate of chilli and offered it to Pearl. Evie rose from the table before the large woman made it around to Evie. She put on the pot of coffee, ready for a battle. She poured herself one cup and claimed the territory on the front patio. Cade could help himself for all she cared, he seemed to be doing a lot of that lately. Eventually he made his way out to the porch and Evie clenched her jaw. Patience was a hard lesson.

"I'm sorry for what I said earlier."

"Which part?"

She blew the steam across the surface, her insides still boiled.

"All of it,"

"I know what you're trying to do Cade and it won't work. I'm built of stronger stuff,"

I know, Cade thought. He'd seen it. He rested his coffee cup on the rail and shoved his stinging hands into his pockets.

"You think you can bully people, push them away. Your father might not have taught you any manners, but I know my father would have. "

"That's not fair Evelyn,"

"And you're being fair Cade?"

Again he didn't answer. The woman seemed to cut him down in seconds.

"You can insult me all you like, but you don't scare me Cade." Cade's head hung, his lips thin. Again as if a curtain had been pulled back and she was given a sneak peek at the man

149

beneath. "I'm here for one reason only," The curtain dropped, the image concealed.

"I hope you don't forget that when you staying at the Blue Bell Inn."

Evie's jaw dropped, "You can't kick me out of – "

"I'm not Evie. Rick booked rooms for you and Pearl for the Dance. All the Ranchers stay or camp in town."

A question buzzed in Evie's mind, she couldn't form the words, Cade's words had taken her courage and replaced it with panic. This time it was Evie who tipped her coffee over the railing.

Chapter 18

Evie ambled down stairs in the morning, Cade absent, Pearl and Maybelle in the kitchen.

"He rode out this morning, promised me he'd made that cutting competition come hell or high water."

Evie nodded and collected her plate. She'd been clear with Cade last night, and now he sulked. And he had the nerve to call her outbursts tantrums. After all he was the one who told her leave that night in the stable. He didn't offer any heart-felt words, no promises of affection, not a single ounce of emotion. How could she reconcile her feelings if his side of the ledger was empty? The problem was Evie knew she wanted to. The audacity of Richard Kline still irked Evie as she threw herself into the errands around the Homestead, with the help of Diego and Tomas she pulled out her mother's old desk and added a few nails, and a coat of oil.

"I guess we should ask them to move it upstairs before they retire for the afternoon,"

"Nonsense Pearl, it's yours keep it. I just wanted to repair it, make it last another few years."

"You're too kind Evie."

Evelyn snorted, "You have a short memory Pearl. Did you want another coating of sugar in your tresses for tomorrow?"

Pearl laughed, "Come on, Jorge is back,"

Together they fed the Angus bull and the indignant dairy cow. Evie threw a glance over the stables, Maverick still absent, while Dawnee's foal pranced around in fresh straw.

"Have you picked a name yet?"

"A few, but it's hard to tell him when he's not here."

Evie cleared her throat hoping her tone didn't sound too morose.

151

"He'll be in Town tomorrow. He has to be! Staying at the Blue Bell, how fancy!"

Evie smiled, how Pearl would regale the sights of New Orleans, St Charles Avenue, and the French Quarter. Besides Rick had unlikely booked a room for Cade and she'd shirked from asking.

"So I don't look the fool, what are the rules of this cutting competition?"

"Oh right, well Cade and Maverick will face a herd of cattle. The Hands will keep them bunched up, but Cade has to cut one from the middle and one from the outside in a couple of minutes. He doesn't really do any of the work other than hold on."

"Who does then? Tomas, Diego?"

"No, Maverick. Cade has to drop the reins, it's all in the training."

"Okay,"

As they wandered back, a Piebald gelding trotted up the drive, Richard Kline sitting high in the saddle.

"What can we do for you Mr Kline?" Maybelle said.

With her hands on broad hips, Maybelle looked as if to barricade the porch against invasion. Evie and Pearl came alongside.

"I came to extend the invitation to Miss Evie-lyn and Miss Pearl for their accommodation at the Blue Bell for the night."

"You shouldn't have Richard," Evie interjected, "Really, I can pay your for the –"

"It's no hassle, at all. Already paid for, I have an account there. It'll give you ladies a chance to freshen up before the Dance," Kline's eyebrows raised.

Evie paused over his last sentence, "Right well thank you for the offer,"

"You ain't going to turn the man down are you?" Maybelle interrupted, "After all, I haven't stayed one night in the Blue Bell,"

"You," Rick coughed, "Miss Maybelle, I meant – "

"How exciting, I'll better be packing my best for the Festival then. How wonderful!" She clasped her two hands together.

Evie's lips rolled inwards, "Well since you are so excited Maybelle I don't know how I could turn the man down."

Rick stepped forward two fingers raised, "I only booked – "

"Well I don't mind bunking in with Miss Evie-lyn unless you can't afford another room Mr Kline,"

"You did say you had an account?" Evie added.

"I did, didn't I," Richard Kline regarded his boots.

"And we can all be early for Church on Sunday!" Maybelle wiped her hands on her apron and returned inside.

"I'll send over my driver tomorrow to collect you and your things in the morning. We'll have lunch at the Blue Bell,"

"Wonderful," Chirped Pearl

"Wonderful," Evie parroted.

Saturday morning came with a chill in the air that stung Evie's cheeks. She'd seen the Hands wearing bright coloured shirts and busying their horses, boots shined to perfection. Evie jostled in her burgundy silks, a slice between her ribs seemed to be missing as she scanned the outbuildings for the man with the darkest shadow. Diego and Tomas completed loading Rick's wagon with the woman's belongings, while the others packed swags in their tacks. Cade strode out of the stables, and Evie's ribs ached. Pearl fussed beside her in soft yellow,

"Cade!" Pearl stood tall in the wagon bed.

Cade exhaled. He'd love nothing more than to avoid Evie at all costs unfortunately Earl didn't teach him to be a coward. He put one foot in front of the other until he came alongside the wagon,

"You look pretty as a daisy Pearl," Cade said, "I won't miss you in the stands," and he wouldn't miss one smudge of dirt on that dress from a young cowboy's hands either. Cade's eyes skimmed over Evie. The deep claret coloured silk twisted Evie's fair beauty into a savage glory that turned his throat dry. He needed to say something to compliment her. The haughty look in her green eyes told him otherwise, "Nothing to distract away from your finery Miss Maybelle, Miss Evelyn,"

Why did his voice have to quaver? Well if Rick laid a hand on her shiny silk, Cade was certain the other side of Evie, the grubby little cherub from the Ranch would sock him one. Unless she so desired. Cade's cleared his throat.

"Well we'll see you in there, Cade wont we?"

"You better be trying my chilli, Boy!"

As usual Maybelle sat splendid in colours too bright for the Texan sun, royal blue and cerise, a metal tub with her prize chilli resting precariously on her lap.

Cade whistled through clenched teeth, "Sure, if I get around there, I will. Don't forget to offer Mr Kline a taste,"

"Something tells me this is too sweet and too fiery for Mr Kline,"

"Right well so long as you are polite,"

"Are you lecturing me on manners Boy?"

"No Miss I ain't," Cade chortled at the matriarch.

"Cheer loud Miss," Tomas said as he slapped Kline's grey ghost.

"For the Double E I will, Tomas," Evie said as she affixed her matching bonnet.

Cade tried to ignore the snarl that came with her words. What the hell did that mean? Exactly what you think it means. Business is more important than anything else for a *lady* like Evelyn Lockwood. She had a future to secure and it wasn't with a Hamerton.

"I can't wait to see the pie eating contest, and the −" Pearl rushed.

Evie let her spine meld to the wagon. The confusion over Cade had to be unravelled, she could ignore him until the calves were weaners, but something about the twist in her gut told her it would be impossible as well as unpleasant. Why did he have to look so clean? It's the cream shirt against his suntanned skin, or was it the pale Stetson against his brown curls? He'd called her selfish, and immature, inconsiderate and stroppy. To a point, Cade was right, but she was more than that! He'd laid hands on her, not unlike what he'd probably done with Bethany. Evie's rejection had turned him sour, exposing his shallow morals. Why did his cheeks colour when Maybelle mentioned her chilli? She wanted to grab his leather vest and shake him till he came to his senses, whether that involved wrapping his arms around her or someone else.

Evie pushed her cold cuts around her plate, the whole town seethed with festivities, Stetsons and ruffles at every turn. Cheap perfume and spicy cologne clogged the restaurant at the Blue Bell. Kline prattled on about something to do with Windy Hill Ranch and the owners failing health. Old George would need a loan soon, or Kline would buy out his herd. Evie exhaled.

"I'm bursting at the seams, Evie," Pearl whispered,

"Of course it's the biggest day of the year for Dew," Jesse Kline took over narrator.

Evie spied the short stocky friend of Cade's loitering at the door.

"What's say we explore it then," Evie stood up as Kline took care of her chair.

He wiped his hands done the front of his red gingham shirt and then bent his elbow, "Of course,"

Evie spied his arm, as she refixed her bonnet. A weight dropped into her toes.

"Thank you," she managed.

Marcus Kearby dipped his hat in greeting, "Miss Lockwood, Miss Pearl are you heading over to the shooting pits?"

"No," Evie scoffed, "Why do you ask?" A small part of her wondered if Cade was there.

"I hear they are looking for more ladies to compete against Miss Jewel Daniels."

"Surely you can handle Miss Daniels, Kearby you don't need us to help you wrangle that cowpoke's bast-"

Kearby cleared his throat.

Evie's cheeks coloured, "Who is Miss Daniels and why is she a problem?"

Kearby pulled his hat off his dark strands.

"They won't let her compete against the men and she's a crack shot. They need four competitors. She's coaxed, well brow beaten one into competing already, however no other ladies are interested in picking up a rifle."

Pearl's eyes flew wide, "Is there an age limit?"

Kearby grinned around his immense jaw, "No Miss Pearl there ain't,"

155

The dark haired girl smiled at Jessie whose pride reflected in Pearl's excitement. Pearl snagged Evie's wrists, "Come on Evie. Imagine if we win!"

"By the sounds of Miss Daniels it's very unlikely anyone else will win Pearl." Evie tried to extinguish the nerves that raced through her body. On the ranch with Cade she'd clammed up, frozen in place, the phantom a memory threatened to ruin the day. She regarded Kline's awkward slimy grin. The day was already ruined, Evie thought.

"Evie-lyn, there isn't much time for us before the cutting competition," Kline said.

Evie's lips kinked, "Alright, show us the way Mr Kearby,"

"It's Marcus Miss Evelyn,"

"Then it's Evie, Marcus,"

Evie picked up her hems and hurried after the stocky man. This Jewel Daniels sounded marvellous, Evie wouldn't mind loosing if only she could keep her composure. As they approached the shooting pits, Jewel Daniels stood, no more than five foot tall, with a bounty of cherry curls adorning her round freckled face. She slung a shot gun over the shoulder of her hickory brown shirt the other hand tucked into the pocket of her brown denims. When she spied Evie and Pearl she stomped forward in calf high boots embroidered with red roses.

"So you found some!" Her pale blue eyes danced sunshine across the pair, "They don't look dressed for it, but I suppose you'll do."

"Um, thank you I guess," Evie glanced at the other competitor, a sturdy girl in riding skirts, with a chestnut pony tail drawn over her thick shoulders. She wore her weapon better than she did the dress, and glanced at Evie and Pearl with unrestrained fear, "Miss Daniels brow-beat her?"

"Clara is as sweet as pie and as brave as a beetle." Pearl whispered.

Evie nodded her head to the bench of three male judges that seemed less than impressed and not a bit surprised with being delayed by Ms Daniels. Evie approached the low table covered in firearms and ammunition. Evie unwound the ribbons in her bonnet and set it on the table. She selected one, the woodgrain gently scratched her palm, the smell of powder thick in the air.

"Miss Evie-Lyn," A husky cat-call echoed from the other side of the barrier.

"Oh Miss Sampson," Evie mumbled. "So nice to see you,"

Pearl ungraciously rolled her eyes.

Jewel stretched upwards beside Pearl, "Not that one, it'll be too heavy for you, this one girl."

Evie smiled, the girl wanted to win fairly, she turned to Bethany.

"You're just in time, come on down,"

Bethany's brown peepers popped as she spluttered, "I don't think so, a lady –"

"Lady!" Jewel snorted.

Evie bit down on her lips and cleared her throat before she could talk, "Don't tell me you're afraid?"

"Afraid's got nothing to do with it, Evie-lyn,"

A cream coloured Stetson made its way slowly through the crowd. Evie's stomach cramped, her lungs iced over.

"Looks like there's quite an audience Bethany,"

Bethany's chocolate curls swivelled from side to side until Cade's frame appeared next to Richard Kline. Jesse shot out his hand to shake, for a moment Cade looked like he would refuse, until he gripped the boy's hand. Jesse's white shirt quivered as he retrieved his palm now slated in red. Such a bully!

Evie mused, "I supposed you're right, a lady of leisure doesn't need to shoot. A ranchers wife on the other hand –"

Evie knew why she baited Bethany, in fact it had nothing to do with the voluptuous brunette in her puffy peach ruffles, she did it to bait Cade. Immature? Yes. Inconsiderate? Most definitely. Then how are you redeeming yourself in his eyes? Evie blew a wisp of hair from tickling her nose and decided it didn't matter one lick.

"Yay!" Jewel hollered before she stuck two fingers between her teeth and whistled.

The crowd cheered as Bethany Sampson found herself inside the shooting pen.

"If I ruin my dress –"

"It won't be a first, so you can't blame me," Jewel winked.

"Watch your tongue Miss Daniels, or you and your Daddy will pay"

"Bethany!" Evie coughed, "No cheap shots please!"

Jewel winked again and stood at the marksman line. The metal targets stood in groups of five and staggered down the line, first the shape of a chicken, then a pig, a turkey and finally a ram.

"You're allowed two shots at each target, move from left to right. If you miss after two move onto the next. Ready girls!"

Evie was definitely not ready. Jewel shot first, the click boom thundered in Evie's chest, the tink-tank of metal on metal screeched up her spine. All five chickens laid flat with 5 shots. Bethany stood at the line next, Jewel coaching over her shoulder. Two chickens fell. Clara laid down four. Evie walked to the line. Richard Kline tucked a thumb into his belt, Cade leaned forward his forearms and one boot on the railing. Evie jammed the butt of the rifle into her shoulder. She inhaled slowly, the sights came into line. Her finger curled around the trigger. Instead of rusted tins on a crooked fence-line, Evie thought of Cade. Well specifically his horses. The first shot resounded in Evie's ear drums, her arms trembled. The tiny metallic frame fell to the straw. A cloud of smoke parted and Evie lined up the second target. Coffee. At the end of Evie's round, the five chickens were down. Pearl stepped up to the line. Evie took a second to glance up at Hamerton.

"Now that's a man I wouldn't mind hitching a wagon to," Jewel mumbled.

Evie's eyes met chocolate brown, Bethany's lips thinned.

"I mean, look at that jaw." Jewel winked at Evie who turned back to the audience. Marcus Kearby clung white knuckled to the railing beside Cade.

"He cuts a striking figure," Evie teased, "I heard he wants to be a Ranger."

"I know, how damn honourable of the man!" Jewel sighed.

Pearl shot four clean targets, the last chicken taking two shots before it gave up.

"Looks like we got ourselves a competition, Girls!"

"I'll say," Bethany mumbled, her gaze briefly scanned Hamerton before returning to Evie.

Chapter 19

By the time they shot for the ram, Clara had three turkey's still standing, Pearl had two. Bethany had three turkeys and two pigs still upright, while Evie and Jewel had levelled their targets. Evie gleamed with pride even if it had taken two shots to drop her last turkey. The crowd cheered as each girl took their place. Pearl hit one ram, Clara one, Bethany none. Evie brought the rifle up for her attempt, her shoulders and forearms ached. Freckles. The tiny target bounced of its hay bail and onto the dirt. Callouses. The next one down. Shirtless. The ram stayed upright. Evie rested her shoulders for a second before she drew the rifle level. Axe. Metal spun end over end. Denim. The ram mocked her. The muzzle dropped and Evie blew a strand across her nose. It was no good. Hamerton, suntanned, shirtless in stretched denim would not be shaken from her mind. She dropped the four next shots. The garnet crowned Jewel strode over and relieved Evie of her weapon.

"Damn Girl, what broke your concentration?"

Evie let her head fall backwards on her neck and laughed, "Nothing."

A thought spiralled out of control, like a cotton thread on the wind. Evie had more words for Cade than she had targets. Hardworking. Protective. Loyal. Strong. Irritating. Rogue and definitely easy on the eye. Evie took her place in the shade while Jewel shot, each little silhouette tumbled backwards, five shots not one more.

"Bravo!" Evie clapped, her shoulders too weary to drag her hands above her belly button.

The crowd applauded as the Judges stepped forward, Evie shook their hands as they pinned the red ribbon of second place to her burgundy gown. Pearl waved her emerald green third, Jesse Kline by her side. Evie spied her bonnet and walked between the milling judges and competitors, by the time Evie arrived at the small table, Cade spun the tiny bonnet in his hands. Evie halted.

"Don't you be going anywhere Evie!" Jewel hollered.

Marcus Kearby grimaced at the girls' abrupt tone.

"And why is that Miss Jewel," Evie straightened her spine.

"Cause, I'll be wanting a rematch next year, you hear," Jewel prodded Evie's shoulder with a finger.

Evie's gaze darted to Cade, his eyes downcast, bowed lips thin.

"I'm afraid I'll be returning to New Orleans as soon as the stock is ready,"

Jewel plonked two hands on her hips, her tongue rolled around the inside of her cheek as she eyed up Cade.

"Is that so? Well you come on back here next year, for a visit anyways," said the curly haired imp.

"Thank you for the offer," Evie slowed her words, the tang itching to be free.

"Well done, Evie-Lyn," Rick's arms curled around Evie's shoulder, "Knew you could do it,"

Cade handed Evie's bonnet to Rick, "Did you now?"

"Yep."

Cade snorted.

"What Hamerton? Evie-lyn's always shot like a dream, even when she was little one, why I remember this time when you –"

Evie inhaled and held her breath, the fog lifted, "It misfired."

Rick tugged down on his leather thong and inhaled through his teeth, "Well yeah there was that time."

"You told Earl I fell out of the tree."

"Well he was going to skin me alive, Evie-lyn!" Rick's narrow cheeks huffed and puffed, "As it was he shipped you off the next week, what would he have done to me!"

"Oh gosh," Evie snatched her bonnet, the dust kicked up her heels.

Cade's palm slapped onto Rick's chest so hard, spittle flew from the smaller man's lips.

"Hamerton! Damn you!"

Cade's fingers wrapped in red gingham and he drew Rick's vulpine face up to his nose, "Leave her alone."

Rick's fingers dug into Cade's grip, his clenched fist drove for his abdomen, but Cade twisted, his knuckles grazed his hip. Rick grabbed Cade's collar and threw his weight backwards. His knee aimed low.

Kearbey's palm tapped Cade's shoulder, his voice a harsh whisper, "Cade."

Cade relaxed his knuckles and Rick splattered on his rump, the crowd sniggered, some hollered.

Rick rushed to his feet, "I'll -,"

"No you won't," Cade opened his arms, his chest and chin exposed.

Rick grabbed his hat and dusted the dirt off the brim, "I'll beat you fair and square Hamerton, you can't stop me from competing."

Cade regarded the wide eyed onlookers, "Good luck, Rick."

"Don't go wasting any of them right hooks on him. He'll keep. Come on," Kearby said.

Cade pumped his fists and grit his teeth, a glimpse of burgundy raced through the crowd followed by sunshine yellow.

Evie's shoulder snagged on the corner of a building. The vision repeated, she aimed at the bent targets that stood atop the crooked fence. Her sights arced over the first tin, Kline stood somewhere behind, she pulled the trigger, the impact tore all sound from her ears, the fog exploded in her eyes. Evie sucked down bitter air, timber sizzled in her palms. Kline stood over her and shook her, his face twisted in panicked anger. Rick grabbed her by the scruff of the collar and dragged. Words tumbled over and over, he pointed to the tree. Next she stood in front of Earl, he knelt down, his grizzled cheeks flat, he ran the back of his hand across her cheek, smearing the residue into her many tears. Evie fell against her father's chest and cried louder than she ever had done before. His voice boomed over her shoulder, the boys scattered, as he scooped her up and carried her inside.

Evie shivered as she exhaled, trying to dam the tears that threatened. Memories of the fear, the shame and the comfort collided into a whirlwind that lashed her senses. It wasn't Rick's fault. It's wasn't her father's fault her sent her away. Earl had honoured the wishes of her mother, up until the back fire, he'd held on to Evie as long as he could.

"Are you alright?" Pearl said as she threw an arm around Evie's shoulders.

Jesse Kline skidded to a halt, not far behind.

Evie's finger tips wicked away the dew, "I am."

"Rick's is just the -,"

"It's fine Pearl, with all the powder and the heat. I just needed some fresh air."

Jesse started tossing some pebbles at the ground. Evie recalled her first meeting with Kline, he'd told her then she'd fallen out of his tree. But Earl was gone, there was no need to keep up the charade. Only to impress Evie and by lying, Kline had managed to do the opposite.

"Let's go." Evie managed.

Evie had worked through a dozen ways to skin a cat by the time she found Richard Kline back at the shooting pen. It wasn't his fault, that Earl had shipped her off to her high society aunt. It was Rick's dishonesty and all over sneakiness. Kline dusted off his thighs.

"Evie-lyn I probably should apologise for what I said, I didn't know it would upset you."

Not for lying though? Evie mused.

"Thank you Richard, I became overwhelmed with the heat. I feel better now, and I did make a promise to drop by the chilli tent for Maybelle."

"Of course," Kline licked his lips, his brow furrowed.

So nobody could stand Maybelle's chilli. Evie smiled and walked on.

Kline whimpered and hooted, slapping his thighs and guzzling a pitcher of water before he finally sat still. Evie grinned at Pearl. Maybelle beamed. Jesse took each spoonful slowly, his courage stronger than his tastebuds, his lips turned blue before he conceded. Pearl clapped with glee. At the end of the judging the dark skinned woman stood to receive a red ribbon. A lady named Divine took first prize.

"Divine intervention more like it, she wins every time," Maybelle moaned as both woman glared at each other and then smirked.

"Well, you did the Double E proud Maybelle!" Pearl said as she hooked her elbow through the larger woman's.

"Right, I might take a spell around the Festival before the real competition starts!"

Richard Kline spluttered through another glass of water, "I'll see you in the stands then. I'll be looking for you," He dropped a soft kiss on Evie's cheek without warning.

Evie froze.

Maybelle's back hand swung and missed, "Mr Kline!"

"For good luck!" he coughed and dashed off into the sun.

"Damn that man, well you know what you gotta do for our Boy then!"

"Maybelle!" Evie squealed.

Pearl covered her mouth and giggled. Jesse avoided eye contact.

"Come on," Pearl grabbed Evie's wrist.

A crowd milled around the sawdust covered arena, a three tiered stand had been set up on one side an awning barely covered the occupants, parasols and fans quivered in the soft breeze. Evie followed Pearl who followed Jesse through the rear gated area. Manure, fur and hay coated the steamy air, the young cattle bayed and mewed sprinting away from the fences in waves. Evie squinted ahead, until she spied the hitching lines.

"Pearl, what are you doing?"

Evie tried to retrieve her hand as Pearl's fingers curled tighter, "Nearly there."

"Nearly where?"

Pearl's fingers relaxed, the girl spun to the far side of a chestnut Stallion, "Good luck Maverick!" Pearl dropped a kiss on the horse's nose, a creamy brim popped up the other side.

"Pearl?"

"Good luck Cade," The ebony pony tail swung against her slender back as she dropped a sweet kiss on Hamerton's surprised cheek.

"You're missing half the competition and beside, you shouldn't be back here."

"I know but *we* came to wish you luck," Pearl said.

Jesse's hand curled in the girls palm and they disappeared behind a row of horses. Cade circled under Maverick's thick neck, the stallion's nose pressed against Cade's shoulder. Evie didn't know what to say, she spied the young bulls being herded in a separate pen.

"So not brave enough for Rodeo?"

Cade shook his head, "I tried it a few times, I never understood the point of just hanging on. There's a lot more skill in breaking and training a horse. And patience, you've got to have a lot of patience."

Evie swallowed hard. Maverick's rump met the fence, blocking Evie's retreat.

"So you came to wish me luck? That almost sounds considerate,"

Damn that girl! Tiny flames licked Evie's insides, she straightened her spine. Maverick's hooves danced around Cade's boots which inched closer to Evie's. Maverick snorted and huffed, Cade's palm captured Evie's waist. Evie broke off counting the freckles that danced across his twice-broken nose.

"I surprise myself sometimes."

"Did you wish Rick the Tick good luck?"

"Accidentally."

A crease appeared between Cade's brows, his hand dropped, "After what he said?"

"He stole a kiss from my cheek when I wasn't looking, what was I supposed to do?"

A thin smirk crossed Cade's face, "Your cheek?"

"Yes," Evie huffed, "Besides it's not really his fault Earl sent me off to live with Aunt Eustace. My mother wrote in her journal a long time ago, that she intended to do exactly that whether my father liked it or not." Evie found a line of shade between Maverick and Cade and sheltered against the tall horse.

"I didn't know that, why?"

"Because she knew, I mean, she thought that," Evie spluttered, "… that as I grew older, there would be nothing for me in Dew Springs."

164

Evie's cheeks darkened and she loosened the strings on her bonnet. She was supposed to furious at this man, how did she end up feeling guilty all of a sudden.

"Some way to wish me luck Evie."

Evie ignored Cade's jibe, what did he care if she left Dew Springs forever? He'd have the Double E all to himself. Evie would just be the notch he never got to add to his belt.

"Rick wouldn't have known what my mother intended. The misfire would have been the sign my father took at the right time before I got even more out of hand."

"You're right about that," Cade snorted, "So Rick's forgiven then?" he said as he brushed his palm down Mav's shiny chest.

"I made him taste Maybelle's chilli," Evie rolled her lips inwards.

"You're a cruel woman Evelyn Lockwood."

Evie laughed, her shoulder coming to rest against Maverick's flank, she tried to ignore the comforting masculine flavours that danced across her palette.

"He deserved it for lying to me. The first day I arrived at Dew Springs he told me I'd fallen out of his tree."

Cade bit his tongue, he wanted to say I told you so, like an itch that he couldn't scratch. He let it pass and focused on the red ribbon tied to Evie's dress. Lying. Was Rick's lie justified? What about his own lies?

"How did Maybelle fair at the cook-off anyway, did she beat Divine?"

"Nope, second place. So far the Double E is doing well." Evie challenged.

His fingers found the ruby satin and tugged, Evie gasped, as he ran his fingers down her ribbon.

"So I see."

Emerald gemstones glittered like dawn across the meadows.

"You better not let us down then."

His life's struggle uttered from the sultry lips of his tormentor. Cade tilted his head, *us?*

"Not to rain on your parade Darling, but this event is all about the horses," His arm traced down Maverick's spine until Evie's heart shaped face came in line with his bicep, his fingers grazed the brand on Mav's rump, "If I win, it'll be the Slanted Hammer on top." The woman didn't even turn, her neck tilted back, chin raised, her chest surged. A rush of energy traversed Cade's spine, he cupped her cheek, dragging his thumb down her bottom lip, "Are you going to wish me luck then?"

Evie's grip entwined in his leather vest as he brought her forward, she stood on tiptoes to reach him, lips pressed for the briefest moment, his tongue darted forward to taste the apricot and peaches that taunted his dreams.

"After this Hamerton I'd be surprised if you - ,"

Cade broke away, Evie straightened her bonnet as Maverick snorted. Richard Kline appeared on the other side of the stallion's saddle.

"Oh Evie-lyn, what are you doing back here?" Rick questioned.

"She came to wish me luck."

"Luck?" Rick's tone softened, "Well I guess this contest will decided once and for all whose most adequate to handle Evie-lyn's stock."

Evie concealed her cringe and strode forward until she came in line Maverick's nose, she dropped a sweet kiss on the horses' muzzle, the chestnut beast closed his eyes and pushed forward until Evie almost overbalanced. The horse snorted, his hoof coming down close to Rick's boots.

"Watch out there Evie-lyn, doesn't matter how well trained they seem, their still a beast at heart."

Cade's polished sapphires churned to blue diamond, a vein in his jaw tensed.

"I guess you don't want to break their spirit. Good luck gentleman," Evie added.

She lifted up her skirts and hurried to a safe distance. Evie initially had wanted to pit these two men against each other to drive her value in the homestead. Somehow the homestead had been replaced by her, and Evie knew who she wanted to win. Questions remained over the price and what Evie would get in return.

Evie spied Pearl sitting low on a fence bar, Jesse stood in front, one leg on the cross beam, his hands clasped hers. Jesse reached out and ran his fingers down Pearl's dark locks. Pearl's gaze met Evie's and she stood upright; Jesse chastely behind, his cheeks rosy red. Evie smiled, some chaperone you've been!

"Well thank you Pearl for that little detour, shall we find some seats now,"

Cade eyed Rick over the saddle of Maverick, forcing the shorter man to stretch to glare at him eye to eye.

"What do you think you're playing at Hamerton?"

"You said at all costs Rick, I'm just playing your game."

For a second Cade wondered if he had drawn ahead. Evie had told him in no uncertain terms, that she would not be involved with someone like him, she had no intentions of staying in Dew Springs. There was nothing here for her. Despite all that, her haughty demeanour had softened, she enticed his kiss. She kissed Maverick too you idiot.

"Nice try. Evie's going to the Dance with me, and by tomorrow morning, I'll be working on another Kline legacy."

Cade scoffed, "You reckon Rick? I think you've got a snowflake's chance in – "

"And you think a Hamerton is what Evie wants?"

Cade whistled between his teeth softly and Maverick stopped his front hoofs back and forth until Rick shifted back.

"You've got some brave words."

Cade stepped underneath Maverick's neck, the hooves ceased. Rick backed further away. Something soft seemed to stir under his ribs, normally he'd have Rick on his back, his fist in his narrow face, but right now Rick didn't seem worth the effort.

"Four Star Ranch, time to shine!" An official hollered from the arena gate.

Cade snorted, "Good luck Rick."

Chapter 20

Evie shoved her thick strands underneath her bonnet and cursed for the third time on her choice of wearing a dark colour in the Texan sun.

"Pardon Evie?"

"Nothing Pearl, now tell me again how does this work?"

Pearl reiterated the rules as Richard Kline entered the arena atop his Piebald gelding. Pearl broke off her explanation to whistle with fingers between her teeth at Jesse who sat atop palomino mare, the young man took his place with three other Hands at the open ended section of the arena. Kline stood in front of the shifty herd of juvenile cattle.

"He's got to get two in the time limit, 2 and a half minutes, points off for using the fence, or quitting the cow too early, or picking too shallow."

"Okay," Evie nodded.

Kline drove his gelding into the bustling herd, he snatched the reins until his horse seemed to hone in on its target.

"Damn, he picked a good one first up."

Kline let his horse meander through the crowd, until the steer balked. Kline dropped his hands to the pommel of his saddle. The Piebald danced from side to side, mirroring the steers movements, the geldings head lowered, his hoofs dug into the sawdust, he sprinted left then right until the beast snorted and turned its back. The crowd cheered. Kline picked up the reins and headed back in, Jesse neared his horse to the mob.

"Jesse and the other one have to hold them there, so they don't mess up Rick's work."

Evie sat wide-eyed in the glaring afternoon sun to watch Kline make his next selection.

"He's gone easy this time, which he is allowed to do, no sense making it hard second time around."

The calf baulked to the clear area, Kline's hands dropped. His horse danced from side to side, the back legs shifted backwards.

"He's going to have to watch out." Pearl mumbled.

No sooner had the words left her mouth than the rear herd startled, Jesse steered his mount to block them. Kline was too far back, one steer escaped. Kline's Piebald pranced in front of its original target until the calf relented and sprinted off to find its friend.

"He disturbed the back herd, they should deduct points."

"Is that bad?"

"Yes," Pearl whispered.

Kline chastised Jesse, the boy's head hung low.

"It's not that Boy's fault, Rick should have stayed forward." Maybelle hollered.

Half the crowd around her nodded in agreeance, the others clapped as Rick's score of 72 appeared on two white placards. Evie turned to the patron beside her.

"What's the highest score so far?"

"That's it there Miss," A grizzled old cowboy mumbled.

"Okay well let's see how the rest fair," Evie added wistfully. A wad of bees seemed to hum inside her belly.

Windy Hill Ranch competed next, Taylor Stone the representative for a man named Old George, his score of 71 earned a gracious clap from the audience. The Blue Cow Ranch entered the arena as Evie's patience had worn thin; she clapped whole heartedly as Shelton Murphy sorted through the cattle to a score of 71.5.

"Cade Hamerton, Double E Ranch."

Evie pressed her palms to her stomach. Pearl stood up and whistled, Maybelle hollered louder than the rest. Evie watched the crowd. Along the fence line, Marcus, Shelton and Taylor clapped, Rick across the other side stood, one hand scratching his chin.

Maverick trotted into the arena, shaking his head to the loud applause, Cade ran a gentle hand down the Stallion's neck. Tomas, Fernandez, Diego and Julius brought their mounts into position. Cade turned Maverick on a dime and the tall horse sauntered, no stalked through the herd. Cade tugged Maverick's reins once, a steer from deep within the herd balked at

Maverick's muzzle. Cade snatched the pommel of his saddle as Maverick stepped to the left. Cade's cheeks paled, his knees slipped. Evie stood as his saddle strap hit the sawdust.

Pearl clutched Evie's arm, as the bulky man twisted trying to counteract the unfastened saddle and the dancing stallion. For a second Cade stood in the stirrups, his white knuckles in Maverick's mane, his knee's clenched the horse's muscled flanks and his boots gave way. With one arm, he tugged the saddle, the tack landed at Nieve's hooves and Fernandez scooped it up in one swift movement. The crowd stood on their feet as Cade held on. Maverick countered to the right, the baby bull gave up.

"What happens now, he'll get a reset won't he?" Evie cried.

She couldn't sit down as she watched Cade drive Maverick through the herd.

"He'll have to choose hard to –" Pearl started, "And he did."

Cade drove the largest steer from the pack to the front, Maverick snorted, his heels dug into the sawdust, knees straight. The steer snorted, and pawed the ground. Maverick reiterated his demands, and stepped forward, the bull dropped his head, Maverick did the same. To the left, then the right and back again Maverick countered. Cade's eyes dead ahead, his roped forearms locked at Maverick's withers, the reins slack. The steer snorted, and shook his head, before turning tail. The stand trembled as the crowd stood, the applause deafening. The judge's placed their heads together, one pointed at the sheet and then threw his hands in the air. The middle Judge stood, the white numbers faced the audience. Hats threw in the air, boots stomped the timber and Evie craned her neck.

"It's 78!" Pearl squealed.

Once the crowd simmered, Evie spied Richard Kline marching up to the Judges, he threw his hat down on the table and pointed a finger at the middle judge.

"They'll be nothing in the rules about losing a saddle, I bet," Maybelle chuckled.

"Not this year anyway," Evie's grin vanished as a dark shadow slivered up her spine. Rick's eyes blasted Hamerton where he stood with his comrades.

"Ronaldo Garcia, Stillwater Ranch." The announcer demanded.

Evie and Pearl sat through the next three competitors holding hands. 75, 71, and 69. Evie found herself on her feet clapping as Cade stood to receive his ribbon. The voluptuous figure of Bethany Sampson marched into the arena, and up to Cade to pin a blue ribbon onto his chest. Evie blinked twice, her hands froze as Bethany threw her arms around Cade's neck, his hand on her waist, his head titled down. The crowd applauded.

Cade tried to unwind Bethany with some dignity, his palms pushed against her hips, before his lips found her ear.

"If you don't move Bethany you'll end up on your rump, like the discarded –"

"I just wanted to congratulate you, Cade," She whined.

The curvaceous brunette moved to second place and then Kline at third place giving each man a chaste peck on the cheek. His eyes scanned the stadiums, burgundy silks missing. A cowpoke laid a single row of flowers across Maverick's neck, his teeth instantly sampling his new decoration. Cade found the Double E Hands and thanked them.

"You forget to tie your saddle Boss." Diego jeered.

"Ci, and after Miss Evie wished you luck too!" Tomas added.

"Las cuatro estrellas estaban desesperadas,' Fernandez threw the saddle down at Cade's feet.

The other hands nodded.

"Desperate. Kline. That doesn't sound right," Cade's jaw cracked.

He'd been too busy filling his hands with Evie to notice what Kline had done at Maverick's side. He picked up his saddle and turned the leather over in his hands. Still intact, not sliced or cut. Cade knew sabotage was not beneath Rick the Tick, but would the man risk Cade's life? If he broke his neck, would the Double E revert to Evelyn? He needed to check the fine print. Hopefully Evie hadn't. He led Maverick back to the hitching lines, a group of Ranchers milled between the ropes.

"Say Hamerton, you train anymore like him?"

"You know I do, Peter otherwise you wouldn't be waiting here."

"Alright Hamerton, no need to get a prickle in your moustache I'm here to talk business."

Cade nodded. He didn't have a moustache, but Peter Stillwater owned the third largest Ranch in Dew.

"Go on Peter, I'm listening."

By the time Cade had finished, he'd shaken hands with all four Ranchers, the details of the deals included providing the horses, breaking some of their newest, training others and studding at least five mares from Maverick.

"You're going to be busy soon Old Boy."

Multi-coloured petals drifted to the ground from between Maverick's whiskered lips. Which brought Cade back to the present, Evie. Bethany had bored a tunnel through any good work he'd achieved earlier. He should be angry, irate, disappointed maybe for her comments that nothing in Dew Springs could hold her. She'd still given him a kiss, or had he taken it? He rested Maverick and entered the crowd of the Festival, he stopped when greeted, his eyes scanned the crowd for errant blonde strands and sizzling burgundy.

Evie tossed her bonnet onto the covers and blinked until her lashes dried.

"Bethany is like ashes in the wind."

"Pearl!" Evie hollered.

"Well she is!"

"There is nothing to get upset about Pearl. Right now I need a bath more than I need to hear any more about Cade bloody Hamerton."

Evie submersed herself in the hot water, until any trace of Cade's caresses had been scorched from her skin. She resurfaced just in time to pick up Pearl's last line of conversation.

"Jesse said Rick ripped into him about that calf, I bet it was Rick who undid Cade's saddle."

"Pearl!"

"Sorry."

Evie shook her head. She could only imagine the girl sulking behind the wooden screen. Evie picked up the bar of soap and tossed it over the barrier. A splash cheered Evie up.

"Hey!" Pearl giggled.

The bar plopped back in Evie's tub, a spray of water injected up Evie's nose so fast, she snorted.

"Did you get to um …wish him luck, at least?"

Evie leaned back, her neck on the rolled edge, "Yes."

Pearl's voice filtered through the slated timber quieter than before, "What was it like?"

Evie wondered whether this conversation had tiptoed into dangerous territory, she didn't want to be thinking about the man let alone reminiscing about it with Pearl.

"Well, I won't be asking Maybelle and I can't ask Cade!"

This was not what Evie meant when she thought Pearl needed lady-like guidance. Evie sighed, "Like double strike lightening…."

Pearl hummed.

"….in the middle of a prairie fire. And looking down the barrel of a tornado,"

"How so?"

Evie ran a finger across her bottom lip, "All the air disappears from your lungs, the strength taken from your knees," Evie pined, "And all you want to do is be swept up in it."

Silence echoed through the bathroom.

Pearl finally spoke, "Wow Evie, are they all like that?"

Evie couldn't answer without her chest constricting. No, they certainly were not.

"Time we got out, don't you think? Especially if, I'm to do your hair, and mine, in time for the dance."

Evie tucked and curled and pinned and tied until Pearls' luscious locks had been piled into a neat bun at the nape of her neck, a whirlwind of curls cascaded down her cheeks, scar hidden, her blue eyes accentuated by the ebony curtain that framed her petite face. The girl's beauty radiated from within, her pink dress fell in ruffles about her slender figure, the canary yellow sash ruched around her narrow waist.

"Oh Pearl, you look like cherries in the sunshine."

"Can you see it?"

"Not one lick, and I've already told you Jesse doesn't see what you think he sees. Jesse looks at you like the desert does the morning dew."

"Like a bird without a song."

"Yes Maybelle, exactly,"

"Like tea without sugar."

"You mean chilli without sugar." Pearl added.

Evie clicked her tongue, "I've had enough of chilli and sweet tea, thank you."

A knock on the door made them all jump. Maybelle rose in her vivacious lime green to greet Kline.

"Why Evie-lyn you look just like a dream," said the Rancher, his silk shirt as slick as his smile.

"Thank you Richard."

"And Miss Pearl and Miss Maybelle."

Jesse Kline loitered in the hallway, his eyes wide, cheeks coloured, "Pearl, you look like an Indian Blanket after the rain."

The group fell silent, as Pearl blushed to match her dress.

"Thank you Jesse, you look very fine tonight too."

Evie's heart skipped to a faster beat as the group departed the Blue Bell towards the Hall. Colourful tea light candles suspended daintily from the acacia trees, strung from roof top to roof top like a diamond necklace. Evie straightened her hair, the skin on her arm crawling as she took Kline's elbow. Her gaze ran from corner to corner, searching the party-goers, for a cream Stetson. A fiddler accompanied a piano on the stage, streamers and more tea lights lined the ceiling and the tables. The ladies jostled in a plethora of coloured ruffles and sashes, like tea lights in the wind. Evie ran her hands down her pale blue dress, the soft fabric slipping through her fingers like patience. If Cade didn't come what did that mean?

"Mr Robert Wrucker this is Evie-lyn Lockwood."

Evie regained her wandering eye and commenced the round of introductions. Rick almost passed over Taylor Stone and Bethany Sampson who stood awkwardly with an older couple. The younger man turned to greet Evie.

"Miss Evelyn Lockwood, these are my parents, Walter and Gertrude Stone, you've already met Ms Sampson," Taylor's freshly shaven cheeks hardened, "Kline."

"Evening folks," Richard circled his arm around Evie's waist, she launched forward to greet the Taylors.

"Pleasure, Evelyn. I can't imagine it has all been fun and fiddlesticks for you out at your Daddy's farm, but rest assured the Double E is in good hands," Walter Stone said.

Richard scoffed, "If you think so."

"Where is Cade, honey?" Mrs Stone turned to her son.

Evie missed the reply as Bethany sidled closer to Evie, her voice dropped to a whisper.

"That man has left a trail of broken hearts and torn petticoats in this town, I should know."

Evie's teeth ground down, she lifted her voice a little, "That is neither impressive nor intimidating Miss Sampson. And considering how it casts you, I'm surprised you'd even bring it up."

Bethany's peach skirt twisted against Evie's pale blue, her top lip peaked as she spoke, "What are you saying?"

Evie paused, she didn't want to embarrass the girl. Cade had called her immature, she should try and hold her tongue for once. The image of Bethany locking her arms around Cade's neck at the Cutting stand, popped into Evie's mind.

"I'm not sure if I failed to hitch a wagon to a horse that I'd be telling all and sundry how I couldn't."

The Stone's gasped, Kline rubbed the back of his neck. He'd shifted his attention to a more ancient cowboy who Evie assumed was Old George from Windy Hill. Kline grabbed the older man's elbow and stepped further away.

Bethany lowered her voice, "He ain't even worth it. You'll find out soon enough."

"I beg to differ, Bethany."

Taylor's brown peepers widened, his brows raised.

Evie baulked, she'd said too much, "I mean he must have been at some point, if he wasn't then what does that say about you?"

Peach skirts swished as the voluptuous brunette sped across the hall.

Evie eyed her company, "I'm sorry, it's just, I mean I –"

Mr Stone leaned forward, and whispered, "That woman has been trying to hitch a wagon to a few horses of late," his steel coloured eyes tracked to his son and back to Evie.

"And that's not counting the ones she rides bare back into town."

"Gertrude!"

"Mother!"

Evie took her hand away from her mouth, once she regained control, "I am sorry."

"I suppose I should go after her?" Taylor mumbled.

"You stay Taylor, I'm the one who has upset her. I need to apologise, I figure you've ended up with the raw end of a bargain somehow and it's because of me."

Taylor fell into step with Evie as they skirted the filling hall, he tugged his collar free from his neck, clearly the stiff fabric itched his suntanned skin.

"Well she wasn't supposed to be my date and nor was Kline supposed to be yours," Taylor added.

"Well,..." Evie flustered, "I know."

"I've stepped out of line, I apologize."

Kline stood with Old George, the elderly man backed into a corner. Well Cade could have asked her?

"I wasn't asked by anyone else Mr Taylor and I'm supposed to be chaperoning Pearl."

"Oh that's right, where is she?"

Evie turned around, her selfishness had let her down, she come over to interrogate Bethany instead. Evie stalked around the edges of the dance, irritation riding her neck like a rash. She reached the far side doors where a circle of ladies giggled and gossiped.

"Miss Lockwood," Taylor started, "I feel I ought to..."

"What Mr Stone?"

Evie paused as a hush settled over the ladies, their gazes suddenly drawn to a figure that entered the hall. Evie followed their path to the striking figure, a pale mint green shirt stretched across his solid chest, the sleeves pinched near his arms. The silky fabric bunched around Cades' narrow waist into the cleanest pair of brown denims Evie had seen. The cream Stetson twirled in his fingers, his russet curls neat around his furrowed brows. The normal rogue locks now restrained. Even Evie sighed in unison with the ladies at the door. Pools of sapphire assaulted Evie, a stampede of butterflies traversed her spine.

Taylor eyed Evie and back to Cade, "Never mind," he grinned.

"Are you taking off with my date Mr Stone?"

"Not know Richard."

Evie dashed from the hall scanning for peach and yellow ruffles.

Chapter 21

Evie heard Rick's boots echo off the steps as he rushed after her. She turned left into the darkened exterior.

"Listen Evie while I've got you, I ought to warn you."

"I'll find Bethany," Taylor mumbled and turned right.

Evie clicked her tongue, her strides falling short of leaving Kline in her wake.

"I saw you with Cade at the stock yards. I know you don't know much about this town or who you should spend your time with. I need to warn you that, Cade Hamerton is -" Kline ran his arm around Evie's waist again.

She stopped and pushed him back. Kline straightened his spine.

"I mean to say, that Hamerton won't treat you like the lady you really are."

Evie hid her smirk in the half dark, I'm not a real lady. Ricks fingers searched for Evie's, and she snatched them back.

"He's just like his Pa, heavy handed with his horses, with his booze and with his women."

Rick's hand landed on her shoulder, his thumb across her throat.

"Evie?" Taylor had come full circle, no Bethany to be found.

Ricks voice raised, "I've seen those bruises on your arm."

Taylor's brown eyes shined like sinking stones. Evie shook her head, No. Not Cade?

Evie cleared her throat, "Those marks are from Dawnee, the damn horse was labouring and I got in the way!" Evie spat, a twang sliding through her words but she didn't care.

Rick tried to push Evie further down the darkened patio, her boots stayed planted, "And I know Evie, that the apple don't fall too far from the tree."

"Rick," Taylor warned his tone thicker than before.

179

"That's not fair to your father Rick I heard he was a great man." Evie said

Ricks jaw dropped.

Taylor coughed loudly, "I think it's time we left Evie, don't you?"

"Yes, excuse us Rick, I was looking for Pearl so if you don't mind -,"

Kline's voice raised, his laugh shallow, "Yes of course, Evie let's go."

Evie's heels thundered down the patio, the light from the main door calling her forward. Taylor hounded Rick's footsteps, as the Four Star Rancher shadowed Evie.

"You should heed my words, Evie-Lyn."

Evie stopped, "Cade was not raised by his father, he was raised by mine."

Swirls of peach and brunette appeared through the doorway, Bethany's cheeks stained red, brown eyes narrow. Taylor squared his shoulders as if to steel himself for the battle. Evie gave Taylor a reassuring pat on the forearm.

"Bethany," Taylor called, as he eventually caught up with the dark haired girl.

Rick cleared his throat, in one movement his fingers wound around Evie's wrist and she stumbled back off balance.

"That's not what I meant and you know it." Kline's face hovered inches above Evie's, her forearms pushed his chest, "Levi Hamerton was as rotten as they get and –"

"No one's arguing that Rick."

Cade stepped out of the shadows, Rick released Evie, the pressure on her elbow tingling back to normal. Her trembling fingers scraped the sleeve of her dress upright, the blue shadowy skin now covered. Taylor paused mid-apology, Bethany's neck stretched. Evie saw two figures emerge past Cade as he stepped up to Rick, Pearl and Jesse waivered at the doorway, their heads turning to follow everyone's gaze. Cade stood almost chest to chest to Rick, the smaller man's narrow shoulder's widening in false bravado.

Rick laughed, his lips thinned, eyes narrow, "Then you should've be happy that he swung when he did."

"Cade?" Pearl gasped.

"Pearl!"

Rick clicked his tongue, "She should be used to disappointment, from you Cade. You couldn't protect her from Levi Hamerton then, and not even when he's dead. Is that what you think of when you look at her face? Do you see your future? Come on Evie-Lyn," Ricks arm slithered around Evie's shoulders.

"That's it!" Evie's snapped as her elbow collided with his ribs.

Kline's fingers clamped down on her collarbone, a slice of pain made her knee bend.

"Don't be a fool!" Kline spat.

Rick suddenly stumbled back by another force, his knuckles clenched, he twisted and grabbed Cades shirt. Evie watched Cades fist connect with Ricks narrow cheek bone, the man went down. Cade gripped Kline's collar, Richard now splayed on the ground. Cades fist landed again and again. Like a hail storm, panic battered Evie's senses, Cade wasn't going to stop. She dashed forward, her hand grabbed Cades forearm, a weight collided with Evie's chest, the air exhaled, Cade turned to register what his elbow had struck. A barrage of male scents overwhelmed Evie as Marcus and Shelton came out of nowhere to help Taylor capture the assailant. Cade stood, and shrugged off his friends. He stepped back, his eyes cold and defeated.

In that moment Evie felt the curtains drawn back, Cade whole and damaged stood before her. Her feet wanted to move forward to the man she now saw. Cade was exposed, raw and hurting. Evie clutched her chest, as his pain sliced through her. She needed to lessen his pain, to share this weight, the guilt and the sorrow he'd been shouldering for so long on his own. The pieces fell into place. Pearl was his sister, Levi Hamerton the man Cade had chased from the Double E. The man Cade had nearly killed.

Evie's heart ached, as the silhouette of Cade disappeared into the shadows. Pearl! She needed to find pearl. Cade would have kept their father's death from her for protection only. Bethany Sampson helped Rick to his feet. A crowd began to mill around the injured Rancher. Evie heard snippets of "Hamerton up to his old tricks" followed by "Can't control his temper" and then "Just like his old man,"

Evie stormed past the injured Rancher, she needed to find Pearl.

"Thank you Evie-lyn," Rick called.

"Don't thank me Rick, you deserved more than that for your despicable behaviour and you know it! I wouldn't spit on you if you were on fire. Don't even think about stepping one foot on the Double E or I'll shoot you myself."

A snigger reverberated through the crowd, someone hollered, "We've seen she can do it!"

"And another thing, if you call me Evie-lyn one more time, I'll slap a month of Sunday's off your sly face before you can say Southern hospitality!"

The crowd cheered, Evie ignored Cade's comrades, no doubt blaming her for Cade's outburst. She'd come with Rick the Tick, she'd pushed him to his breaking point. By the time Evie made it all the way back to the Blue Bell, her anger only subsided when she ran into Tomas and Fernandez at the entrance,

"Ci he took off on Mav," Tomas nodded.

"Thank you Tomas, I don't suppose you know where he was going?"

"We thought here, Miss."

Evie eyed the double storey hotel, lamp lights bright in the front two rooms. Evie hurried upstairs and leaned against the door. She heard Maybelle and Pearl's voices as they packed their rooms.

"Are you alright?" Evie whispered as she tiptoed over the debris.

She stole a spot next to Pearl on the single bed and threw her arm around the younger girls shivering shoulders. Pearls cheeks had been scrubbed red, her eyes lined in ruby.

"I'm fine Evie, I just want to go home. Levi Hamerton was no father to me." The girls' sobs became lost on Evie's shoulder. When the tremors ebbed, Pearl lifted her head, "I worry about Cade. He does everything to protect me, it's not his fault he was only young at the time, almost as old as Jesse is now. He's taken the responsibility of what happens to me since then." Pearl said. He took care of Pearl and then of her father and now Maybelle and Evie, "He takes care of all of us, but who takes care of him?"

"I told you," Evie kissed Pearl on the side of her head and whispered into her hair, "Let me worry about Cade."

"I figured since Mr Kline has an account he won't mind having three empty rooms on his bill," Maybelle said as she slammed her case of clothes firmly shut.

Evie smirked, "I have a better idea."

Evie stood on the Blue Bell stoop, Tomas and Fernandez discussing Evie's idea at length in rushed Spanish. Eventually Fernandez clapped his hands and stood beside Evie. Tomas nodded.

"Ci, I'll tell the others, they will thank you very much Senorita!" Tomas said as he took the three hotel room keys.

Fernandez hitched the stocky Pluma to the Double E wagon.

"Thank you Miss Evie, we'll see you tomorrow morning at Church!"

"Mmmmhumph!" Maybelle chirped.

Evie spied Jesse dip his head to Pearl's cheek and then hover inches from her lips. Evie turned her back and climbed into the wagon, as she slowly counted to ten.

"Come on Pearl, I've had enough of Dew for tonight!" Evie hollered.

"Miss Evie," Jesse stood at the rail, "I apologise for my cousin's behaviour, he is hot-headed and stubborn and downright selfish at time. He means well, I think."

Evie shook her head, "It's nice of you to be so loyal Jesse. Your cousin may not be welcome at the Double E, however if you feel like popping by sometime, don't be a stranger." Evie winked.

Jesse's young face beamed. He gazed at Pearl, Fernandez tapped the reins and Pluma shifted forward.

Evie's eyes strained in the moonlight shadow, a single lamp adding to the thin silvery pool, in which, Fernandez could guide Pluma over the terrain. No sign of a lone horseman tearing off across the fields. Would the man be skin deep into whiskey or would he wrap himself in the flesh of a woman to ease his pain? Evie gave up and sat back in the wagon. She snuggled into the one blanket, Pearl's coming to rest between Evie's shoulder and Maybelle's.

"You did good tonight, Miss Evie."

"I don't think so."

"You did, and don't let anyone tell you otherwise."

"Maybelle, do you know why is there so much hostility between Cade and Rick?"

Maybelle picked a thread from her lap and eyed Fernandez, she leaned closer.

"A while back Earl and Cade argued over that dang Bull of his and some trouble. Next minute Cade marches over to the Four Star for a dust up, that Boy came back darker than midnight in a coffin. Then your Pa gets ill. I mean real sick. For some reason, Cade picks another dang fight with the Four Star! I'm speaking out of turn here."

"Please Maybelle, I need to know."

"Well I can't tell ya much more, but Cade came back that second time, looking like he'd raised hell and stuck a chunk under it. That Boy sold all his horses. Back out on his bones. Then your Pa up and passes, Lord Bless his soul. Cade,...." Maybelle scrubbed her cheek on her shoulder, "Cade has been fighting in one shape of another for most of his life. I've never seen that Boy so lost than on the day of ya Pa's funeral," Maybelle sniffled.

Evie wiped the tears from her eyes. She could fill in the blanks herself. Earl had loaned money from Rick. The loan that doubled in payments almost brokering the Double E. Cade, the boy who had been perpetually followed by a dark cloud had turned into the man knee deep in struggle, until Dew Springs forgot his father's name. No wonder Earl left him the Double E, Cade had unselfishly saved it. Earl had saved Cade. It didn't seem fair.

Rick the Tick had tried to financially bury her father, as well as vilify Cade at every opportunity. Increasing the pressure until eventually Cade would snap and "prove" how like Levi Hamerton he really was. Evie sniffled into the blanket, and on top of losing Earl he'd lost his father, to the hangman. Another mark added to the dark side of the ledger against Cade's name. Evie balanced the columns in her own head, Cade still came out on top. She let her internal tally continue until the timber tilted under her numb rump. Maybelle shook Pearl awake as Pluma

slowed to a standstill and Fernandez helped them down one by
one.

"Gracious Fernandez," Evie said,

"Ci, Senorita. *Alguien tendrá que traer a la Srta. Maybelle de
vuelta a la iglesia mañana, y por casualidad me gustan sus
punqueques.*"

Evie tilted her head, her ears sluggish.

"I never said nothin' about Pancakes Fernandez," Maybelle
grumbled.

The older cowpoke, winked at Evie and lead Pluma away.
Evie regarded the stable, the normal russet roof now eerie blue in
the half-moon light. Was Maverick tucked away in there?
Fernandez would alert Cade to their return if he was. Evie looked
up to the darkened interior of the homestead. Empty. Maybelle
walked around the lower half, a lamp sprung to life on the table,
another in the kitchen. Chitto bellowed from the rear and Pearl
dragged herself up the stairs. Evie threw her arm around the
girl's shoulders. Maybelle bid goodnight and retreated to her
bedroom, on the other side of the kitchen. Evie squeezed Pearl
one more time.

"Please Evie, if you see Cade, tell him I'm not mad. Tell him,
I have already forgiven him for whatever blame he's heaped on
himself. Evie will you, please."

Evie squeezed the girls frozen fingers, "I will."

Pearl scooped up Chitto, the solid pup licking her face, his
teeth nipping the cherry pink ruffles that now sagged over her
narrow shoulders. Evie tiptoed up the stairs, a lamp light splitting
into shards of darkness as her fingers traced the open door frame,
Cade's bed empty. A horse whinnied and Evie returned down
stairs, the patio still in darkness. Evie kicked off her boots and
stretched her stockinged toes. If Cade was coming back tonight,
he'd have to walk through the front door. Evie didn't need to
wait on the porch. What she was going to say to him, past Pearl's
apology, Evie didn't know. She needed to apologise, she needed
to thank him. She needed to tell him.... Evie shook her head and
turned the lamp down low. A hideous patchwork throw became
her blanket, the arm rest her pillow.

Boots scuffed across timber, a cupboard door squeaked the
noise muffled by something soft. Evie's eyes fluttered open to

the silvery darkness, lime green satin and dark denim marched past, a wave of sage washed over Evie. The screen door squeaked and Cade cursed in hush tones.

Evie unwound herself from the couch and tiptoed forward. Cade stood at the railing, he had a pitcher of whiskey in one hand, his teeth tugged the cork free. He tipped the malted liquor over his splayed knuckles, his shoulders shuddered. He took a step backwards, the chair groaned as it took his bulky weight. Cade placed his Stetson on one knee and poured himself a shot of the dark drink. Evie pushed gently on the door, his sapphire gaze stung, her courage fled.

Cade looked at the shot glass, "Once a year, I pour myself one. Just one."

Evie's stockings snagged in the timber as his thigh disturbed her ruffled skirts, "When?"

"Usually at Chri-," Cade let the words die.

A length of rope tightened around his ribs. He looked at Evie, her blonde hair in messy loops, strands straightened down her slender neck. Ruth's favourite patchwork throw covered the splendour of her pale blue dress. Cade's tongue had thickened when he'd spied Evie across the Hall tonight. Her usual savage beauty, gleamed to a loud intensity, had softened to a glorious deep melody. As if the blonde scamp he once recognised as Evie had blossomed into a woman, rather than impersonated one. He ran his gaze down to her stockinged toes, the knot around his chest loosened. He'd struck Evie accidentally when he'd flattened Kline. Damn Rick the Tick! He owed Pearl and Evie an apology. Evie inched closer.

"At Christmas." Evie whispered.

Cade didn't move. Slender fingers curled around his, the glass came free. Evie threw back her head, the dark liquor gone in one swift movement. She licked her lips and shivered before she sat down in Earl's rocking chair, one hand remained, finger tips traced his raw knuckles.

"Please, Cade."

Cade took his hand away, and regarded the blisters in his palm. The phantom rope twisted under his ribs. He closed his eyes and exhaled slowly. Evie sat as still as a lizard on a rock, waiting. The pain ground through his bones, the weight frustratingly stubborn.

"Levi Hamerton brought my mother and I out to the Double E when I was a baby. It didn't take long for her to realise he wasn't going to change his ways, so she took off. When he didn't have her to rage against, he took it out on me."

Cade heard Evie wince. He swallowed hard, and pressed hard on his cut knuckles.

"Edwina did her best, keeping me out of his way. Earl sent him on every drive he could. Without liquor, Levi was supposed to have been charismatic, a joker. When you came along, I think Earl realised more of what was going on, because I spent more and more time with him and your mother than I did with Levi. They had arguments over it."

"Why did my father not just send him away?"

"He did eventually. We never spoke about why then and not earlier. I figured Earl thought, if we were here, in sight, then he could protect me." Cade shook his head, his shoulders arched.

"Go on,"

"It got bad." Cade inhaled slowly, "Just after you left, it got real bad." His finger absentmindedly ran down the bridge of his nose, "Earl had enough and sent Levi on his way, a full pay in his pocket. He was broke before he left the Nine Lives Saloon the next day. They ran him out of town."

"You stayed,"

"I did. I don't think Earl would have let me leave with Levi, but after he'd lost you, he saw an opportunity. I worked hard, if I could just stay out of trouble, I'd might turn out alright. Levi had tried to teach me the only way you gained respect was having people fear you. Earl showed me another way."

"And Pearl?"

"When I was fourteen, Levi dragged himself back here with empty pockets, a new wife, half Mexican, maybe Indian and a baby daughter. Figured Earl would take him back if he saw how he'd changed. I think Earl saw straight through him. I did. He used Pearl and her mother as a bargaining chip,"

"Emotional blackmail to a man who'd already taken in his eldest child," Evie whispered.

The scent of sweaty hair, and blood coiled at the back of Cade's tongue. He shifted to the far side of the chair, the space between Evie and himself increased.

"He took me to task one day, over something stupid." Cade flicked the brim of his hat, "I pushed back, harder than I had before. Earl stopped him," He rolled his cheek between his teeth, the sting of those blows echoed through his mind, "So he took it out on Pearl." Out of his peripherals Cade sensed Evie's tension, yet she remained still. He wriggled in his chair, his gaze regarded his boots, his chin almost to his chest.

"You ran him off the Double E?"

Cade just nodded.

"The other day you told me you almost –"

"Levi came back to Dew Springs, I found him in the Nine Lives Saloon before he could make it out the Double E to plead his case."

"What happened?"

"I beat him to within an inch of his life,"

Chapter 22

"Earl bailed me out. I never saw him again. I never told Pearl."

"Cade, it's not your fault,"

"If I hadn't stood up to him, if I'd just taken the blows –"

The words tumbled over his lips, like a loose thread unwinding, coils of tension wracked his muscles. Levi's face swum before his eyes, bloodied and bruised, the flesh tore across his lips and brow, dirt caked into the open wounds. The anger and finally shock swirling through Levi's blue gaze, like the shards of a broken mirror.

"No, Cade," Evie crept to his side, her face at thigh height, her hands clasped to his, "Don't you dare blame yourself for this. No child should have to suffer what you did."

"It doesn't matter what happened to me," Cade cleared his throat, "Pearl has to walk around with his mark on her face for the rest of her life, because of me, because I chose to fight back at that moment."

"No Cade. Your father is responsible for his own actions, you can't take on his failings. Pearl knows that, she loves you, she told me you would blame yourself for tonight as well. You've done everything in your power to protect her, like someone should have done for you. You're father's sins are his own. Let them rest with his soul as it is judged."

"Earl did his best Evie,"

"He should have done more, even my mother should have –"

"I said Levi Hamerton was a charmer when he was sober, he always found a way to shift the blame. It was an accident or I was a wayward child and I deserved it."

"No child deserves that."

Cade shifted forward, and leavened Evie off the floor, she sat back in her chair.

"I know Darling." His ribs expanded, his shoulders almost feather-light.

"What happened to him?"

"He stole some horses. Even Earl said the man was a natural when it came to breaking and training horses, he could enter a paddock with the wildest Bronc and it would come to him. I don't remember him ever raising his hand against an - ." Cade swallowed, "So now you know, Evie. Kline hit the nail on the head, I've got a temper Evie, Pearl's scar is my fault, at any point, I'm just one step away –"

"Nonsense," Evie barked.

She fidgeted with her skirts, her feet curling up under the pale blue ruffles and out of sight.

"What?"

Evie shuffled the blanket back over her shoulders, "I don't know a lot about patience, except that I have none of it Cade and you have it in buckets. You've been pushed to extremes, through no fault of your own. A lesser man would have bowed under the pressure at lot earlier. Besides, Kline deserved to be put in his place." The warm liquor loosened her tongue and heated her insides. Although sitting this close to Cade, his heart open, wounds exposed, she couldn't trust herself not to throw her arms around his neck. Kline felt like a safe topic, "I know about the loan to the Four Star."

Cade sat back in his chair, his knees higher than before, "I tried to do something, unfortunately the name Hamerton isn't worth the paper it's written on, not like the name Kline."

Evie rose from her chair, the railing paint crackled under her grip, "Knowing my father he would have thought to burden the risk himself. That should tell you Cade how much he cared for you. It's not good business sense, for you to keep your stock, but I see how Earl thought he would pay his debt and interest with the Angus cross calves."

"Except Kline doesn't work like that,"

"He doubled the payments, I know. Why didn't you tell me earlier?" Evie heard her tone sharpen and she exhaled with each step she took.

Cade smirked, "You told me you thought Kline was a smart business man,"

Evie stopped her advance, pale blue ruffles encroached on brown denim.

"I've said a lot of things lately I wish I could take back."

Cade slowly tilted, his elbows coming to rest on his knees, his Stetson twirled between his hands, "Really Darling? All of them?"

Evie's tugged away his Stetson, "Not all of them Cade," her palms returned to Cade's wrists, pools of blue tilted upwards, his bow shaped lips kinked, "I am sorry for all my harsh words. I should have thanked you for saving the Double E, for looking after my father." Cade's hands retreated, her hemline snagged and his palms cupped her calves. Evie stumbled over her words, his shoulders bunched under her fingers, "I took Earl away at Christmas time," Warmth spread up her calves as his hands stroked the sheer stockings at the back of her knees, "I called you arrogant and boorish and -,"

"I am Evie," Cade whispered, his callused palms scratched her thighs, a shudder echoed up Evie's spine, "I don't want your pity," his voice husky, "I don't need your sympathy,"

Evie tilted forward, Cade's curls tickled her hands and she clung to his neck.

"I'm trying to apologise, to be proper and courteous,"

Cade's shoulder's tensed, Evie's bare feet raised and she landed on his lap, her knees pressed together at his belt buckle, her skirt ruffled and bunched around her. Cade's lips parted, his grip tightened, until he brought Evie's nose to his.

"I don't want the Duchess Lockwood tonight, Honey,"

Cade's mouth clamped down, Evie's lips parted by rote, her tongue seeking the hot nourishment she desired.

"Damn you Cade," Evie whimpered as she broke away.

"That's more like it."

Cade's lips reverberated against her jaw and down her throat. Evie gasped as his palms, slithered to the top of her thighs, she wound her fingers through his hair, his masculine scent penetrating her scenes, his caress gentle and deliberate. Evie arched her back as his teeth tugged at the thin ribbons surrounding her décolletage. Her chest swelled to meet the dance of his kisses across her tender flesh. Like a furnace had been hidden from Evie, her hands dove into the collar of his shirt, the button's falling like leaves under her trembling ministrations.

Cade's heat radiated as she scratched her fingernails through the soft covering of his chest. Evie's skirts billowed, Cade's bicep locked around her ribs, threads of quicksilver pumped through her veins, as Cade found the line of buttons up her spine.

"You know you're beautiful Evie,"

"Cade –"

"But tonight, to me, you looked like all the flowers of spring decided to bloom all at once,"

Evie snuggled against his chest, "When I saw you arrive, there was nowhere more I wanted to be than by your side."

Cade's lips found hers, his tongue sought its mate. Golden flames licked Evie's insides, her ribs expanded, each breath shallower than before. Cade broke away, sultry cerulean challenged.

"And if I'd asked, would you have chosen me?"

Evie dipped her forehead to Cade's, the words seemed to spring from her lips, before she could restrain them, "I told you, I would give you first option,"

A deep chuckle rose from Cade's throat as he seized her lips, another button surrendered, her neckline sunk. Cade's kisses ran down her throat, his knees shifted and Evie's followed, ruffles suddenly breached as his palm slid between her thighs. The moist fabric met his fingers, and Evie melted. Cade's strokes ricocheted through her body, every nerve ending scorched, her skin swollen and pleading for release.

Cade inhaled the sweet heady scent of Evie's apricot skin, his tongue tasting and savouring all that he could of the woman who moaned atop his lap. His desire, strained against denim, his restraint slipping at every gasp as he stroked the hidden silken folds of Evie. He released another button, the satin chemise dipped. He covered the plush curves of her breasts with kisses before seizing one hardened bud between his lips. Evie rocked against his palm, spiking his carnal demands, and soothing his soul with the barest of movements.

Evie's hands slithered across his chest, and Cade surrendered, he cupped her buttocks and slid Evie over his tortured arousal, the feel of her supple flesh yielding to his pressure thundered through his muscles.

"Not here, Cade, please," She whimpered.

The sound of his name from her lips sliced through the haze of pleasure. He rose in one movement, Evie in his arms. He scooped up a lamp in one hand before they ascended. The steps creaked under foot,

"I can walk you know," She giggled against his neck,

"I like the feeling of you in my arms way too much Evie,"

Evie ran a string of kisses down his cheek, "You're are all spikes and thorns on the outside Cade Hamerton, but on inside, you as soft as a day old lamb,"

He fumbled with the door knob, his orientation out of kilter.

"Who are you calling soft?" Cade scoffed.

He slid Evie down his frame, his arousal snagged between her thighs.

Evie's lids became heavy and she arched backwards, "I mean sweeter than stolen honey"

Cade set down the lamp, the gentle glow dancing across Evie's porcelain features, now flush with colour.

"Sound's delicious." He said as he brought Evie flush against his own. The remaining buttons slipped free. Cade stood back as the soft light caressed Evie's exposed beauty, the chemise puckered around her rose bud nipples, a deep blue bruise marred her upper arm, another barely concealed on her upper thigh between frilly lace and stockings. Cade coveted her slender arm, "What happened here?"

"Dawnee," Evie's hands grabbed her elbows, she shifted away from the light.

"Oh Darling," Cade stepped forward, until his knee struck the mattress, Evie between his thighs, "I'm sorry, I didn't know,"

He pressed his lips to her bicep, his knee dug into the mattress as he lifted. Evie's light frame sunk into the linen, and Cade had never seen such an enticing sight, all sweet cream and gold, with eyes that dared him to release the wild carnality that lurked deep inside. Cade kicked off his boots, as Evie's lips sought his. Her tongue moist and demanding retaliated against his plunder, his shirt pealed back by hands not his own. He drove his knee forward, until Evie's thighs gently parted.

"It's feels better already," Evie mumbled.

The mint green satin slipped from her fingers, the sensation of Cade's hard frame contradicted his tender caresses that sizzled across her skin. An arch throbbed in her lower abdomen, fulfilment loitering just out of reach. Cade leaned his weight backwards and Evie took a moment to watch her fingers trail across his sculptured bare chest. She wanted all of Cade. The man, she'd witnessed tonight, raw, open, and hurting had transformed into the other half of her own heart. His deft caresses awoke her hunger, his kisses brought more thirst, until Evie's demand increased, her patience tested.

Cade dug his fingers into the top of her stocking and slowly tugged, the sheer material slid down with ease, tendrils of desire wove into her veins. His strong fingers curled around her upper thigh as he kissed the tender bruise.

"And this one?"

Evie arched into the mattress, she wanted to rush, to have all of Cade now, "Yes,"

Cade pealed the other stocking free, his palm cupped her most intimate flesh, "What about now?"

Evie could only whimper as he kissed upwards across her belly, his teeth dragging her camisole as his fingers slid back and forth, turning her loins into molten liquid. His tongue held one of her peaked centres, drawing it and the satin into his sultry mouth. Her fingernails dug into the tensed muscles at his back, her thighs twitched to clamp onto his hips. Like a tornado had started to form, but Cade kept her at arms' length. She wanted the danger, the tumultuous ride of being swept up in its powerful current.

"Oh God yes, Cade,"

His weight shifted down as his hands drew her camisole over her head, he kissed one breast then the other as he rose to his knees.

"Do you know what it does to me," Cade's voice hoarse with need, "To hear you say my name like that?"

Evie fought for breath, as his fingers found her waist band, "Tell me Cade."

He slid the sheer material from her ankles, and Evie shied into the covers, he pulled her arms back, one by one, until she lay naked beneath him.

"I'm exposed, Evie," Cade lay down against her side, and traced his finger from her throat, between her breasts to her belly button, "I'm unprotected and you're there, inside the boundary beckoning me forward," His palm cupped her hip and she twisted to face him, "Taunting me, to step into wildfire,"

Evie seized his lips, gentle at first, the pressure and pace increasing as Cade's weight settled over her. The fine dusting of his hair scratched against her bare breasts, his denim knee separated her naked thighs.

"I saw you like that tonight," She pushed back the curls from his forehead, and kissed the tiny freckles across his nose, "I don't want to get burnt either Cade," she kissed across his chest, "I know within those flames, there is something I've never seen before and I'm not sure I'll find again. I'm scared Cade," His fingers stroked her slick feminine flesh, her next words came in garbled gasps, his teeth nipped her throat, "So let's tumble into the flames together."

"Together" Cade withdrew slightly.

"Yes," Evie whimpered.

She registered the heavy thunk of belt buckle hitting timber as Cade returned to her arms. His hardened flesh pressed against her outer thigh and for a second Evie flinched.

"Evie?"

"Cade, please,"

Evie crawled into his arms, his powerful embrace wrapped around her, his sage scent sweet along her palette. She raised her chin as his lips ground down onto hers, and she met him in kind. Evie embraced the tornado of sensations that coursed through her body, the aching in her loins, the demand for release that built in her abdomen. Cade dragged her thigh across his hip, the full length and thickness of his arousal pressed against her slick flesh. A shiver of anticipation and trepidation squirmed up her spine. Evie froze.

"It's alright Honey, I'll be patient,"

Cade kissed her jaw line to her ear, he rocked backwards, his rigid flesh caressed her silken folds, Evie trembled against his bulk. He thrust forward again until Evie's flesh parted slightly, his tip driving along the outer edges. Evie arched her back, her pelvis tilted. Cade's fingers curled around her neck, his tongue plunged into her mouth as he slid backwards, a thousand goose bumps dashed across Evie's skin. Evie rocked forward, sliding along his thick shaft, tendrils of pleasure warped her senses, her flesh ached, her veins sung. Cade's thumb rolled across her nipple, as he retreated, his engorged tip parted her delicate folds. Evie's groan captured by Cade's kisses, his breaths deepened, his heart thundered under her fingertips. Evie rolled forward once again, the slick heat too much to bear.

Cade withdrew and nibbled her throat, "Make me your man Evie,"

This time Evie rolled her pelvis back along the immense length of Cade's desire until his tip rested gently against her threshold. Evie sunk downwards, the pressure firm, her flesh unyielding. Cade's hand clasped her hip. Frustrated, Evie tried again, she wanted nothing more than to quench the thirst that ravaged through her body. Her own desire and Cade's, demanded release.

"Cade please," Evie wriggled against Cade's sex.

"What Honey?" he chuckled,

"Don't make me wait, Cade," Her teeth scored his jaw line.

Cade scoffed as he sucked her lobe, "To make you mine, Evie?"

Evie kissed his cheek, she bit his ear lobe, "I already am."

Cade growled, his palm pressed her knee into the mattress as he hovered above, and pressed his advantage. Cade's patience peaked as his tip parted Evie's velvet edges, her maiden flesh stubborn, the woman more than willing. He winced as the pressure increased, knowing his painful success, only moments away. Silently he begged for forgiveness as he thrust forward. Evie flinched, her lips pursed. Cade paused. She felt so damn good beneath him, too good. The coy apricot scent flayed his nerves, her words slicing through his chest like a barbed arrow to a wound he thought closed. Evie cupped his buttocks, Cade smiled against her soft lips, slowly and carefully, inch by inch he made Evie his own.

As Cade advanced, Evie surrendered, caressing the taunt ridges and valleys that writhed up Cade's back. His power surged forward and Evie all but wilted, a flower in the desert sun, she clung to him, as a barrage of carnality strummed through Cade's body. His kisses met with hunger and demand, Cade withdrew only to have Evie's embrace tense and pull him back. Cade checked himself and inhaled slowly, it did no good as Evie clamped onto his hips and ebbed and flowed with his movements.

"Evie you'll ruin me," he moaned.

Her laugh lost against his neck, her hard centres collided with his chest and he slid to his side and pulled Evie with him, her breast coming to his lips like a magnet. Evie mewed and purred. Cade tugged her blonde strands through his fingers, stroking her curved back as her slick heat threatened to overcome him. Cade could feel the flames, like thorns piercing his blood, she had always been his woman. No matter what came with the dawn, this moment would not be taken from him. Cade thrust forward slower, as Evie enveloped his manhood. Like double struck lightening, every part of her body collided with his in a shower of sparks. Cade's caress found the epicentre of Evie's pleasure, her arms encircled his neck.

Cade rocked inside her, Evie wailed as every movement slow and deliberate unfurled more tendrils of arousal that commanded satisfaction. Her body hungered for the man, all of him, without care or concern, without protection or safety. Her thirst demanded to be satiated. She knew that Cade was the source of that fire; that no man would be able to start a blaze that would burn as brightly or as fierce. It would be unleashed and Cade was the only man who could quench it.

"Take me there, Cade,"

Like the gusts of a tornado battering her senses with sweet pleasure, the frequency increased as did the intensity until Evie released, letting the storm take her to new heights and depths. Cades scent mingled with her own, as his body wrapped Evie in strength and affection. Evie's chest ached, her ribs burned, Cade now the beholder of Evie's last possession, the object only one man could hold. Cades gentle caresses stirred her from the pleasure haze. Did she hold his heart, like he did hers?

197

Cade tensed as Evie's convulsion racked his body, her pulsating flesh almost destroyed his resolve. He licked a dainty line of beaded perspiration from between her breasts, her heart vibrated through his tongue, as her fingers kneaded his shoulders. As her trembles subsided, Cade drove forward, her blonde hair askew on the pillow, her eyes heavy lidded, the green centres clear and bright. He savoured her lips as he drove deeper, the taste of Evie sinking further into his soul. Evie's cries of pleasure tore through his heart, as she wound her limbs around his body. Never had a woman come to him so honest and alive, without limit or pretence. Her heart was open, pouring healing light into Cades' wounds. Her curled Evie underneath him, as he thrust deeper. Evie nipped his neck, her gasps for air hammered into his chest, was he was hurting her?

"Into the flames Cade" Evie whispered.

Cades muscles tensed, his willpower depleted, Evie pulsated around his hardened flesh. The world tumbled around him, from the highest height he fell, Evie his woman, this moment theirs. Instinct warned him, he withdrew, his hot seed spilling over Evie's thigh.

"Cade?"

He gathered his breaths, as he cleaned.

"Trust me honey that's one investment you'll be happy I didn't make,"

He drew the sheets around them, Evie snuggled into his chest, her quivering lips pressing gentle kisses to his neck.

"If you say so," she mumbled as sleep claimed them both.

Chapter 23

The dawn broke over the homestead like soft sleet running from the fire and Cade stretched. His bicep now weighted down, lean limbs tangled; a familiar apricot clung to his skin. He didn't want to move for fear of Evie's regret crystallizing, her possible rejection crushing. He could enjoy the last few moments of bliss that Evie had come to him and soothed his soul.

Solid clunks and clangs rose muffled through the timber flooring as Cade tried to reconcile his surroundings. Evie lay splayed across his arm, her blond hair like golden rays crisscrossed the linen to his bare chest. Earl's clothes hung limp in the crooked cupboard, a solitary bed table in one corner. Cade grimaced.

Evie stirred, a wall of solid muscle curved around her back, thick thighs between her knees. Maybelle's breakfast ministrations infiltrated her peace. She rolled in the linen, her palm tracing gently over fur lined muscle, leather and moss tickled her nose. Tentatively she snuggled against Cades bulk; her lips grazed his warm skin.

"Evie?"

"Mmm?" Evie curled a single curl behind his ear.

"Evie are you awake?"

"I am now," she mumbled another string of kisses ended on his chin, "Is something wrong?"

Cade hesitated, "Would you tell me if there was Darling?"

Evie leaned back, and straightened her legs, other than a slight tenderness, she felt wonderful. She regarded their predicament, Earl's bedroom chosen in darkened lust filled haste.

"Of course," Evie rolled her forehead against his chin, "I've never imagined so much bliss, Cade and I don't regret one moment of it," She hesitated, "Do you?"

Cade sighed, "Other than our choice of bed, not a single moment," his lips pressed against her nose.

Maybelle's grumbles reached Evie's ears, and she leaned back, her arms struck the bed head as she stretched, the linen receding past the upper curve of her breast.

"I don't want to get up,"

Cades arm snaked around her bare waist, as the rest of his body circled her, his lips pressed against her ear, as his ample desire throbbed against her hip.

"I already am," he said.

"Should you save your energy?" Evie teased.

She entwined herself in his grip, his palms traversing her narrow waist, dragging the linen down past her hip, his fingers kneaded her buttocks, pulling her tight against him. His lips captured hers, his teeth nipping, tongue tasting and savouring.

"To convince Maybelle," Evie ran her hands down his muscular frame enjoying the tiny tremor that resulted as she traced the outer V of his inner hip, "that we can skip church."

Cade chuckle burst across the tender skin of her throat, "I'm with you Honey," his fingers sought the golden curls that had already coated in moist dew drops of Evie's arousal, she gasped as he stroked her melting velvet core, "I for one," his tongue flickered the hollow in her neck, suckling her swollen breasts one by one as his knee drove apart her thighs, "Intend on doing," his lips grazed her abdomen, "all my worshipping," he nibbled her waist, "right here," Cade kissed the tender flesh at her inner thigh.

"Cade!"

His moist tongue tasted her slick heat.

"Oh sweet hallelujah," Evie mumbled as she fell back amongst the pillows.

Cade enjoyed drawing forth more tremors and gasps until his own desire to be sheathed inside Evie, exceeded his patience. He leaned back on his haunches, Evie's hips meeting his own, he thrust forward, dainty teeth sinking into his shoulder. Together they moved, until Cade's nerves shredded into oblivion, tumbling as one over the precipice, their bodies glistened with a thin sheen of sweat. Cade let the sheets catch his seed, whatever

Evie desired from him physically, he was more than happy to oblige, but until she said otherwise, that's all he would offer.

"Honey," Evie said as she sat up from the bed.

The sun heating the floor boards, and turning her blonde strands to corn silk ribbons.

"Pardon?" Cade stretched, the scent of Evie still lingering on his skin.

Evie stood, wrapping the linen around her slender physique, pert breasts hidden, sumptuous hips concealed.

"That's what I want to name Dawnee's foal."

"Then so it shall be, Darling."

He rested his hands behind his neck as he watched her pick up her clothing he'd discarded.

"Come on, you know she won't let you get away with it." Evie said as she tossed Cade's denims onto the bed.

Evie watched with a newly blossomed hunger as Cade stretched, the powerful muscles across his chest tensed, his thick arms curled, roped forearms twisted. His bow-shaped lips kinked to one side, freckles shimmered. He was hers. Evie spied the ruffled sheets. Well almost.

Evie dressed in her own room, still puzzling over Cade's decision to guard against their union. Didn't he want her to be his woman? Apparently a few women had tried to hitch their wagon to this particular beast and without success. What made her any different? Foolishness came over Evie, and she shook her head. No, her decisions were her own. If he rejected her, of course her heart would break, but at least she would have known real pleasure, the real intensity that can burn between a man and a woman.

Evie tucked her hair up into her bun and regarded the cerulean blue dress that gleamed back through the mirror. The length of the sleeves the only reason, she'd decided on the shiny fabric and not because the colour matched anyone's eyes, or the way it hugged her breasts, Evie reminded herself.

A gentle knock trembled her door.

"Evie," Cade whispered.

Evie quickly cleared the rainbow disarray that heaped onto her bed, paper and fabric spilling between bed and window frame.

201

"I'm coming," she mumbled.

The door opened and Cade stepped in. His curls had been tamed, a crisp beige shirt covered his broad shoulders, blue denims tightened around his thighs. His clean scent stirring all too recent arousing memories, Evie inhaled.

"I just wanted to say, ... " Cade's head dipped down, "I mean after last night," His eyes travelled down her neckline and back up to her eyes, "I mean, I need to talk to Pearl, and I think that I should....," The apple in his throat bobbed, "The others might ..."

A spike of irritation ratted Evie's manners. She turned back to the mirror. He needed to speak to Pearl, yes. He'd fought Rick the Tick in front of half the town. The last thing he needed was a clinging woman ruining his reputation any further. Is this what he told Bethany? Evie swept a strand back from her forehead, her lids began to fill. You're being immature and inconsiderate. Pearl has just lost her father, her brother is trying to warn you to give them time to heal.

"I understand Cade, it's fine."

She blinked fast as boots narrowed the distance, Cade's arm wrapped under her ribs, his lips sunk to her throat.

"Just for now," his words silenced by the kiss he sunk to her neck, before he broke away, "You kept these?" He picked up the tiny wooden owl and spun it between his fingers,

"Of course," Evie tilted her head, "Why do you ask?"

"You know your father taught me how to make these. In the end I started marking their eyes black to tell mine apart from his."

A wave of recognition crashed into Evie, the little wooden figurines on Pearl's window were most likely from Cade. Evie's mind cast back to the ones she had left in New Orleans. More than a few wooden statues stared back at her with blackened eyes.

"I'm sorry that I have to tell you, I have quite a few black pipped ones in New Orleans,"

Cade chuckled, "I suspected as much."

"I will not be delayed!" Maybelle hollered from below.

Evie clicked her tongue and brushed past Cade, hoping to make it down stairs before he said another word. Maybelle sat splendiferous in the rear of the wagon, Fernandez and Pluma just as impatient. Evie stormed to the side and began her ascent, Pearl's fingers dragging her upwards. Cade stepped down the front stairs, his eyes narrowed at Evie already seated. Evie turned away as the man neared his chestnut mount. Well if he didn't want a clingy female messing things up, he'd have his space.

"Morning Evie," Pearl smiled, her hand squeezed Evie's.

"Morning," Evie tried on a genuine smile.

The younger girls' radiance lifted the fog that soured Evie's mood.

"Did you sleep well?" Pearl asked.

The timber jolted under Evie's rump, the tenderness caused her to gasp. Stones of cerulean struck her gaze. Maverick snorted.

"Well enough," Evie answered, "How about you?"

"Better than expected," Pearl turned to Cade.

He drew the tall horse alongside the wagon after they crossed the tiny bridge. Maybelle clamped her hat down as the first gust of Fall whipped around the party.

"Standing room only, I reckon. Half the Rancher's will still be in town." The larger woman called.

"Great," Evie mumbled.

She twisted away from Pearl, the mid-morning sun overbearing the tall silhouette that shadowed their journey. Another confrontation with Kline loomed. Perhaps with Bethany as well? Evie shifted in her corset and regretted it instantly. How had she woken this morning, enveloped in pure gold and now every buzzing fly, every strike of leather on tack, every creak of wood on steel, grated on her nerves. She had been the balm to his wounds, but now he'd shut the door again. By the time Fernandez halted Pluma, Evie's uncertainty had reached its zenith. Her boot skidded backwards off the step as long fingers trapped her waist. As the ground came underfoot she shoved Cade's hands away, hoping the lingering heat would disperse. She pined for Cade's affection, for some sign that their union had been with purpose and for love. Without a word, she followed Maybelle to the double doors. Give him some space, don't be so selfish, she scalded herself. Be patient.

Inside, the walls lined with men, hats in hand, some wearing yesterday's shirt, others with foreign perfume under their collar, a lot with sore heads, and even more with blood shot eyes. Maybelle had found a half filled pew on the far left, and they filed in, the larger woman first, then Pearl and Evie on the edge. A hush rumbled through the crowd and Evie refused to bend her neck to watch Cade enter the church. A sliver of concern spliced into her ribs. How could he bear it? Evie froze as beige sleeves appeared in her peripheral, oak moss leaked into her senses. Mumbles turned into greetings as Evie recognised the square jaw of Marcus Kearby and the tooth-pick laboured voice of Shelton Murphy.

Cade watched Evie's spine solidify as he shook hands with Marcus and Shelly.

"Kline's nowhere to be seen," Kearby mumbled.

"I heard he offered Old George $7 dollars a head."

"He's the last thing on my mind at the moment," Cade answered.

Evie's heated caresses ghosted across his skin, her luscious lips now petulant and thin. Why had the woman suddenly turned as cold as mountain ice? Her ear turned slightly to listen to their conversation. Cade rested his boot against the wall, and tucked his fingers into his belt as he eyed the congregants. Evie had swatted him away when he tried to help her at the wagon and now she stone walled him. Cade swallowed, like lead tumbling down ashes, a slice of anger slivered under his ribs. So she like him between her thighs, but surrounded by Dew Springs, Cade Hamerton was still beneath the Duchess Lockwood's boots.

The air in the church sweltered to obscenity and Cade's irritation had plenty of time to boil. He'd warned her he needed to speak to Pearl, to give her time to heal, and now since Evie took second place, she immaturely pouted. He needed to look after his family first. The sermon dragged to a timely end as the noon heat baked the ground, Cade's strode out of the hall without a backward glance.

"Hamerton!"

Cade marched over to Peter Stillwater where he stood with two of his three sons, their heads swivelled as Evie's gleaming aqua frame glided over the emerald grass.

"When you going to bring that brute of yours out to Stillwater."

"I'm surprised you're still keen Peter," Cade grimaced.

"Nonsense, Kline doesn't worry me. He's always been too big for his hat," Peter Stillwater jammed a cheroot past his lips, the red glow wavering as the bitter taste permeated the air, "Besides some fillies are worth fighting over,"

"Pa!" The older Stillwater boy turned to his father, the younger son's gaze tore across the crowd.

"Tell you what, Hamerton, you come out this afternoon and inspect my herd. I have a few green ones that need some work as well as a few fillies your brute could service. You pick,"

"Serious?"

"Serious as the business end of a .45."

"Alright,"

Cade spent the next few minutes coming to an agreement on prices before Stillwater surprised him again.

"I'll be interested in seeing what stock comes out of your heifers too, mind you," Stillwater resettled his hat on his head, "If that Angus is worth the money, I might be interested in a Bull or two,"

Cade nodded, "You'd have to speak to Evelyn about that, the Angus Breed is hers."

"I won't mind having a word with her," the younger son's green eyes sparkled towards the jewel amongst the calico pebbles.

"Settle down Callum. You bring that stallion of yours over this afternoon," Peter Stillwater shook Cade's hand and made his way to Evie.

He'd wanted to raise the capital to buy Evie out, however as he watched the Stillwater's greet Evie, he wondered about the future. Did he still want to buy Evie out now? Evie needed money to buy her life and a husband in New Orleans, would she still sell? She raised a narrow eyebrow, her chin tilted, back straight as an arrow. Cade shook his head. His family first. Jesse stood beside Pearl at the far corner of the church, almost out of sight of prying eyes.

"Pearl,"

"Cade,"

"Mr Hamerton," Jesse's hand shot out, which Cade reluctantly shook.

"Give us a moment will you Jesse," Cade said.

"Of course,"

Jesse hesitated for a moment and plonked his hat back on his head, before he stumbled in retreat. Had he meant to kiss the girl in front of Cade? Too much courage can be a dangerous thing, Cade smiled.

"Boys will do anything to impress a girl," Cade said.

"Is that your excuse?" Pearl threw back.

"Maybe," Cade sighed as he twirled a blade of grass through his fingers, "I need to apologise for not telling you earlier."

"It's fine, I understand," Pearl softened her tone. How had she grown from an innocent teenager to a compassionate young lady overnight, "I know you would have thought you were protecting me. I am a big girl you know,"

Cade snorted, "Pearl you're only 15"

"Almost 16!"

"That's still young,"

"You don't owe me any apology Cade. I'm lucky that I have you at all."

"Don't try and soften me up," Cade smirked.

"I'm not! I'm telling the truth!" Pearl's blue eyes popped. The same colour blue as his own eyes, the same as their fathers'. "And don't let that go to your head, Mister. The only good thing about Levi Hamerton is that he gave you a wonderful little sister!"

Cade threw his arm around her shoulders and pulled her into his chest, "I suppose there is that."

"I know you don't want to talk about him, but can you tell me what happened?"

Cade released her, "He stole some horses. They caught him and hung him."

"No, Cade," Pearl twisted her thumb in her fingers, "I mean, about him, about your mother, about mine?"

Cade discarded the blade of grass, the invisible rope twisted against his ribs. Some part of Pearl still held onto the notion that Levi Hamerton might have some redeeming qualities. He didn't have the strength or the know-how to tell her without disappointing her and no part of Cade wanted to sing the man's praises either.

"I will sometime."

"Sometime is fine Cade."

"Tell me about this boy Jesse," Cade said.

He threw one boot against the outer wall of the Church and watched as Jesse Kline loitered near the tables of refreshments.

"Umm, he's nice, I mean, what do you want to know?"

Cade registered the panicked tone of the girl, "Will I have to remind him that I'm your big brother, with a rifle and a shovel,"

Pearl squealed, "Don't you dare! Besides after what Evie said to Rick the Tick, Jesse is no doubt terrified of the pair of you."

Cade titled his head, the sun blinding one eye, "What did she say to Kline?"

Cade listened to Pearls third person relay of the events of the night. Afterwards he left her to share in cups of punch with Jesse by her side as Cade made his way over to Taylor, Kearby and Shelly.

"Yeah he pointed out some marks on her arm, she set him straight. She also said you were raised by her Daddy and not yours."

"I heard she threatened to shoot him if he set foot on the Double E ever again!"

"Where did you hear that?" Cade turned to Marcus Kearby.

The shorter man took a sip of a bottle of sarsaparilla and shrugged his shoulders. An awkward looking damsel caught Cade's eye. Layers of skirts kicked along the ground, the ginger curls piled atop Jewel Daniels freckled face.

Kearby turned back to the group, "Ah Taylor told me,"

"Yeah, yeah sure I did," Taylor smirked, and winked at Cade.

Jewel Daniels took a wide birth around the other patrons, trying not to over balance in her hooped skirts. Cade would bet she still had a pair of cowboy boots on under the ruffles.

Shelton Murphy twisted the tooth pick from one side to the other, and lowered his voice, "I don't see what the problem is Hamerton, hurry up and bed her then."

Cade could feel the colour draining from his cheeks, as if the crosshairs of a rifle, if Cade moved a single inch, they'd pull the trigger.

"Oh," Shelly grinned.

"Come on boys look where we are, keep some dignity,"

"Shut it Kearby I want to hear this,"

"Shelly," Taylor reprimanded his friend, "Although seriously, Cade I had to spend half the night apologising to that Bethany Sampson, tell me my hard work was worth something,"

"It ain't like that," Cade said.

Slowly he tipped his bottle to his lips and eyed Evie circling with more townsfolk. Shelton and Taylor hooted until shushed by Kearby. Cade's throat constricted as they drew the gaze of those around them, including Evie.

Evie's neck heated as Cade's friends smirked and chuckled into their drinks. She concentrated on what Peter Stillwater had offered. Surprised Cade had even sent the man over to her, surely Cade would have tried to broker a price man to man. After all he'd chastised her for settling the Double E debts. The calves were her inheritance, yet she didn't have a brand. Surely if the stock had a crooked hammer on their rumps, and he'd have to drive them up the trail, then Cade would want some say in the price. Evie shifted back to the present, a cool breeze easing the moisture that stuck her corset to her ribs. A chocolate braid bobbed ahead of Evie, pink lace scuffed the flattened grass. Evie inhaled slowly, her gut clenched.

"Excuse me Bethany,"

"Oh Evie-Lyn," The brunette's brown eyes glistened, "Hope this morning finds you well."

"Same to you Bethany," Evie cleared her throat, "I do wish to apologise for my comments last night,"

Bethany licked her sugar coated fingers and grinned, "Do ya now?"

Would the dark haired girl make a scene in front of the whole town? How would a cat fight fair against Cade's reputation? Evie shook her head and swallowed her pride.

"Yes Bethany, it's wasn't fair or proper of me to say such things to you, I –"

"Save it Honey," Bethany leaned forward, and tilted her head, her gaze ran up and down Cade's tall frame, "We ain't even racing in the same league."

Chapter 24

Evie blinked at the curvaceous brunette, Evie's composure waivered. Bethany hadn't finished either.

"If you're standing over here and not over there, then ask yourself have you really won?"

"I should have saved my breath," Evie sighed as she slowly released her balled fists.

Bethany's cherry red lips curled at the corners, "Although, one day I might have to thank you,"

"How so?"

"I found a more prosperous horse to saddle my wagon too, Honey."

As if the sun had shaken loose the shackles of a storm, a rush of warmth spread through Evie's chest. Here stood a woman not unlike the Evelyn Lockwood who returned to Dew Springs not so long ago. Bethany's exterior had been polished and preened for appeal, the woman's inside deceptively shallow. Evie wanted nothing more to do with the façade of love, the empty promises of a passionless union.

"I wish you all the luck you deserve Bethany," Evie grinned.

She rounded on her heels, Cade's pale Stetson peaked above the crowd. Evie's smile widened for a moment as she held his sapphire gaze.

"Oi, Evie," Jewel Daniels barked, "How do you walk in these dang skirts!"

Evie laughed at the red-headed cowgirl waddled awkwardly towards Evie.

What the hell did that mean? One moment Evie looked like she could freeze hell with one look, then after a run in with Bethany, Evie's stiff frame, had melted, throwing Cade a smile that rivalled the dawn. Shelton elbowed Cade in the ribs, as

Marcus slunk into his black Stetson when the girls met under the shade of the trees.

"Beat's me Cade, I can't imagine Bethany saying anything good,"

"She never does," Which added another edge of Cade's nerves.

"Well whatever it is, it's not my fault Cade. After Rick hit the deck, she took off." Taylor said.

"If the girl is smiling I say that's a good thing," Shelton pipped up.

Marcus cleared his throat, his eyes still at his boots, "You know as well as any of us Shelly, that if a Texas girl is smiling she's about to do something crazy."

"And if she's laughing, she's already done it." Cade finished.

Evie's lilting laugh erupted across the green, echoed by Jewel's. Marcus froze. Cade's boots spurred into action, he took a wide berth around the crowd. Evie looked beautiful the dappled shadows playing off her peaches and cream colouring, her narrow shoulders relaxed as she conversed with the rough cowgirl. When Cade stopped just to the right of Jewel, the tiny spitfire, tilted her head.

"Yes Hamerton?" Jewel asked.

"I wanted a word with Evelyn, if you don't mind Miss Daniels."

"Don't you Miss Daniels me Hamerton,"

"Fine Jewel,"

"Hang on, you'll be driving them new Angus up the Chisholm when they're ready."

Cade's gaze met Evie's, her viridian gemstones darkened.

"I might," He said.

"What's she paying you for that service?"

Evie's brow's furrowed, clearly she hadn't calculated any fee for Cade's effort. The way the sun resonated off her flushed cheeks, the sly kink to her heart shaped lips, he'd probably do it for free. Perhaps Evie had wrangled a bargain of her own.

"That's still under negotiation," Cade finally answered, "What's it to you?"

"Just wanna see how you get them Angus and them, what did you call them Evie, wicked Hammers are gonna handle on the trail,"

"The slanted hammer," Cade corrected.

A rush of colour lined Evie's cheeks.

"You want to be part of the Double E drive? Won't you be needed at the Crooked K?"

This time it was Jewel's turn to blush, "It's seems I won't be needed," She shoved her hands under her arms and lowered her voice, "They ain't even sure if they've got the numbers." Cade knew the girl was worthy of a spot, not only could Jewel shoot the eyes of a mouse a hundred yards away, she was more than competent in the saddle, "I don't wanna be at the drag with all them greenhorns and I sure as hell ain't cooking,"

Cade laughed, "Sure."

"Then you may take your Evie," Jewel said.

The diminutive cowgirl, scooped up her hemline and strode away, red roses painted on leather, peaked under the ruffles. Cade, careful of the eyes they drew, paced towards the wagons, thankfully Evie followed, her apricot scent tickled his nose, bringing forth memories of liquid heat and svelte curves. Cade stumbled, his hands itched to be filled with her feminine warmth. He scratched for something to keep her in his company.

"I have to head over to the Stillwater Ranch this afternoon."

Evie fingers came together across her waist, and she nodded. She had to be patient, the words spilled out of her mouth.

"I saw you speaking with Pearl, how is she?"

"She says she fine." Cade paused as they edged closer to a row of wagons, "She wants to know more, I don't know –"

Evie couldn't resist and put her palm gently on his forearm, "I will keep what you told me to myself, I won't interfere."

Long fingers trapped hers and the distance between broad beige and Evie's swelling chest reduced. A spark of energy raced through her system ending in her abdomen.

Cade's hand slid around her waist, "Thank you,"

Evie's fingers trembled against his solid chest, the noise of the townsfolk reduced to a hum, the thundering of Cade's heart, echoed in her own chest.

"Bethany – "

"I wished her luck in her endeavours," Evie scoffed, and took a step back.

Cade nodded, his lips seemed poised to say more, a spike of fear drove into Evie's abdomen and she turned on her heels, safely to the edge of the wagons.

"Don't take too long at Stillwater, Cade."

She strode into the sunlight, the bright light stinging her eyes. She had no idea what she was doing, only the why. Her heart yearned for Cade, for reciprocation of her feelings. Patience.

Evie found Maybelle and the Double E hands, small talk failing to keep her interest as she watched Cade's broad shoulders twist through the crowd. Her mother had worried that Dew Springs had nothing for her daughter's future. Evie had to agree. Financially, Dew would dawdle along waiting for prosperity to land on its doorstep, New Orleans seethed and bubbled with opportunity. With opportunity came risk. What opportunity would Evie miss if she turned her back on Cade? A life filled with long days and even longer sunsets, laughter, love, passion. What risk would she take if, that man didn't love her?

The ride back from Town Evie had pondered her predicament and now, as the afternoon sky wound down to violent peach and peaceful violet, Evie wandered out across the Homestead yard. She'd discarded her shiny dress for the comfort and practical denims and gingham. She headed over to Jorge, his snout coating her fingers in slime as she fed him and the dairy cow their usual corn husks. Evie peaked in to see Dawnee and the newly named Honey as they tested the air with their muzzles. Dawnee ran her nose over Evie's palm, as Honey hid behind her mothers' flanks.

"Are you happy Dawnee?"

The mare tested Evie's sleeves for molasses before turning away in disappointment. Evie surrendered to bed no clearer on how patient she might have to be.

Cade unsaddled Maverick and stabled the three green geldings and two mares from the Stillwater ranch. The damn Roughie herd had found every hole and divot, forcing Cade to take more care to reach the Double E well after dark. He'd have a week to break the geldings, same as Maverick to enjoy his harem. Cade took slow steps to the homestead, a low amber glow bleached into the empty patio.

Cade tiptoed up the stairs, with the single lamp. He spied his opened door opposite Evie's. Both vacant. Cade took a breath before he crept forward, to the bedroom at the end of the hall. The door slightly ajar, soft breaths beckoned him forward. Evie lay tangled in the bed sheets, one bare leg askew, the tangerine lamp light licked over the lace hemline of her night dress. Slender arms curled around a pillow, her golden strands swept backward from her narrow neck. Cade stood there for a long time, letting the scene sink into his bones and hope grow in his heart. Evie his woman, his lover, his wife.

Was it possible? Did Cade Hamerton deserve happiness? A lifetime of rejection and anger weighed upon his shoulders, would his temper get the better of him, would Evie cut and run, did she even want to stay? Cade ran his hand through his hair, did she love him, like he wanted to love her. His heart had closed more than a decade ago. He didn't have the answers. If what he held now was fleeting then he could still dream for now. Cade turned down the lamp and slid out of his boots. His woman, his lover, his wife. He shucked his shirt and denims and walked to the far side of the double bed. He crawled in under the sheets, his arm encircled her slender waist. Evie murmured something incoherent, her fingers speared through his, and she dragged his grip tighter. Cade closed his eyes and inhaled her sweet apricot scent, tomorrow he'd ask her. Cade pressed a tender kiss to the nape of her neck, before sleep overcame him.

Evie woke amidst a wonderful dream, leather and masculinity clung to her skin, yet the bed was empty. She dressed in denims and red checks, looping her hair into a messy bun as she descended the stairs. Pearl already sat at the table, picking pieces of pancakes from her plate to feed the puppy at her feet. Maybelle whistled a ditty in the kitchen, the scent of batter and sugar salivated Evie's mouth. She entered the kitchen to a fresh pot of coffee, and a chipped ceramic plate shoved in her hands,

"You're welcome," Maybelle said.

"Thank you," Evie mumbled, the uncertainty twisted her stomach and although mouth-watering, Evie doubted she could finish a mouthful.

"I've packed you a lunch, so don't go wasting any of my good food, ya hear,"

Evie strolled past the benches, "Packed a lunch?"

A sneaky kiss pressed against Evie's cheek, a warm palm slid down to the curve in her back, fresh juniper invigorated Evie's soul.

"I figured we'd ride out to see the stock,"

Evie took a second to recover, as Cade scooped up the next plate and strolled to the table. Pearl's lips thinned into a poorly concealed grin. Evie cautiously took her seat and eyed Cade's sapphire eyes.

"Is that so?" Evie said.

"It is the second day of Fall Evie, calving season," Pearl added.

Evie still confused chipped a slab of butter onto her pancakes, the gooey lump melting just as fast as Evie's heart.

"I have some work for Stillwater and this might be the last chance I get for a while, unless the Duchess has got something else to occupy her time with?"

A shiver of apprehension slid up Evie's spine, they were up to something, she knew it. Patience Evelyn, she warned.

"I suppose the Duchess could spare a few hours."

Evie pulled Earl's second best hat down over her eyes and let Nieve pick the path behind Cade's second favourite horse, a caramel gelding named *Picaro*. Apparently Maverick had to spend some time with his new ladies all with Dawnee just across the paddock. Evie snorted.

"Something funny?" Cade asked.

"Ranch life," Evie mumbled, "So which way are we headed?"

Cade pointed to the hundreds of hoof prints in the paddock, "West,"

Evie nodded, "Are there any cliffs to avoid?"

"Nice, Evie," He smirked.

"How about some gentle hills, think you can handle that?"

Cade's eyes ran up and down Evie's physique and she fought the quivers that resulted.

"You know that I can Honey,"

"Come on!" Evie hollered as she drove Nieve forward.

She heard Picaro's hooves thunder across the ground, Evie clapped her hand over her hat. The cooler air whipped around her ears, flattening her shirt to her chest. Evie squealed as she pushed Nieve faster, she grabbed two hands on the reins. The sunlight beamed down on her forehead as the wind tore invisible fingers through her hair. Cade's mount closed the distance, her hat in his hands, he smirked. His words teased across the void.

"Hold on, Evie" Cade said and then whistled two sharp bursts, the third longer than usual.

"You're cheating!" Evie howled as the dainty horse pulled up.

"Are you going to have another tantrum?" Cade laughed.

"Not a tantrum, Cade."

Evie released her balled up fingers and straightened her back. She flicked Nieve's reins. The horse stood firm until Cade issued a shrill half whistle, then the pale animal continued at a more sedate pace.

"I'm not sure I like the sound of that." He said.

"So, Kearby owns the Crooked K ranch doesn't he?" Evie said.

As they rode, she pondered Jewel's predicament, and why the girl suddenly wanted to work for the Double E. Whatever had transpired between the renegade cowgirl and the soon-to-be-Ranger sparked Evie's curiosity.

"His father does, yes. Kearby wants to be chasing outlaws and Stage Coach villains instead of stuck in Dew Springs." Cade jaw clamped shut.

Evie contemplated Jewel's plight, as they strolled between pockets of groves that lined a long grassed filed. Clearly Jewel cared for the man yet didn't want to keep him from his dreams. Evie still had to broach the question of this fee, she'd owe Cade for driving her cattle to Market. Evie watched the long grass fold under the hooves of Nieve, until a small brown lump shifted in the green. Evie tugged on the reins, and halted the horse, as the brown lump lifted it's head, glistening black babbles blinked at the intrusion.

"Um Cade," Evie whispered The man had disappeared behind a thin strand of trees, "Cade," Evie dared a little bit louder. Eventually he turned Picaro around, Evie threw up her hand as she calculated the caramel horses trajectory, "Stop, go around."

Cade eventually drew alongside Evie as low mewing noises echoed from somewhere out of sight.

"Congratulations Evie." Cade said.

Evie's throat constricted, as the newborn licked it's lips and tasted the air. Evie sucked in a sharp breath, manure and beef lingered in the air.

"Now, let's get out of here before the Mamma see's us."

Cade's fingers tugged on Nieve's reins and the mare followed Picaro instinctively around the grove. Evie wiped back the moisture that lined her lids, as Cade weaved the two horses as wide as he could from the herd. Evie stood in her stirrups as the sight of another calf suckled at its mothers udder came into view.

"They're gorgeous!"

"First calves on the ground, Evie you're going to have to decide soon."

A chill rode Evie's spine and she kept her gaze on the fringes of the heifers, searching for more offspring.

"The Wicked Hammer brand or the Double E?"

"Isn't it the slanted hammer?" Evie corrected.

"I like Wicked better,"

Evie resisted the urge to cool her cheeks with her palms. A wave of disappointment and impending doom cast over her mood. The goal of the day had been achieved, marking the beginning the countdown of her departure.

"Where will you drive them up, the Chisholm or something?"

"The Texas Road, to Abilene. Well they're getting a bit hesitant about Texas Fever lately, they might let the Angus slip through. As usual they'll want their share."

"A fee?"

"Yeah, and the Indians are getting a bit twitchy crossing their land up there, the last time, Earl had to pay more than he cared to mention just to get to the other side. I don't have any horses to sell, with four Hands, myself and now Jewel, it's hard to say."

"In Earl's journal he had the beasts down for about $40 a head."

"True" Cade shifted in his saddle, "I heard a single beast can fetch $100 if you're brave enough to head west to mining country."

Evie let the rhythm of the saddle lull her thoughts, "How many Ranchers will be driving cattle to market?"

"Pardon?"

"Excluding the Four Star, how many Ranchers around Dew Springs would be driving their cattle to market when they're ready? I mean Jewel said the Crooked K weren't sure and Old George at Windy Hill was doubtful."

Cade ran a long finger along his jaw, a thin line of growth peppered his cheeks.

"A fair few, at least a dozen or more. Why?"

"How much would you pay Jewel for the drive?"

"What are you getting at Evie?"

"Maybe nothing, Cade, please how much?"

"If we went North about $40, if we went West to Dodge, probably $50, although if she offered to cook, I might reconsider."

"Okay,"

The thought hadn't fully formed in Evie's mind, so she closed her mouth and calculated a price per head, per cowpoke, per beast. She tallied up the numbers again until she realised Cade hadn't turned for home. The word sizzled on her tongue.

"Where are we going?"

"I want to show you something," Cade said, his voice low and soothing.

Evie rolled down her shirt sleeves as the sun peaked, the noise of crickets dimmed as their horses approached the thick line of emerald that snaked through the field. Evie watched Cade's shoulders tilt and sway with ease as Picaro descended into the trees. The saddle rocked underneath Evie's hips and memories of a night wrapped in pleasure ghosted across her skin. She blinked through the hazy sunshine, her eyes adjusting to the cool shade as Nieve entered the grove. Splashes and bubbles reached Evie's ears as the cooler air soaked through her shirt. She fanned the collar of her gingham, not entirely sure the weather had anything to do with her temperature. Cade dismounted, the denim stretched around his thick thighs and Evie bit her lip. Pools of sapphire met her gaze and Evie shivered. Each step he took seemed with measured accuracy until her stood at her ankle.

"Do you want a hand?"

Evie nodded, her words trapped as she hooked one knee over the pommel, Cade's fingers grabbed her thighs. She slid off the leather and into his arms, her fingers locking behind his neck, her thighs around his hips. Cade's lips grazed hers, she parted her lips in anticipation only to have Cade press a tender kiss before drawing away. Evie's lifted herself upright until she faced him nose to nose, she titled her head, the gentle pressure all the more alluring.

"I could get used to this," Cade mumbled.

Evie hovered over the puckering denim, his arousal ignited hers, and her teeth nipped his bottom lip, she soothed it with her tongue.

"Really?" She prodded.

Cade groaned against her lips, his willpower fleeting, as his tongue searched for hers, Evie tugged buttons from their loops as Cade stepped backwards. Evie's boots struck the soft grass as Cade lowered himself to the ground. Evie curled upon his lap, his shirt pealed back and she kissed his neck, brown curls tickling her nose. So could I, she thought.

Evie rocked forward her patience already stretched thin, the heat started to climb, her desire ached. Her shirt lifted from her waist band, her belt buckle fell aside as Cade's hunger peaked. Evie gasped as his fingers tested her molten core.

Cade groaned as Evie's slick heat met his caress, his woman already wet and waiting for him. His other hand tore down the middle of her shirt, buttons popped, her erect nipples peaked through the satin chemise, demanding his attention. He sucked the nub hard against his tongue as Evie fumbled with his belt, hastily freeing his hardened flesh from its denim trap. Suddenly the woman lifted and tugged, her denims snagged on one heel,

"My boot!" Evie lamented.

"Don't worry about your boot, Darling,"

Evie laughed as she righted her footwear and added, "I wouldn't want to get pricked by a thistle,"

Cade chuckled, "A thistle?"

He lifted her upright. Evie gasped as Cade brought her down on his manhood, her flesh stretching to accommodate as much of him as possible, bliss traversed her spine and coursed through her veins.

"I love being wrong," she pined.

Chapter 25

As if the ground quaked underneath Evie she held onto Cade as the tremors rocked her body, in one swift movement Cade's arm curled under her buttock and she rose, his seed spilling on his washboard stomach. Evie's brows furrowed, yet inside the pleasure haze she bit her cheek. What did it take to have all of Cade? She rested her head against his chest, his undone shirt tickled her nose. Cade's heart thundered against her ear drum, his breaths fought for calm.

"Hold on," Cade scoffed.

Within seconds, he'd shucked his shirt and denims, lifting Evie into his arms.

"What are you doing Cade?" She hollered.

With one hand, Cade tugged off one of her boots then the other. He strode forward to the river's edge.

"If you want to keep that shirt dry, I suggest you take it off,"

"Cade!"

"Alright then."

He stepped into the water and Evie jostled out of her clothes as the cool water lapped at her ankles.

"It's so cold!"

"Not where I'm standing," Cade uttered.

His lips seized hers as they sunk lower into the water. Evie cupped a handful of water and tossed it upwards, Cade enveloped Evie's shoulders and leaned her lower and lower in the water until she gave up, squealing she clutched his naked frame. The sun streamed through the leaves as they adored each other in sweet languid caresses. Reluctantly, as Evie's finger tips began to pucker and her bottom lip wouldn't stop trembling they left the cool water. She pulled on her sun baked clothes as Cade spread out a saddle blanket and opened Maybelle's picnic.

"Chicken?" Evie paused as she peered at the roasted poultry legs.

"Ah, one of your hen's stopped laying."

"Oh," Evie's energy had been severely depleted and she sunk into the honey baked meat with resigned hunger. Ranch life. "Wait a minute," she mumbled around her morsel, "That's my inheritance!"

Cade scoffed until he coughed and cleared his throat as Evie laughed.

"I don't know what to say Darling, it's delicious."

Evie laughed again and bit into a hard biscuit. After lunch Cade stretched out, one thick arm behind his head, he pulled her onto his chest. Evie succumbed her fingers dreamily traced over his bulky chest.

"So what we're you thinking about the other Ranchers?" Cade probed.

Evie propped her chin onto his ribs and stared into his eyes, the sapphire blue ringed in thick lashes, his freckles like cinnamon atop a donut.

"Well you're driving the Double E herd – "

"Your herd, Evie,"

"Right, and hoping to get somewhere near $40 a head, but we won't have a lot of wieners, not as much as the Four Star Ranch."

"And that doesn't count if Rick the Tick buys George out of his stock,"

"How much did he offer?"

"$7 a head."

Evie flicked his shirt between her fingers, and schooled her thoughts to calm.

"And Rick would sell them for $40 or less?" she asked.

"They'll be in worse conditions by the time Kline gets them there,"

"And neither you nor I have enough money to buy them, and you're not selling any more horses!" Evie jabbed a finger into his ribs.

"I'm not?" Cade's brow raised, "Fine, but what does that matter?"

"How many animals do you think you could handle with the five of you?" Evie asked.

Evie bit her cheek, if she stayed at the Double E, there was no way she was waiting back at the homestead for Cade for six weeks but she was also not a wrangler.

"A thousand, maybe more, come on Evie you're on the edge of a cliff and I don't like heights."

Evie laid her ear against his chest and chose her words carefully.

"Well what if the Windy Hill and the Crooked K paid you to drive their cattle to Kansas?"

"What?"

"Think about it. Kline will broker Old George if he managed to buy his cattle for $7 a head, he was talking about a loan and coming in underneath. What if Windy Hill could get their cattle sold for $39 a head, or even $38 a head?"

Cade remained silent, his chest rose and fell in slow breaths.

Evie continued, "It's only a $1 a head profit, but 150 from Windy Hill, 400 from the Crooked K, how many does Stillwater have? Would the Blue Cow Ranch hire a contract drover?"

"You expect the Ranchers to hand over their cattle to me, not only to get them safely to Market but to sell them and bring home the profit? Me, Levi Hamerton's son?"

A lick of anger speared through Evie's chest, how could he expect Dew Springs to excuse his name, to see that Cade was a man, self-made and honourable, if he couldn't.

"Yes! Not only did they watch you win that cutting completion, saddleless mind you. They know the Double E standard, they're more than curious about the Angus calves. You'll baby the fresh stock to Market, because their new and untested. The town respects you Cade, whether you see it or not."

Cade's muscles leeched tension and Evie eased her palm across his chest.

"It was just a thought." Evie said.

Cade closed his eyes, he'd supposed to be asking a more serious question than how many head of cattle he could drive to Kansas, yet Evie's words had his thoughts spinning end over end. With so many sons lost to the war, reconstruction, barb wire springing up here and there, Indians and quarantine, and even rail freight charges, cattle was becoming more difficult to turn a profit for some of the smaller Ranches. If he was driving Evie's Angus anyway, could he manage that many beasts? He'd have to take a closer look at the numbers. The sun dipped behind a cloud and absentmindedly he ran Evie's silken strands between thumb and forefinger.

"Wait a minute Duchess, is this a ploy to avoid my fee as Trail Boss?"

Evie's head lolled against his chest, her words coated with sleep.

"How many biscuits is that?" She mumbled.

Cade laughed as gentle as he could, a cool breeze washed over his cheek, as Evie's hand slowed to a stop against his chest. His shoulders relaxed and he let the afternoon take him.

Something cold stung Cade's cheek, the small warmth that curled at his side began to stir, a horse snorted. Cade's eyes snapped open, the grey afternoon confusing Cade as to how long they'd slumbered. Evie unravelled her limbs and stretched before she curled back up against his side.

"It's cold." Evie whispered.

"Yeah, come on, rains coming," Cade climbed to his feet brining Evie with him. He searched for the sun through the silver lined clouds, "It's not that late, we'll make it back before the sun is over the stable, but I don't know how dry we'll be."

He whistled and Picaro and Nieve wandered over to the tree.

"I hope Maybelle has stopped plucking my inheritance."

Evie hooked her boot in the stirrup as Cade jolted her upwards. The words voiced in his head, fear kept them in his throat. Evie lowered herself gingerly on Nieve, Cade's chest ached, she narrowed her eyes at his concern.

"I'm fine Cade," Evie's cheeks flushed in colour, "A *warm* bath wouldn't go astray though," she winked.

Cade ran his hand down her thigh, "If we make it back before dark, Honey I'll run it for you."

He'd hoped to ask her as soon as they stopped, Evie had other ideas and he didn't have the willpower to argue. Just ask her damn it! On the return journey, they scouted the calves again, the herd moving cautiously closer to the homestead. Cade ran through his options resolved that before the night was out, he'd have her answer, whether he liked it or not. As they neared the stables, Pearl's slender shape came dashing through the house yard, her hands wrung in her apron.

"Pearl?"

"Hiya, Cade, umm Evie," Pearl's cheeks drained of colour, "I thought I should let you know, that your Aunt," Pearl sucked in a deep breath, "Your Aunt –"

"Evelyn!"

The stately Aunt Eustace waved a handkerchief from the porch of the homestead.

".… has returned." Peal finished.

Cade's stomach sunk, his muscles coiled and bunched, something about the narrow eyed gaze and wide grin, of Earl's sister warned Cade that her homecoming didn't bode well. At least you can be honourable and ask for Aunt Eustace's permission to wed her niece.

Cade took hold of Nieve, which left Evie free to greet her Aunt. Evie dug her toe into the damp hay as she loitered at the stable door, her eyes down cast, fingers clenched together. She pressed a palm to her abdomen and glided across the lawn to the homestead. Cade brought Picaro into his bay as Fernandez took the reins.

"*Un conejo conoce una pista de zorro igual que un perro de caza*" the older man commented.

"She's not a rabbit and I'm not a fox, Fernandez," Cade replied.

"Ci Boss, *¿Entonces que estás esperando?* "

Cade sighed and left the Hand to unsaddle Picaro as he trudged his way to the homestead. Fernandez was right, what was he waiting for?

Evie hugged her Aunt on the patio, the older woman's grey and yellow hemline caked in dust, her handsome face weary.

"I thought you'd be there to collect me from the stage, didn't you get my letter?" Eustace asked.

Evie shook her head. Cade's mind raced back to the two envelopes he collected when he picked up the dresses.

"Then you mustn't have received Lewis Myers offer either," The Aunt added.

Cade's gut cramped, the liquid evaporated from his mouth, his ribs compressed as Evie bolted inside, with every rushed boot step up the stairs, another nail drove under Cade's skin.

Evie rummaged through wrinkled satin that had slipped down between bed and window, two envelopes sat crumbled amidst the bold fabric. She recognised her Aunt's elegant script and placed it on the bed. She regarded the next envelope, bold, graceful loops and flourishes crisscrossed the parchment. Evie held her breath. Her fingers suddenly leaden. Evie let her hands fall to her lap, the wall supporting her back, legs curled underneath, she sat on the floor. She stared at the envelope, against the backdrop of denim, her shirt wet from the last drizzle of rain. Evie stood.

An unusual calm settled through Evie's skin. She tossed her wet strands with a towel as she changed into dryer clothes, the unopened correspondence on her bed. What did Myers offer? Did it even matter now? Cade! Evie peered out the window, broad shoulders stalked back to the stable as the drizzling rain set in. After all they had shared and she'd childishly run up the stairs to a promise she no longer wanted. What had Cade offered her? Nothing. Why? Evie paced back and forth before Eustace interrupted her wondering.

"Well Evie, what do you think?" Eustace asked.

Evie handed the letter to her Aunt who crooked her slender neck, one eye narrowed, she ran a painted nail down the seam,

"My Dearest Miss Lockwood,"

Evie almost groaned. Dearest. Miss Lockwood.

"It is with sadness in my heart, that I learn of your subsequent losses with your fathers passing and the railroads like so many of our contemporaries have suffered. As to your current predicament, I am confident that notwithstanding, any compatibility or objective issues, we will be able to negotiate an amenable agreement with regard to our respective futures, upon your return to New Orleans. Yours Sincerely, Lewis J Myers."

Evie threw herself face down onto the bed. Was that a marriage proposal or a business deal? Weeks ago, she would have partially swooned at the notion of Myers. Now she knew what made her tremble at the knees and it didn't live in New Orleans.

"What's the matter, Evelyn, I thought this was good news."

Evie didn't know what to say, if she told Eustace about Cade, would her high society Aunt drag her back to New Orleans?

"I'm fine, I just need time to think."

"About what Dear?"

"The first calves have arrived, they need to get to Kansas for sale,"

"You're sounding like your father. Let this Hamerton buy you out and be done with the heat, and the dust and the drought."

Evie lifted her head off the covers, "It's raining Aunt."

"Is that sass?"

A rush of heat curled up Evie's neck, "It's not sass, it's the truth."

"Unless there is another reason you're wanting to stay at the Double E?"

Evie bit her cheek, "No Aunt, it's just good business sense. The calves will sell for $40 a head or more, if I sell to Hamerton now, I'm lucky to get $7 a head. And not all of them are born yet."

"I see."

Evie didn't look at her Aunt, instead she plucked stray threads from the coverlet.

"Well I better make myself comfortable then, Maybelle was airing out Earl's room, I better see if she's done –"

Evie's cheeks coloured. Within seconds of her Aunt's arrival she felt 16 again, running around New Orleans trying to find adventure with no courage and even less freedom. Evie listened to her Aunt's steps tiptoeing down the stairs. Evie would have to thank Maybelle. She pressed her palms to her cheeks. She picked up Myers' letter and discarded it as soon as she'd started the first line.

Cade waited until total darkness before he returned to the homestead, he'd tested his luck with the Stillwater broncs and had both onside, even in the rain. Maybelle had a beef stew and hot biscuits ready as he entered the kitchen. He scooped up a plate, only to have it taken away by Pearl and placed at the head of the table. Cade winced but took his place. Aunt Eustace sat to the left, Pearl and Maybelle on the right. Evie took the final chair at the opposite end and pushed the stew around on her plate for the best half of the meal. Aunt Eustace prattled on about New Orleans and the Panic, the ruins that had been left of the stock market, the riots and the rebuilding.

"Don't mind me saying Ma'am but doesn't sound like a mighty safe place to be," Maybelle added.

"Nonsense, the elite are far away from Downtown."

Cade couldn't take his eyes off Evie, her cheeks flat, lips thin. She'd clearly had more than a sufficient offer from the shipping magnate and she struggled with how to tell him. His chest ratcheted a notch tighter. He shouldn't have waited. Any offer he now made would pale in comparison, and appear a desperate bid to trap her.

"So Mr Hamerton, tell me what you've had my niece doing in my absence."

Pearl's fork clattered to the ceramic.

"I beg your pardon Ma'am,"

"Well last time I left Evelyn was in silk skirts and now I see her back in plaid and denim,"

"Back to denim," Evie's lips curled slightly at the corners, "Well riding atop *Nieve* in skirts was damn uncomfortable."

Pearl's stew sprayed onto the plate, as Evie scooped up her unfinished dinner, the resounding splash brought Pearl up from her seat to follow.

Aunt Eustace graciously stood.

"Never you mind Ma'am, I'll put on a pot of coffee, Cade boy show the woman some manners," Maybelle said as she picked up Eustace's plate.

Cade lead Aunt Eustace out to the dark porch while they waited for Maybelle,

"Clearly my return has not been to everyone's pleasure," The stately woman said.

The night air clung like an icy blanket to Cade's skin, "She's thriving out here, you'd be proud of her. She birthed a foal, won second place in the shooting competition."

"I heard she threatened to shoot that Mr Kline!"

Cade scoffed, "She did. Tried to plant a half dead possum in my saddle bag too."

This time Aunt Eustace laughed, a husky trickle that eased Cade's shoulders.

"Now that definitely sounds like Evie, I wonder Mr Hamerton, will you buy her out?"

"I don't have the capital."

"I will lend it to you."

A squeal tore through the night air as Maybelle delivered two cups, the steam curling in the darkness, a temporary reprieve for Eustace's inquisition.

"Thank you Dear," Eustace clutched at the coffee and smoothed her silver hair back into place as Maybelle left, the older woman turned back to Cade, "Well Mr Hamerton?"

"Please call me Cade," he said, his chest as tight as a drum.

"Only if you call me Eustace and not Ma'am, it makes me feel twice as old as I want to look,"

Cade nodded, "Why do you want to buy her out?"

"If Evelyn needs to leave the Double E behind and the only thing that is keeping her here, is those damn cattle, I will buy them."

"If she needs to leave?"

Aunt Eustace put down her cup, and ran her fingers along her temple, "Tell me Mr Hamerton did my niece manage to tame that beast?"

"Jorge?" Cade's gaze instinctively went to the fence line. He'd been missing from his afternoon corn husks.

"No Mr Hamerton,"

Cade put his cup down, his chest suddenly frozen in place. He inhaled slowly, his voice steady and level.

"Eustace, I intend on asking for Evelyn's hand in marriage. By the sounds of it Myers has already done that."

"Something like that, yes Cade." Eustace harrumphed.

Cade leaned back on the patio railing and considered the stately woman's last words. He should just ask Evie and be done with it, hear her rejection and close the door on heartache.

"Do you think you can provide for Evelyn's future, can you give her everything she needs and everything her heart desires?"

The bitter coffee stung his tongue and warmed his throat, before he could surmise his thoughts, Eustace continued.

"If you are unsure, then how is Evie supposed to know,"

"I know the weight and measure of the man I am Eustace, it's just how your niece values a man,"

"And that is up to neither of us, Cade. I will abide by Evelyn's wishes, whether she decides to invest her heart in her future is up to her," Evelyn stood, and smiled thinly, "Goodnight."

The screen door creaked, the noises in the kitchen now silent. He let time stretch out until his rump became numb, Evie didn't join him. He tiptoed up the stairs, only to see Evie's door closed. Cade quietly let the latch click in the door, before he sat on his own bed, the sheets cold, the scent of apricot craving in his blood.

Evie tossed and turned, her empty stomach echoed her aching heart. She owed Aunt Eustace an apology, and she owed Cade an explanation. She rubbed her nose against the pillow hoping some miniscule amount of his scent lingered on her skin. The pitter-patter of droplets pushed her into sleep.

Chapter 26

The rain continued in a slow drizzle that penned Evie in. Cade had already taken off to the stables, and Evie thought of hopeless excuses to make her way over there. Even Maybelle tried, with a hot lunch, but Cade arrived and ate on the porch without stepping foot inside. Evie picked through the uneaten bucket of corn husks. Chitto let out a whine. Was Jorge hiding from the rain?

At supper Eustace listened to Evie's idea about contract droving, with raised eyebrows and lip twitches that neither approved or disagreed with Evie's calculations. Pearl nodded appreciatively and swore to secrecy that she wouldn't discuss it with Jesse. If Rick got a wind of it, he'd throw some mud in the water just to spite Cade. The man himself arrived only to yawn his way through supper. Evie watched him fall asleep with coffee in hand.

Evie spent another restless night tossing and turning, her thoughts as uncomfortable as her sheets. What would Myers give her? What did he actually offer? Financial security, wealth, a life of society balls and a facade of love, hoping that maybe one day he might love her for the woman she is? In reality Myers offered her no gain for little risk. And what of Cade? He offered adventure, strength, protection, honesty, passion, love. She could end up destitute, broke, fighting for survival, but she's still have Cade and the love they shared. All the risk and with the greatest reward. If Cade loved her? If Cade opened his heart to her. As the sun rose hampered by the grizzly clouds, Evie braced herself as she entered Eustace's bedroom.

Aunt Eustace sat preening her fabulous bouffant, "Yes Evelyn," she said.

"I found my mother's journal."

"Oh."

"Did you know what my mother had planned?"

Eustace put the silver comb on the wonky little table, "Towards the end before your mother passed, I heard them discuss it. After your mother died, I know it weighed heavy on your father."

"Did you push him to it?"

"No Honey," Eustace twisted on the stool, "I will admit that I did often say that the Ranch was no place for a little girl. After the tree incident –"

"It was a misfire, of a rifle, from Richard Kline."

"Oh,"

"Kline lied to Earl, so he wouldn't get a hiding."

"Well come to think of it, you did look a little more, full of soot than a simple fall from a tree." Eustace said as she tapped a finger to her crinkled lips.

"I won't be returning to New Orleans." Evie stammered.

As soon as the words passed her lips, her shoulders slid down her back.

"Oh," her aunt patted the coverlet and Evie took a seat, the springs squeaked, "Have you received a better offer?"

Evie bit her lip, no. Cade had said nothing. The man was patient to a fault and there was more than that, like an iron chest, the man's heart lay locked away. She would need a giant hammer to crack it. The rain splattered on the roof and she regarded the empty fence line.

"Not an offer per se, but I have given away my heart Aunt, and I don't want a refund; regardless of how difficult the investment may be in the future."

"Men are an investment all of their own kind. Some pay off in a large lump sum, they are the shallow kind and the investor never learns the true value of the man. Or you can choose one rich in all aspects, kindness, respect, laughter, loyalty, trust and love. Let it grow and mature, renew it when necessary, don't take needless withdrawals and make regular deposits. In the long term, these investments will pay dividends for the rest of your life." Eustace said. A sigh escaped Evic's lips and her fingertips whisked away the droplets. Aunt Eustace tugged back a stray strand of blonde, "They are the rarest investments to find, I never had the luck to find one and I'm not sure I would have had the courage to take the risk, even if I did. Your father and mother had been lucky enough. Have you made an official bid yet?"

Evie walked to the window the rain splattering against the pane, "No."

Tomas sat astride his bay, and pulled up abruptly, just before the stable doors. He leapt out of the saddle, his eyes wide. Evie held her breath as the small Hand gestured frantically to Cade. Briefly Cade looked up to the homestead.

"Something's wrong," Evie mumbled. Evie dashed to the stables, the water stinging her eyes, "Cade what is it?"

He pulled a leather slicker over his shoulders, his eyes trained on the horses.

"The river has risen and the herd are on the wrong side, they could be cut off or worse," he said.

Evie gasped, "The babies!"

"I know Evie, why do you think I'm heading out. Tomas came back for help, the others are already out there and struggling to turn them, and Jorge is out there."

"What?" Evie wracked her brains, when had she last seen the giant bull at the fence line.

"He's stuck Evie, if I can get him out I will,"

"What do you mean if?" Evie snapped. Cade reached for his shotgun and Evie's stomach rolled, "No Cade!"

"I won't stand by while an animal is in pain Evie,"

"I'm coming,"

Evie stormed to the saddles, for once Cade didn't object.

"It's your investment Evie you should be there."

"It's Jorge!" She spat

Cade shouldered the saddle, and nodded to the caramel gelding's stall.

"You take Picaro, I'm not risking your neck on a Stillwater Bronc,"

"Then who will you take?"

"Mav,"

Evie exhaled slowly, the blood sped through her veins until shivers ran up her spine, if Cade was taking Maverick, the situation was serious. New born babies and Jorge the gentle giant were at stake. It was heavy lashed obsidian that she thought of, not dollar signs. Cade's jaw looked like it could chew barbwire. She ran the belly strap and threaded it through the buckle.

"You want to check it," She threw him a half smirk.

Cade's top lip curled slightly, "I trust you."

Evie dashed to the row of slickers than hung up near the entrance, Evie turned to see Cade checking Picaro's belly strap, just as Pearl opened the stable doors, her ebony locks drenched with the rain.

"What's wrong Evie?" Peal asked.

"The herd are about to be marooned or drown and Jorge's is in worse trouble,"

Pearl nodded, "What can I do to help?"

"Pray they have enough horse power and I have enough will power to drag that beast out of the mud."

Pearl didn't say anything as she looked past Evie to Cade, "I will."

Evie wiped the back of her hand across her brow and sucked in the droplets that course down her lips. A dribble tracked past her collar and down her spine. Tomas led Cade and herself west as fast as their horses could travel safely over the sodden earth. Picaro compared to Nieve was a faster but bumpier ride. As they neared the creek bank, Evie stood in her stirrups, her throat closed as she saw Fernandez thighs deep, a bulky head and shoulders barely above the mud.

Evie brought Picaro to a halt and clambered to the ground, her hands filled with mud until her boots got underneath, and she tore forward. Cade pulled Maverick alongside and unwound a rope, his arm snatched at her elbow.

"Evie you'll be crushed."

She shook him off, "Cade I can't stand by and watch. You need Fernandez on the horses more than you do me," she snatched the rope from his fingers, "Tell me what I need to do."

Cades fingers ached as they released her, "It needs to be behind his ears and the knot under his chin," he said as he tied the rope blinding fast.

"Boss, -"

"Go Tomas, help the others turn them away from the river bank,"

"Ci"

Evie looped the rope around her forearm and dashed forward, Earl's second best pair of boots, slipping out from either direction.

"After this you'll owe me a new pair of boots!" She hollered.

"Actually you'll owe me Evie, this is your beast I'm dragging out."

Evie's thigh dipped in cool slop. The slicker dragged behind and she stripped it off and threw it back.

"I've already paid for those services!" She shouted.

Cade scooped it up, shaking his head, hoping the cool rain would ease his colouring cheeks.

"Concentrate Duchess!"

Evie went on hands and knees and scrambled forward, Fernandez dragged Evie the rest of the way. He took the rope and looped it around the beasts' ears. The massive head lolled to one side, Jorge's, nostrils caked in mud.

"Head up."

"Yes" Evie carried the weight as best she could, without sinking further, she half curled herself underneath his chin and brushed away the mud, "Come on Jorge," she cooed, "Think of all the corn husks you'll be leaving Daisy," she ran her sticky palm down the bull's nose and across his cheek, the rain blended with the tears.

Fernandez crawled away, and Evie heard a sharp whistle as the rope took the strain.

"Evie move back,"

Jorge gurgled, froth bubbled at his muddy lips, she released his head only to watch it dip into the mud.

"I can't, he's too exhausted!"

"Evie!"

"Cade he can't breathe!" She screamed.

"Watch yourself," he snapped back.

A whistle sounded, the rope groaned, Jorge's eyes opened, nothing. The whistle broke the air another three more times. Evie turned to see Cade and Fernandez pulling back on the rope with the three horses. Evie's thoughts went to the rifle. She turned back to Jorge.

"Keep trying,"

"I'll try another angle, keep an eye on that rope, it will -"

The rope twanged across Evie's upper arm, before Cade could finish. Evie cursed loudly, and closed her eyes against the sting,

"Evie!"

"I'm fine!"

Cade whistled again, a slow sucking noise reverberated from underneath.

"It's working, something's happening!"

Evie lost track of time, as the tug of war between man and mud continued. She stroked Jorge's nose and whispered words of encouragement, scooping layers of mud off his fur as more of the bull became free. Evie scooted back with each ground they gained, until Cade waded into the mud and grabbed the animal's tail.

"It's time to get back Evie," he directed.

Evie leaned back, her shoulders burning with the movement, her thighs cramped in drenched denim. Cade sent out another whistle, and with both hands on the tail he inhaled deeply, and leaned back. His cheeks filled with colour, against the drizzling rain, his shirt soaked, his thick forearms red and bulging.

"Now Evie," Cade spat.

Evie crawled to the safety of the horses; Fernandez dragged Evie to her feet. She wiped specks of mud from her chin as she watched Cade heave and tug, until Jorge's rump was clear. Beside her Fernandez sucked in deep breaths. Cade whistled and the olive skinned man picked up the rope as Maverick and his helpers walked cautiously forward. Inch by inch Jorge became clear. Cade dropped the animal's tail, and Fernandez slapped Mav's hind, as he whistled. Cade took giant strides as he followed Jorge's journey from mud to solid ground.

Evie planted a kiss on Fernandez's cheek before she waddled over to Cades heaving chest and threw her arms around his neck. He stumbled back.

"Thank you."

Evie kissed Cade's wet cheek before she undid the rope from Jorge's neck and dropped another sweet kiss on the beast's muzzle.

"Give him a minute and we'll get him up,"

A shot rang out across the field, Evie's muddied hands flew to her mouth.

"You go, I'll get him up," Fernandez stammered.

Cade unhitched Maverick and swung into the saddle, Evie close behind. As they closed in on the river bank, Evie's eyes strained to make sense of the disaster she saw before her, one cow was being dragged by Diego and Julius, pockets of the herd crowded on the edge of a mud pit, their flanks covered in muck, calves wide eyed and hiding under their mothers. A handful of cows lamented in the mud, while Tomas stood above another, the rifle pressed to fur, the retort crackled in her ears, and echoed in her chest.

She turned to Cade whose jaw twitched, he flew into action tying Maverick to the lead ropes and starting the tug of war again. Evie trotted Picaro over to one stranded heifer and unravelled the rope. Cade didn't say a word as he handed her the loops. A shout rang out from behind and Evie tensed as she recognized the stocky Piebald horse.

"Relax Hamerton we came to offer help," Kline barked.

"Then quit yammering and get hauling" Cade snapped.

Evie bit the inside of her cheek, perhaps Kline could redeem himself. She eyed the rifle and shook her head. Jesse came beside Evie with more rope.

"Pearl found us heading into town, she said you needed help," the youth said.

"Thank you," Evie managed, her throat as dry as the mud under her fingernails.

Together the Double E and the Four Star stood shoulder to shoulder, knee deep in mud as the hours ticked by until the last heifer was free. The long horn cow waddled to her feet, and let out a long bellow towards the river bank, an island of grass steadily being absorbed by the rising water. The heifer lamented again, the breath from her muzzle misting the drizzling air. Evie turned to the marooned island, a tiny brown form mewed back.

"Oh god!" Evie wailed. The baby tiptoed to the water's edge. Cade cursed and dragged a muddied rope free. Evie caught his bicep, "Cade no, you'll drown."

"It's your inheritance Duchess."

"It's not worth it, I'm not risking you for a sodden calf," the rain mingled with her tears, her words came out strained.

"That's sweet darling, but you need all the calves you can manage to pay for my Drover's fee," he smirked.

Cade tied the rope around his waist, and headed to the river bank, entering with large strides, the murky water rushing up around his thighs, suddenly he sunk chest deep. Evie gasped, he struck out arm over arm until his fingers closed on the wet grass, and pulled himself from the water. Evie watched as the man took a moment to gather his breath before he scooped up the baby animal. He waved his arms above his head and Tomas whistled, Maverick steadily walked forward. Cade kept one hand on the rope, the other curled around his charge. Evie bit down on her dirty nails as slowly Cade made it back to the mud pit on this side. He released the tiny calf as Evie made her way to his side, the baby slipped as it dashed to its exhausted mother. Evie threw herself into Cade chest, his arm coming around her shoulders.

"I don't know how to thank you Cade for saving them."

"I have a few ideas," he whispered hoarse against her ear, "Starting with a bath."

Evie blushed, "I might be able to manage that."

They broke away under the eyes of the Ranch Hands and Cade sighed as he realised he'd have to thank Kline for his assistance.

"Thanks Rick for lending a hand."

"That's what Neighbours are for, although I am disappointed that your comment about warming someone's bed after the dance ended up like this, but then again, fairs fair."

Cades exhausted brain struggled to catch up, "What Kline?"

"You said, you'll have Evie's share at any cost, but I honestly didn't think you'd take me up on that bet!"

"Is this really the time Kline, I'm here thanking you, and all you can manage -" Cade turned his back on the man, to see Evie's white cheeked face.

"What did you say?"

"Only how Hamerton had a side bet, set a challenge to have your share of the Double E, one way or another." Kline said.

"Don't listen to him Evie."

"Anything to win a bet, huh Cade?" Evie's lips twisted.

Cade sighed, "He's a sore loser. That's all."

"So you were playing a game then?"

Cade shook his head, his brain formed words slowly as his fists pumped. He didn't know which way to turn, explain to Evie or just flatten Rick's in the mud. Evie stormed off to Picaro, before he could do either. Cade turned back to Rick but the Four Star Rancher had already made it to his Piebald.

"You're a son of bitch Rick!"

"Seems to me that title is more deserving of you, Hamerton."

Jesse stood beside the spotted mare, his eyes downcast. Anger boiled over in Cade so fast, if his energy hadn't been depleted by the mud he might have killed Kline. The shorter man put his muddied boot into the stirrup, the saddle twisted, Kline slunk back into the mud, the tack landing on his chest.

"Did you check that strap cousin?" Jesse smirked as the Hands laughed in unison.

Cade tipped his hat to Jesse but right now he had to find Evie.

Chapter 27

Cade spurred Maverick on, but the stallion was beat. He let the horse pick his own pace as he followed the hooves of Picaro back to the homestead. Early darkness loitered on the horizon, as black as his mood with Kline and Evie. The man was lower than a worm, but it was Evie's eagerness to believe his words, to turn against what she should already know of Cade. Picaro sat in his bay, his mane drenched. Cade spent the next few hours until sunset, combing out and rubbing down each horse, as the Hands began to wander back in. Cade left the stable after he thanked them for their efforts,

"I'll have another dozen of them biscuits,"

"I don't like your chances, Tomas"

"You'll do fine,"

"I don't bake"

Cade entered the homestead to the salivating scent of beef pie.

"Get that mud out of my house!" Maybelle shouted. Cade tiptoed through the back door, his shoulder colliding with soft feminine as Evie dashed out of his way, "I'll throw another pot in for you boy," Maybelle murmured as she rushed to refill the bath.

Cade stepped out of his muddy clothes and sunk into the hot water. He scrubbed and cleaned as he thought about the words he needed to say to Evie. By the time he vacated the bath the water was cool. He wrapped a towel around his waist and poked his head out the door. A pile of fresh clothes had been laid at the door. Bless you Maybelle, he thought. She'd saved him again by handing him a hot plate and loaded fork as soon as he entered the kitchen. He crammed the food into his mouth as a rush of denim and gingham departed.

"You're about to see another tantrum Boy if you don't do something."

Cade just nodded. He scoffed his plate and helped himself to another his apology and explanation still unfinished. As he finally sat down to the table, Evie rose. Cade eyed her half-finished plate as she disappeared into the kitchen.

"I feel that puppy of yours is going to get fat my dear Pearl," Eustace said as she eyed Cade.

Pearl lowered her gaze, "I'm sorry Cade."

"There's nothing to be sorry for Pearl. We needed the help and I appreciated all the hands I could get out there."

"I didn't think Jesse would bring Rick the Tick."

"It's not your fault."

Eustace cut her pie in tiny morsels before speaking again, "Did Mr Kline make an offer of sorts?"

Cade put down his fork, "No, but he sabotaged the bid all the same."

Eustace's dainty brows furrowed, her lips lined with age and sass, she dabbed at her mouth with the corner of the napkin.

"Well I do believe that until all formal offers are rejected or accepted the bidding continues."

Cade noted her emphasis on formal. He hadn't asked Evie at all. He picked up his plate and cautiously entered the kitchen. Evie stood with her forearms in the sink, her eyes blankly staring out the darkened window.

"Evie, he's lying to you, he's turning his words into mine."

She kept silent, as she swirled the water around the ceramic.

Cade shouldn't have to defend himself. Evie should know how much he cares for her. Have you ever told her?

"Evie you should that I'm not the man who -"

"I'm not sure I know what you're capable of." Evie spat.

A wedge slammed into his chest, his name, the towns slander all came back to haunt him in the words of the one he loved. No, the one he thought he could love.

"You don't know me," he whispered.

Evie's voice came out flat and strained, "I know you're afraid to be more than your father."

Cade reeled, his blood thundered in his ears as he retreated, the table shaking as he stormed past.

Evie threw her hands down into the sink, the warm water splashed up her nose as a sound struggled to escape her throat. What had she done, what had she said? She was in pain, her pride, her bones, her heart! The irony hadn't been lost in the process, the Evie who had hunted eligible bachelors for their portfolios in New Orleans now cried over dishwater and cowboys who bet against her measly inheritance! Hadn't she previously thought to pit Cade against Rick to raise her price? How could she be so hurtful? She heard the front door squeal and Evie took the opportunity to run upstairs, ignoring Pearls shout and later Eustace's gentle knocks.

The morning came with burning sunshine, Evie sat at her bureau, and combed her hair. Dark circles lined her eyes, her cheeks flat. She tuned the little wooden animals in her hand one by one. Patience. She had had enough of patience. He hadn't made Evie any kind of offer. He worried over her splitting the Double E, but he couldn't see how to make it whole if it bit him on the foot. Well, if the man couldn't see it himself she'd have to show him. Damn Cade Hamerton! She dressed in her burnt cherry satin and tied a bonnet over her blonde strands. Tomas didn't need any convincing, needlessly apologising for shooting Cade's heifer and thereby one of Evie's calves. She reassured him on the way to town that she understood. As they left, the Double E, Cade paced a Stillwater Bronc into the paddock. So he'd thrown himself into work, well he'd have more than he could handle soon enough.

Cade tugged on the Broncs reins as he coaxed the horse to follow his lead. So much for Evie's words, she'd called him out and dared him to do better. She wanted Meyers for his wealth, she wanted Cade for her bed. For Earl's daughter, Cade would do the right thing. Besides that, no one threatened a Hamerton. He saddled the Bronc as the wagon rounded out of sight. First he stopped by the Nine Lives and found Taylor and Shelton. Both his friends considered the option he put forth and agreed, if anything to take the pressure off Old George. As he crossed the street he spied Jewel leaving Miss Delvin's.

"Another dress, Jewel?"

"Hamerton what you doing snooping around here?"

"I got a proposition I want you to talk to Marcus when you see him next. Let him think it over and tell him I want his answer by Sunday."

"Alright, let's hear it," Jewel listened with eager ears and nodded, "Sounds fair to me, 11 or 12 ought to do it."

"Right, now you haven't seen Evie have you?"

"I seen her?"

"Come on Jewel."

"She was leaving Franklins office you know that stuffy Lawyer."

"Thanks Jewel,"

"Is there gonna be another wedding Hamerton?"

Cade paused, "Another?"

"I hear Bethany finally landed herself a big time Rancher, no one is saying it but there might be a little Tick in the oven, and it'll be over-cooked!" The ginger haired girl said as she threw Cade an over enthusiastic wink.

Cade smiled, no wonder Rick was more than nasty yesterday. A sliver of panic worked its way under his collar, what was Evie doing at Franklin's office? By the time Cade made it over there, the plump lawyer quivered in his jowls.

"I'm not at liberty to discuss another clients matters Hamerton." Franklin said as he threw his hands up in defence.

Cade climbed onto the Stillwater bronc and headed for home. What the hell was she up to? Cade spied Evie's burgundy dress traipsing from the stable to the homestead, her pout turning into a scowl at the sight of Cade. Something snapped inside Cade, he'd put it all on the line right now, tell her straight what she wanted to hear instead of cowardly hoping she'd come to love him rather than worry about his bottom line. He put the bronc back in its paddock and waited till Evie stormed over, a little kink in his lips at the anticipation of witnessing another Evie tantrum. Half of him wanted to bait her, after a day of curt words and harsh truths he could use a little spice. Judging by the frown in her heart shaped face he'd have to supply the sugar.

"Evie before you say anything, I want you to have, the Double E."

That pulled her up short, "Pardon?"

"I should have done it that first day in Franklins office, the Ranch is yours. I'll sign it over, then you can leave Dew Springs behind."

Evie's lips thinned draining their rosy colour, "Here!" She shoved a document tube forward. Cade took it.

"What is this?"

"I've signed over the Angus and the Homestead to you! All you have to do is sign it!"

Like an axe through Cade's chest, he unfurled the first parchment and read the first line.

Evie's voice caught in her throat, "I just have one request...."

Cade ignored her demands, "Why Evie?"

Her emerald eyes paled to mint green, almost his new favourite colour, her bottom lip trembled, "Because Cade I trust you to...to make.... " her voice heated, "Because my father got your measure a long time ago Cade that you're the right man for this... place.... To keep the Double E whole,"

Cade rolled the documents up not reading the second, and shook his head. The Double E all his with one swoop of a pen; but no Evelyn. She'd return to New Orleans, to Myers, out of harms' way and out of his reach. "I heard you got an offer from Myers," he lowered his voice to a whisper, "I've unfairly taken away part of your future already, I don't want to jeopardize it any further."

Evie's lids began to fill, she rolled her bottom lip inwards as he handed the document tube back to Evie. Cades chest constricted, "I will sign the Double E to you Evelyn's it's yours. I put the word around about your idea, and it looks promising, I'll contract drove until I get back on my feet."

Evie swallowed hard, her heart choked her throat the tears welled, "But I thought that-"

Cade scoffed, "What Evie, I have no shipping lines to give you, no wealth to speak of save a few nags and land that should by rights be yours. I can't give you the financial future you want."

The truth hurt more than anything but he had to be honest. She was right he'd accepted his father's lot in life, not letting himself get over the chip on his shoulder. He needed her to see him for what he really was and the whole heap of nothing that he could offer her. He needed to free her.

"The *financial* future I want," Evie's lids narrowed her slender fingers curled into fists.

"Yes Evie, it's time to face facts, I can't give you what you want."

"And what do you think I want Cade? A business arrangement," She tapped the document tube against her thigh in rapid strikes. "I thought, no I hoped that what we had meant more than that."

Evie pirouetted as fast as a rattle snake, her dark cherry hemline dragged in the mud.

Cade tilted his head, and replayed her last words, had more than that? What could he, Cade Hamerton offer Evelyn Lockwood, he'd give her the Double E, she'd already been offered immeasurable wealth and financial security in New Orleans? A trail of thoughts collided in his head. Evie wasn't a real lady, she was a woman, whole and raw wanting what any woman wanted. A man to love her like she loved him. Cade shook his head, as if strings on his heart had been tuned tight enough to rupture. The clouds parted in his mind, his shoulders eased and Cade squinted at the retreating figure of Evie.

"Evie wait!" She didn't stop. Cade groaned. She wanted his heart but she had it already, "Duchess Lockwood if you don't stop you'll force me to take drastic action!" He hollered.

"Do your worst Hamerton!" Evie snarled back. She had enough of patience, she registered the new brand with Franklin and had it ready to give it including all her stock to Cade and he'd gone and ruined it all. Something cool and heavy splattered against her hip, springing moisture up her spine. Evie turned to see a ricochet of mud decorating her dress, and Cades hands covered in muck. The rage boiled over, a tiny laugh escaped her lips, "You didn't!"

"Free shot Duchess!" Cade opened his arms.

Evie heard footsteps on the patio,

"If you don't Evie I will," Pearl called.

Evie spied the Hands peeking out of the stables, oh how she wanted to embarrass Cade. Gingerly Evie bent down to the nearest pond of mud.

"Evelyn!" Eustace called out. Evie paused, how could she explain her way out of this? Eustace snatched the document tube and pointed, "That pile over there is thickest!"

Evie threw back her head and released a rage fuelled laugh as she dashed to the mud pile. It brought her closer to her target, and Cade opened up his arms, his chest exposed. She scooped up a thick pile and tossed it over arm, the spray missed by inches.

"You can do better than that!" Cade hollered.

Evie took a few steps closer as did Cade, she threw her next shot and it landed just shy, a fleck of mud springing his denims. Cade stepped closer, his voice low and deadly, his sapphire eyes alight with mischief

"I'll give you one more try Duchess, make it count." He dared.

A nervous giggle bubbled from Evie's throat as she stepped forward, Cade dropped one knee to the mud, his hands clasped her stained thighs.

"Evelyn Lockwood, I can offer you nothing other than my shoulders for your burdens, my ears for your worries and my eyes to watch over you. I give you my hand to walk alongside you and when you ask me, I will lead. When you tire I will not hesitate to carry you. This is all I am Evie, I will give you all of me from this day until to my last, I will give you my heart Evie, if you'll keep it safe."

Streams of tears tore down Evie's cheeks as she sunk into his embrace.

"That's all I want and all I'll ever need."

Cade's lips seized Evie's and she relaxed, the world's problems unable to touch her within Cade's arms. He savoured her lips, with nothing held back, as the crowd of onlookers cheered and whistled. Evie felt gravity dip and turn as the mud claimed her dress, Cade's arms refusing to release her.

Evie's teeth nipped Cade's ear, "Now how about that hot bath?"

Evie had stormed into Miss Devlin's that day unable to wait any longer than a week for her lace covered wedding dress. The Church had filled on either side, as hooting and hollering threw colour up Evie's neck. As they exited the Church, a burst of firecrackers sizzled in the air. The Pastor chased Shelly and Taylor from the rear of the building, as Marcus set off another batch on the other side.

Evie relished the moment Cade swept her up on Maverick and rode for home.

"It was nice of Rick to pay for Maybelle and Pearl and my Aunt to stay at the Blue Bell." Evie said as Cade carefully carried her over the threshold of the homestead. Our home, she thought.

"It's the least he could do," Cade placed Evie gently at the top of the stairs, "But there is something I've been meaning to ask you Mrs Hamerton."

"Go on," Evie tugged her blonde hair to one side of her neck, as button by button Cade traversed her back.

"What was your one request?"

"Oh!"

Evie escaped her husband's warm clutches, and rummaged through the drawer of the bureau and pulled out a cylinder of documents. Cautiously Cade read the second document in the tube, a registration of Brand, his eyes drawn to the rudimentary symbols.

"The Hammer and Lock"

The paper curled on the coverlet and Cade swept his wife into his arms, "I love it. I love you,"

"I love you Cade, forever and a day." Evie arched her back as Cade peeled away the lace that hid his delights. Evie's fingers undid the neat line of Cade's buttons, her hands slithering across his chest, her teeth nipped his ear, "So does this mean I can void your Drover's fee?"

Cade laughed, as Evie pulled free his shirt, "I don't know Honey."

"I know it's a *large* fee." Evie whispered as she kissed his neck, "I'm more than happy to make regular repayments."

Cade drove his knees between her thighs, the lace and satin chemise rolling upwards under his fingers, "I'm sure we can come to some sort of agreement," he kissed and sucked the tender skin of her neck, "After all I am a gentleman."

Evie laughed, and wrapped her legs around his thighs, his hefty hardened flesh meeting her plush feminine heat.

"No more than I am a lady,"

The End

Epilogue

"What do we tell Marcus?" Evie said as she hugged Jewel for the fifth time.

Over the long trail ride to Kansas, Evie had grown close to the petite firecracker who she now farewelled. The red-headed dynamite had found a spot in a travelling sharp-shooter show. Jewel Daniels was farewelling Dew Springs forever.

"Tell him, he'll know where to find me." The ginger haired girl squeezed Evie one more time before Evie climbed back into her saddle.

"Take care of them for me, will you Cade."

Cade nodded, "You know I will. Stay out of trouble Jewel."

"Don't know what you mean Hamerton, but I'll do my best!"

Evie waved goodbye as she sat astride Nieve the poor mares belly swelling under the weight. Not until three weeks into the drive had Cade worked it out that the mare was expecting. At Kansas, the Hammer and Lock Angus had sold fairly, even the Dew Springs longhorns had done well. Old George wouldn't have to borrow from Kline to stay afloat. The Crooked K and others would be well pleased. Evie rolled her tongue against the roof of her mouth, as the bile climbed the back of her throat. Nothing more certain of her predicament, after all it had been more than six months since their wedding day. Getting the cattle safely to market had distracted Cade sufficiently enough on the Trail. Testing Evie's craftiness in their times of passion so he'd overlook her more curvaceous shape.

Cade stepped Maverick out as the party began their homeward journey. Evie bet she would miss Jewel more than she realised right now.

As the city fell away in the early morning light, Evie slowed her mare down to a trot, Cade halted Maverick and drifted to the rear, Tomas took the lead. Evie blew a curt whistle through her lips and Maverick heeded her call.

"Cheeky girl," Cade said.

"Figured I should learn it so you would stop cheating in races."

Cade laughed and reached out as Evie neared his flank, in one swift movement Evie sat in front of Cade on the giant stallion. Evie wrapped Cades hands around her waist, it's now it never, she thought.

"I was thinking if it is a girl, Eleanor."

"Now that's cheating you can't name the foal before it's born."

Evie drew Cades palm lower and tighter around her belly.

"No Cade not the foal,"

Evie winced as she heard Cade's throat bob, his fingers worked their way under her belt buckle, his long fingers testing the tightness of her stomach, he dropped a long lingering kiss on the nape of her neck, and brought her hard up against him.

"You're fearless. Why didn't you say something earlier?"

"You would have told me to stay home!"

"Wait, you knew before we left the Double E?"

"I didn't want to miss the adventure."

Cade laughed and snuggled into Evie's frame, "I don't have the words Evie. For a long time, I thought I'd never have this kind of happiness, the one that comes with the satisfaction in life, that all is right with the world and the world is ours. You've brought it to me Evie, more than I could ever have believed and now you give me even more," Evie pressed her back against the solid warmth of her husband, his love soothing her soul. Cade's lips whispered against her ear, "And if it's a boy?"

"I was thinking Lachlan."

"Lachlan Hamerton? The Hammer and the Lock or the Double E, Evelyn and Eleanor,"

"Something like that."

"I love it Duchess, now who gets to tell Pearl?"

About the Author

Louise Crouch loves all genres of fiction mixed with a healthy splash of romance. This is her second foray into the world of Historical Western Romance. When she is not writing, Louise spends her time frustrating her wonderful husband and raising their two marvellous children.

Her debut novel was Even Spinster's Need Company which is set in Pennsylvania in the 1870's. Hannah Evans arrives in Franklins Shallows to take up the Headmistress position. She soon finds out not all is as it seems in this quaint town especially the Sherriff, Nicholas Hoffman and his devious family tree. Find it here:

http://loucrouch.wordpress.com

www.ingramcontent.com/pod-product-compliance
Lightning Source LLC
Chambersburg PA
CBHW021224130626
46554CB00004B/1356